Green Eyed

Temptation

Halos & Horns: Book One

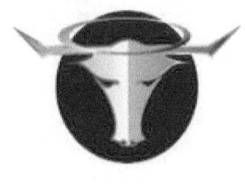

BY
LORI LEGER

DEDICATION

To my wonderful husband, Michael…
You will always be my hero.
And to our grandchildren, from seventeen to under a year,
you are all adored!

ACKNOWLEDGMENT

Special thanks to Kim Killion of The Killion Group
for the fabulous cover design.
www.hotdamndesigns.com

Also to the two tiny bookstores with big hearts that carried my
books long before anyone else did:
Sean and James Gayle of Patti's Book Nook in my old hometown
of Gueydan, La.
www.pattisbooknook.com and

Christy Lepretre of Java Joltz in Jennings, La.
www.facebook.com/Java Joltz

Glossary of Cajun Terminology

Bon Dieu – Good God
Mon ami – My friend
Bonjour – Good day
Sit tois – Sit!
Ici - Here
Comment to ye? – How've you been?
Ca cest bon – It is good
Monsieur – Mr.
Merde – shit
Mon coeur – my heart
Tete dure – hard headed, stubborn
Pere et Mere – Father and Mother
vieille femme – old lady
Vieux verrat! – Old boar
Bouche ta gueule – shut your mouth
Bien bon—very good
Merci beaucoup—thank you very much
Inutile – useless
Arret ca – Stop that
Mais non – But no
Chere – dear
Fais pas ca – Don't do that
Mange – eat
En francaise – in French
Sil vous plait – if you please
Mardi Gras – Fat Tuesday
Laissez les bon temps rouler! – Let the good times roll!

PROLOGUE

Austin, Texas

Black Stetson in hand, his jeans worn and faded, Liam Nash knelt in front of the granite headstone. He reached out with his opposite hand and traced the first inscription.

My Wife and Child, My Loves, My Life . . .

He'd read the words hundreds of times over the last year, but today's visit lacked the overwhelming feeling of loss he usually felt by now.

Resting his hand on the head stone, he lifted his face to absorb the warmth of the sun's rays and allowed a particular memory to wash over him. The image of his beautiful Kimberly the last time he'd seen her alive filled him with a feeling of joy, both sweet and melancholy. It had taken a year of hard work and learning to forgive himself for her death. He could finally smile at the tender memory of Kim, seated in a rocker in the just finished nursery, her hands gently caressing her protruding belly.

He moved his hand to the smaller inscription, as fingertips traced the name and birthday of his infant son. Because Kim had been eight months pregnant when she died, he'd asked the coroner to deliver the baby so his mother could be buried holding her child. She'd waited so long, and it was the last thing he'd been able to do for her.

He remembered well the first time he'd set eyes on Nicholas, nestled in the arms of his mother. His son had his mother's nose and the stubborn set of his father's chin, as well as his mouth and ears. The pain of seeing them together, arranged so perfectly had nearly done him in.

Somehow, he'd managed to survive the wake and funeral. Somehow, he'd managed to be there to comfort Kim's parents, devastated over losing their youngest child and grandchild. He'd even comforted her siblings—his two brothers in law who would never again tease the kid sister they'd nicknamed Kaybee before she even walked. He knew they would be haunted by the tiny, but perfect face on the last 3D ultrasound she'd emailed her big brothers of their newest nephew. Her death created a huge void in the lives of everyone who knew and loved her.

He'd been strong for everyone until the funeral was over. Then he'd tended to himself the only way he knew. He had run as far and as fast as he could, away from everything that reminded him of the wife and child he'd lost.

He'd tried to move on, but learned the hard way that you couldn't build a future while running from a past. Everywhere he'd turned there had been a roadblock, and he'd hurt people. One person, in particular, had been heartbroken. His biggest failure had been to hurt the one person who'd been nothing but good and loving to him.

That sin had prompted him to return here to face his demons. Here, in the place he'd spent the happiest days of his life, as well as the most miserable, he'd found the peace he'd been so desperately seeking. He'd begged forgiveness from his wife and son for not being able to keep them from harm. He'd visited Kaybee's parents, and cried with her brothers. It hadn't come easily…had taken a full year to feel the forgiveness he'd searched for and finally found. It was as though Kim had laid a hand over his heart, freeing him from the pain and guilt that had plagued him.

It had taken five long years of running and facing up to it, but he'd finally accepted it as God's will, and truly believed there was nothing he could have done to prevent it.

He stood up, and dusted off the knees of his jeans before bending at the waist to place a gentle kiss on the headstone. "I love you both," he murmured. "Goodbye Babe."

After passing one hand through his hair, he placed his Stetson back on his head and took two steps back. Finally prepared to get back to his life, he turned and walked away from his past—and into his future.

∼✑

The very same day, Lafayette, Louisiana

"Get in there, you bitch!"

Sarah Richard winced as her estranged husband, shoved her into the bedroom of the grungy apartment he'd set himself up in. She barely managed to keep herself from slamming against the opposite wall. She turned, trying to focus on Troy through the eye nearly swollen shut. Her "husband" hadn't wasted any time giving her a slap the second he'd driven her away from the hospital. Her first phase of the lesson he'd no doubt be inflicting upon her in his own time. She was used to it. Used to running from it. Used to him eventually catching up with her. This time she'd managed to escape him for two months, only to have some well-meaning police officer in the Lafayette, Louisiana Police Department inform him of her whereabouts. After being knocked unconscious during an untimely car accident, they'd found Troy's name listed on the registration papers of her car as the owner. By the time she'd been lucid enough to ask about her babies, he'd removed them from the hospital already. He'd wasted no time in bartering their babies for her silence and submission.

"The twins, Troy. Please. Where are my babies?"

He pointed to a closed door on the west wall of the bedroom. "They're in the bathroom. It's good you're here, because I sure as hell ain't changing anymore shitty diapers."

"You—you left them here—alone?" She flew to the door, her heart thudding wildly as she prayed her babies were safe. She pushed it opened, released her breath in a rush as two heads of golden curls turned her direction. Their immediate cries at the sight of her sent her milk running from her breasts. "Oh, God." Ignoring her own pain, she fell to the floor before them, checking for bruises. "Did you hurt them?"

"Do they look hurt?" His hateful snarl made the hair at the back of her neck prickle with fear.

She turned her gaze on him. "You took them from the hospital twenty-four hours ago. Please tell me you've fed them."

"Sugar water."

"Not even canned formula?"

"Sugar water shuts them up—for a while."

She clenched her jaw, ignoring the pain. "I need to nurse them." She reached for the buttons on her shirt, knowing better than to ask for privacy.

"Yeah. You do that."

He turned, left the room while she nursed her famished twins, feeding them in two sessions each to keep their hunger induced cries to a minimum. Troy couldn't abide screaming infants; he'd made that message abundantly clear on numerous occasions. She still bore the scars to prove it—would gladly collect more if it kept this animal from touching her daughters. With one baby sated enough to fall asleep, the whir of a power drill reached her, making her stomach flip in uneasiness. The tell-tale sound of screws chewing through solid wood told her his plans. She'd seen and heard him install enough locks on her doors and windows to know she wouldn't be leaving this prison anytime soon. Finally, with both girls well fed and sound asleep on the full size bed, she made her way to the bathroom. Thankfully, she found a large bottle of generic aspirin. She popped three with a cup of water and re-entered the bedroom hoping to rest beside the twins.

He stood there at the door, waiting for her, his icy glare dark with fury.

"You're more trouble than you're worth, you know that?"

"Then why go through the trouble of keeping me around?"

"Because you're mine, Sarah. And the day I'll let you go will be the day one of us dies."

She forced herself not to cower as he took two steps toward her.

"And I'm just the right amount of pissed off to make that a reality for one of us." He grabbed her hair, jerked her from the bedroom into the tiny living/kitchen combo area.

"I've got to go to work in an hour, but that's plenty enough time to remind you why you should never—" He accentuated the word with a slap to her head. "Ever—" A slap came from the opposite hand. "Try to run from me, Sarah. You want to scream after I leave?" He sent her an evil leer. "You go right ahead. This ain't the Ritz, babe. A couple of real winners flank this apartment. One is a sexual pervert who got off on a technicality. He likes 'em young." He glanced at the bedroom door for emphasis. "Real young. The guy's a real pig." He pointed toward the opposite wall. "The big guy on this side gets his jollies by cutting on women after he rapes them. Seems he's got a judge in his pocket. So, scream. Knock yourself out."

He wrapped one hand around her neck, gave his brow a curious lift. "How about it, Sarah? Want to make some noise?"

Filled with equal parts terror and dread, she could only shake her head.

He smiled and went to work on her then, making good on his promise to refresh her memory. She prayed for deliverance from his angry fists, but only until she blacked out.

CHAPTER 1

Late February

Angelique Baptiste carved a quick path through the crowded dance floor toward the bar area. She kept a close eye on the tall, well-dressed guy, the same one who'd been ogling her for the last hour. He circled the perimeter of the dancers to reach the bar a few seconds before she did.

She brushed her hair back from her face before walking up to a vacant bar stool. Just as she placed her hand on it, the guy in question covered her hand with his own. His hand, large, but well-manicured and soft, looked as though it had never lifted anything heavier than a fork or a pen in its life. He reeked of money.

Her gaze locked onto a pair of brilliant blue eyes, owned by one of the most gorgeous men she'd ever seen. Angie took a moment to appreciate the physical appearance of the man standing before her. Blond, blue eyed, buff, and looking as though he'd just stepped off of the beach, even though it was the end of winter. She narrowed her eyes, curious as to the source of the tan. Although he was as handsome as any male model she'd ever seen, and built enough to peak her interest, he had the look of someone who spent more time in front of a mirror than she did.

Bummer.

"Excuse me, is this your chair?" she asked.

"It is, but I'm always ready to make a sacrifice for a woman as beautiful as you."

She smiled at the line she was sure had been used on a multitude of occasions. Smooth as a baby's bottom. Just like that, she had him pegged. This guy was obviously a player. A smooth talkin', momma's boy of a player, used to using daddy's money to get his own way.

She smiled sweetly, and pulled her hand back from under his. "Keep your chair. I'm not interested."

She watched him shake his head, as though he was shocked at getting turned down, and waited for his next doomed attempt to pick her up.

"Look, is it a sin to want to dance with the most beautiful woman in the room?"

Angelique stepped back for a head to toe perusal before giving her head a quick shake. "You don't want to dance. You want what I can't give you. I don't play those games." Anymore, she added silently.

The man cocked his head. "And you got all that from two sentences?"

"Absolutely. And more."

"I'm intrigued. Mind if I hear the rest?"

Angelique chuckled. "Trust me, Golden Boy. You don't want to hear what I have to say about you."

His eyes narrowed perceptibly at the nickname she gave him. "Do I know you from somewhere?"

"Definitely not." She turned toward the bartender. "Hey, Bryn, could I have a Grey Goose martini, extra olives? Make it dirty, please." She turned as she heard the man clear his throat.

He swiveled the bar stool so that she could seat herself. "I really would like to hear all about your perception of me, however warped I believe it may be."

Angelique straightened to her full height and lifted her chin to meet his blue eyed gaze. "Don't say I didn't warn you."

He gave her a gallant bow. "I wouldn't dare."

She cleared her throat. "Okay then. You're a player, and you have been for years. You're the type of guy who doesn't give a damn if you leave a date, or a girlfriend, or a wife waiting at home and wondering where you are, while you're out playing touchy feely with another woman. And you wouldn't even care if it's a friend's woman. You're obviously spoiled. You've been raised with a silver spoon in your mouth and are far too used to getting your way. You are selfish, self-centered, and conceited, and that tan—Is that spray-on, or from a tanning bed?"

She waved off the beginnings of his indignant reply. "Doesn't matter—whatever it is, it tells me that you spend far too much time in front of a mirror. I cannot abide a man who primps more than I do. It's not natural, and frankly, it's a huge turn off."

She took one of his hands in hers and examined it. "Soft," she said. "Too damn soft. I bet you've never gotten dirt under those nails, or God forbid, blisters on those palms from anything other than maybe a tennis racquet from that exclusive club you belong to.

And maybe patting your own self on the back. You definitely don't know what it's like to do any kind of physical labor."

Angelique flipped her hair off her shoulder and placed both hands on her hips. "Had enough?"

His eyes widened curiously. "Is there more?"

"Not without having a real conversation, and I doubt you'd be interested after all that. As a matter of fact," she said, checking her watch, "I figure you'll be heading off to find a more receptive audience any second now."

The man crossed his arms and stood there, looking as though he'd settled in for the night. "Mind if I say something?"

She nodded. "By all means, defend away."

"Although I do play tennis occasionally, my sport of choice is baseball and I got plenty of blisters from that, playing from the age of five all the way through college," he said. "Oh, and the tan is natural. I just got back from my time share in the Hawaiian Islands."

She rolled her eyes. "Flaunting your wealth is almost as bad as primping."

"Since when is stating a fact considered flaunting?"

She raised her hand to stop him. "If you'd said, 'It's natural,' and stopped at that, it would have been stating a fact. You threw in the time share in Hawaii. There's your flaunting." She gave him a pat on the arm. "Give it a rest, Golden Boy. Go find some doe-eyed Sorority girl who'll fawn all over you. I'm a grown woman and I prefer real men, not spoiled little boys who refuse to take life seriously." She turned abruptly and bumped her nose into the solid wall of an extremely broad chest, belonging to a very tall, very hunky man. "Oh, excuse me."

The wall of chest spoke in a deep baritone. "Not at all, ma'am. I couldn't help but overhear a little of your discussion. Is this gentleman bothering you?"

Angelique smiled up at the mountain of a man with straight, coal black hair, and nearly black eyes—he possessed the look of someone with Native American in his bloodline. His shoulders were massive and he dwarfed the blond guy, who looked to be well over six feet tall, himself.

"No, he's not bothering me. He's just having a difficult time accepting that he's not God's gift to women." She took a step back to encompass the whole of the big man. "My goodness, you are a tall one, aren't you?"

The man swept off his Stetson and brushed a huge hand through his jet black locks. "Yes ma'am. Six foot and seven inches, to be exact. Mike Harper is the name, and as long as we're talking, would you care to dance with me?" He extended his hand and bowed gallantly at the waist.

Angelique reached out for his hand. "I think I'd like that, Mr. Harper." She turned. "Bryn, hold my drink back there, please?"

Mike Harper turned her toward the dance floor, his hand placed intimately on the small of her back. He paused long enough to cast a grin at the other man, who stood there gaping at him as though someone slid their mud-covered four by four in the parking spot set aside for his Mercedes. "I hope you're taking notes, pretty boy, because I don't give lessons."

Once out in the middle of the dance floor, Angelique slid her arms up around the man's neck. "Can you still see him?"

Her dance partner looked over at the guy. "Yep. He's standing there like he doesn't know what hit him. I picked up a bicycle tire pump off a street this morning. Maybe I ought to give it to him after this dance."

"For what?" She gazed curiously at him.

"I believe he could use it for that deflated ego of his. I didn't catch it all. What'd you say to him?"

She shrugged. "The truth."

He winced and clucked his tongue. "Poor bastard."

Angelique laughed, then looked up into the dark eyes of her dance partner. "You're late, Detective."

He made a face as he sucked in his breath. "I'm sorry about that, Angel. I tried to call you from my truck, but your phone didn't pick up."

"I fried it. Again." She tried her best to avert his gaze, even as she felt the rumble of laughter from deep in his chest.

"What was it this time?"

"It took a bath."

"Again? What is that, the third time you dropped it in the tub?" He shook his head, obviously amazed at her God given talent for destroying cell phones. "Was it insured?"

"Sure, but they'll only replace it twice. I'll have to pay for a new one this time. I've got the parts spread out on my table. I'm hoping it'll work once it dries."

"If it doesn't, I could buy you a new one," he suggested. "I know you help your parents out a lot financially. If you're strapped right now, I could help."

She shook her head. "I've got enough in my savings to cover it, but thanks for offering. So, why were you late?"

"I was walking out the door and got a call about a hit and run two streets down from the precinct."

"Was anyone hurt?"

He shook his head. "No life-threatening injuries, thank God. Some asshole hit a car with a mother and her two small children."

Angelique gasped. "Bon Dieu! Were they hurt?"

"Everyone was buckled up and belted in safely, but the young mom still got some nasty bruises on the side of her face and on her body. She was more worried about her babies, though."

"Did the asshole get away?"

"Nope. We were all pretty determined to catch him once we saw those two adorable twin girls being taken out of their car seats. We had that punk behind bars in thirty minutes. Some rich kid with his learner's permit sneaking his daddy's Jaguar out for a joy ride. As I was leaving the precinct his lawyer pulled up in a high end Lexus." Mike shook his head in disgust. "Far from his first offense, but the little bastard won't see a single day of juvie, I guarantee it."

She gave him a sad smile and brushed his hair back from his forehead. "You and your guys do good work, Mike. If you didn't, a good friend of mine wouldn't be alive."

"Red McAllister?"

"Actually, I was talking about Tiffany."

He smiled. "I can remember the first time Dr. Tiffany LeBlanc walked through the doors of my precinct. She'd come in to provide an alibi for Red. That was over a year ago. I didn't realize you two were that close."

She nodded. "We're getting closer every day. She's helped me so much with my job at the Lake Coburn office."

"How's the new job going, anyway?" He led her off the dance floor once the song ended.

"I love it, Mike. Tiff's insight to the employees and workings of that hospital has been instrumental in helping to get me established pretty quickly." She walked to the bar. "I'll take that martini now, Brynn." When the bartender handed it to her she took a sip. "Mmm, good."

Mike shuddered as he watched her. "I don't know how you can drink that stuff. It tastes like rubbing alcohol to me."

"The olive juice makes the difference, along with good quality vodka. It's my one drink of the night, so let me savor it. After this, it's cola or water." She had set that rule for herself since the Benji Bradford business last year. Angelique knew if she'd been thinking clearly, she never would have let him get that close to her. She was determined nothing like that would ever happen again.

Mike pinned her with his dark-eyed gaze. "So, besides the fact that you're still the most beautiful woman I've ever laid eyes on, how've you been, Ms. Baptiste?"

She smiled up at him. "I've been good. I miss not being able to see my buddy on a regular basis, but other than that, the move to Lake Coburn has been good."

He dropped his head back on his shoulders and groaned. "Six months we've been dating and you still just consider me a buddy. I'm wounded."

Her eyes sparkled with laughter. "We don't date, Mike. We spend time together. As friends. No pressure, no serious business . . ."

"And definitely no sex," he groaned, as he pulled her hips toward his own. "I didn't realize what I was sacrificing when I agreed to this arrangement."

She pushed away from him. "Oh, look now—you were warned well ahead of time. Admit it, Harper. You didn't think I'd be able to resist your fabulous body for this long, did you?"

He flexed his shoulders back, puffing out his broad chest. "Yeah, how can you?" he asked, playfully.

"It's not that easy, you know. You're the first guy I've spent any time with since I started this celibacy thing a year ago." She took another sip of her martini and lowered her lids. "And I can admit that when I'm around you, I can't help but think about how well we'd fit together, if you know what I mean," she mused.

He took a deep breath and released it agonizingly slow. "You're damn right, I know." He cleared his throat before having to adjust himself. "But dammit, I feel in my bones that we'd be great together, Angel."

Angelique gave her head a quick shake. "Don't start, Mike. I have issues I need to deal with before I can have any man in my life. Doctor's orders. Or in this case, therapist's orders. I need to learn to live with myself before I can share my life with anyone else."

He made a disgusted noise. "You are the last person in the world who needs a therapist."

She thought back to the one night stand with Benji out in back of Red's club. That one moment of bad judgment and lack of morals had very nearly led to her death. Mike was the detective working that case, so she'd had to give her statement to him. She'd only admitted to having a quick sexual interlude with Benji outside of the club that night. No one else knew that it happened up against the rough exterior brick of the building. It still shamed her to the core. She looked sadly up at him. "It just goes to show how little you know about me."

Mike reached up to brush a lock of hair away from her face. "Sometimes I wish I could see what's going on in that head of yours. Maybe then I could understand why you're so hard on yourself."

Seeming to sense her need for a subject change, he complied. "How are your folks doing? They still dead set on staying in Lafayette?"

Angelique nodded, relieved to be talking about something else. "My parents are seventy-two and seventy-six, and they're not going anywhere. As long as I can make it over to check on them once or twice a week, they're happy. I told mom I was going to see you tonight, and she said to tell you she's baking fig tarts next week." She laughed at his wide-eyed grin.

"I was just thinking today it was time to go have coffee with her again." He flinched then scanned the screen of his ringing cell phone before accepting the call. "Harper here."

Angelique watched him rein in his emotions throughout the thirty second phone call. Within seconds, she knew he'd have to leave her.

Mike ended the call and shoved his phone back into the inside pocket of his sports coat. "I've got to go back to the precinct, Sweetie. It looks like all hell's about to break loose, but damn, I hate leaving you."

She smiled, determined to make it easier on him. "It's okay. If anyone understands about the demands of a job, I do."

"I know, but I was sure as hell looking forward to spending some time with you." He sighed. "I miss you, Angel."

She raised her hand to his face. "I miss you, too, Mike. But, if it's meant to be, it'll happen. That's my new mantra. Come on, I'll walk you to the door."

Hand in hand, they made their way to the exit.

He turned toward her. "I'll call you during the week."

She nodded and beamed at him. "If you can't get through to my cell, call me at work. You take care, you hear?"

"I will." He leaned down to give her a quick kiss, the only kind she allowed. He scanned the room, as though assessing the bevy of guys available to her, then wrapped her in a big bear hug. "Don't you forget about me." He spoke in a rough voice. "Don't you walk away from me without giving me a real chance to show you how much I want you in my life."

"I won't, Mike." She rested her face against his broad chest. "When my situation changes, I promise you'll be the first to know."

He pulled away from her and walked off, glancing back briefly to give her one last smile before he left the building.

Angelique took several deep breaths and released them slowly. God almighty, this celibacy thing was torture. Once she'd composed herself again, she made her way back to the bar to order a coke before going to join some ladies from work. She wasn't there thirty seconds before "Golden Boy" made a repeat appearance.

"That was dirty. How long have you two been seeing each other?" He slid in beside her.

She glanced up at him. "Who says we're seeing each other? Maybe we just met."

"Nah, you two were struggling to keep your hands off each other. Though why, I haven't a clue."

"How very observant of you," she admitted. "Truthfully, I haven't always had self-control when it came to men, but I like to think I've learned from my mistakes." She gazed into his blue eyes. "Can you say the same?"

He returned her gaze. "I'd like to. Maybe you could help me see the error of my ways."

She gave a hearty laugh. "Honey, that's something that has to come from you. If you're not ready, it won't happen."

"But how do you know you weren't put here, in this bar, at this very moment so that our paths could cross. You may just be my salvation, Ms. . . . ?"

She chuckled. "Oh come on, you can do better than that, can't you?"

He put his head back and laughed. "Okay, I see I'm wasting my time here, so maybe we can just call a truce and start up a friendship." He took a deep breath and released it in a rush before smiling soberly at her. "Truth is I'm in need of a good friend."

Angelique studied him and gave him a nod. "That may be the first sincere thing you've said to me all night." She held out her hand to him. "As long as you know that's all I'm offering here. Angelique Baptiste," she said, taking his hand.

"Tanner Collins," he said, sounding surprisingly grateful.

She cocked her head in concentration. "Why does that name sound so familiar to me?"

He shrugged. "I don't know. Maybe my bad boy reputation precedes me."

"You're not Tiffany's Tanner, are you?"

He cringed at her comment. "We were engaged for two years before she dumped me for Red. Are you a friend of hers?"

Angelique pursed her lips. "I am, although I haven't always been. It seems we have something in common, after all." She chuckled at Tanner's perplexed look. "I used to date Red."

Tanner's brow raised in surprise. "Is that a fact?"

"Yep."

"You two must have parted on good terms or you wouldn't be friends with his wife."

Angelique sucked in her breath. "Yes, and no, and yes again. But that's another story for another time."

"I understand completely. Does that mean you wouldn't mind talking to me about it some other time?"

Angelique studied his face for several moments. "Do you live here in Lake Coburn?"

"I live on the west side of the city."

She made the decision in an instant. "I could use a buddy here, but I can tell you with certainty that we'll never be more than friends. Can you accept that?"

He seemed excited at the prospect. "You've got a deal,"

"Well then, mon ami, what I need right now is a good dance partner. Think you can help a buddy out?"

"I know I can." He hauled her out to the floor for an invigorating country two step, the first of many dances they'd share that night. By the end of the evening, they'd settled into an easy, relaxed banter. It had all the signs of a platonic, friendly relationship, destined to last for years.

Admittedly, a first for Tanner Collins.

∿

The next morning, Angelique fished one blouse out of the washer and put the rest to dry. After draping the blouse over a hanger, she closed the laundry room door and headed for a coffee refill. She inhaled the aroma of strongly brewed coffee, had just poured another cup when she heard the front doorbell's distinctive ring. The clock on her microwave flashed eight a.m. as she walked over to the door, wondering who the hell would be here so early on a Saturday morning.

Angelique opened the door and stood, immobilized by the unexpected, shocked into silence, and staring up into a familiar face. A single utterance laid claim to the world of hurt he'd left her to wallow in.

CHAPTER 2

"Liam . . ."

The visitor swept off his brown Stetson and gave her a sad smile.

"Hello Angel."

Angelique slowly placed her hand to her own chest, hoping to ease the pounding of her heart. She stared at him in silence as a war of mixed emotions battled for supreme domination in her mind.

"You look pale, hon. You're not gonna faint, are you?"

After a moment, she blinked away her confusion, and prepared herself to respond to the man who'd managed to capture her heart and break it in a matter of months. "It's about a hundred years too late for the vapors, don't you think?" She blinked again. "How long have you been back?"

He looked at his watch, then back up at her. "I crossed into the city limits about fifteen minutes ago."

She crossed her arms and raised an eyebrow. "You came straight here?"

He nodded then pulled at his collar while slapping his hat against his blue jeaned leg.

"You look nervous, Liam."

"I am."

"Well, that's gratifying," she snorted. "You should be on your knees begging me not to throw your ass out of here."

He nodded again, keeping his gaze on her.

Angelique thought of all the conversations she'd had with him in her mind. Thoughts of what she'd say if he ever had the nerve to show up on her doorstep again. All of that flew out the window, as she uttered four little words. "You hurt me, Liam."

∿∿

Liam Nash bowed his head, consumed by shame. "I know I did. Can you ever forgive me?"

"I don't know."

He lifted his gaze from his scuffed boots to her beautiful face. "I wish you'd try."

"I bet you do," she said, her voice tight, controlled, even as her eyes blurred with unshed tears.

His heart ached for her, knowing she was reliving the misery he'd put her through a year ago. After four months of steady dating, she'd fallen hard for him. He'd thanked her by freaking out, and leaving town in the middle of the night with no explanation or warning. He'd called her home phone two days later, knowing she'd be at work, to leave her some piss poor excuse on her voice mail. God almighty, why she didn't slam the door in his face, he couldn't fathom.

"I'm not expecting you to," he explained. "I know I don't deserve any time from you, but I was in a bad place, Angel. It's taken me a year to get my head straight. As soon as I did, I came here to explain things to you. You mind if I come in?"

She pulled the door open wide, motioning him inside with a one-handed flourish. "By all means, explain away, Liam," she said, annunciating his name in two precise syllables.

He walked inside and looked around. "This is a nice place." He followed her into the kitchen.

"Thanks. Coffee?" Her tone was dry and clipped.

"I'd be thankful." He sat himself at her kitchen table, stretching one leg out in front of him in an attempt to get comfortable.

"Who told you I'd moved?"

"When the Christmas card came back with no forwarding address I ran a search on you."

"I told the important people." She set his cup on the table, along with the sugar and creamer then sat across from him with her own mug of steaming brew. "I've been here for six months. If you'd called, you'd have known that."

He held up a hand. "I know, Angel. I wasn't implying anything. I'm just surprised that you'd move away from your parents, that's all. I know how you worry about them."

She forced herself to relax her shoulders. "I see them twice a week, sometimes more." She placed her fingertips on her temples. "So, what's this excuse of yours?"

Liam watched as the woman who'd turned his life upside down, looked torn between crying and screaming at him. "I love you."

Her eyes flew open wide. "What did you say to me?"

"I said I love you, Angelique Therese Baptiste." He leaned in closer to her. "Every gorgeous inch of you."

Her eyes narrowed angrily. "What gives you the right to come over here and say something like th . . . "

"I was married once." She froze in shocked silence at his admission. "Seven years ago I was married." He continued in a rush of breath. "We were very happy together when my wife passed away five years ago. We had a nice home, two dogs, a talking bird, and a baby on the way." He tunneled one hand through his hair nervously. "I lost everything I loved in one night."

Angelique brought her hand up to her mouth. "Why am I just hearing about this now?"

"I couldn't talk about it. Hell, I couldn't even look at a picture of Kimberly. That was my wife. After the funeral, I packed up the few things I had stashed in my locker at the police station and hauled ass—all the way to Lubbock, Texas."

She placed her hand on his arm. "What happened to her, Nash? Can you tell me?"

He dropped his head back and closed his eyes. "It was late November, two nights after Thanksgiving. We'd busted our asses getting the house all decorated for Christmas. I put up the lights on the outside of the house and she decorated the tree and the rest of the place."

He gave a bittersweet laugh. "You've got to understand that Kim really loved Christmas. Every damn room in the house had to be decorated. The tree . . . " he paused as his breath hitched slightly. "The tree was her specialty. That thing was gorgeous. She shopped all year long for antique Christmas ornaments. And the lights—I always told her she would burn down the house one day because there were so many lights on the damn thing."

He stopped and gave Angel a crooked grin. "She'd even put a small tree in the nursery because our son, Nicholas, was due a week before Christmas."

He paused again to fortify himself. "I had to go to work that night and, man, was I beat. Before I left the house I went to meet her in the nursery. She was sitting in a glider rocker we'd bought, with her feet propped up, because they were all swollen. I gave her a kiss, and the last thing I said before I walked out was not to go to bed without turning off the tree lights."

Angelique heard his voice catch, and she suddenly knew the horrible outcome of that fateful night. "She left them on, didn't she?"

Liam nodded. "The fire marshal determined the origin of the fire was the tree in the living room. She died of smoke inhalation, but the fire never touched her. We found her body in our bed once they put the fire out. She just went to sleep and never woke up." He let his head fall back and released a long sigh. "I lost everything that day. Even that damn bird she loved so much."

"I'm so sorry, Liam." She leaned forward. "You must have been devastated."

"I wanted to die, Angel. I drank myself stupid for a year, but the morning I woke up in my bed naked, alone, and not knowing how the hell I got there, I knew it had to stop."

He gave his hat several twirls before laying it on the table. "I never had anyone call me about how I'd done something stupid, dangerous, or worse. I figured it was Kim watching over my dumb ass until I got smart enough to realize the stupidity had to cease and desist."

"I can't even imagine surviving something like that." Angel spoke in a tearful whisper.

"I eventually went back into law enforcement and after two years the loneliness drove me to date again, if that's what you want to call it. I figured as long as I didn't commit to anyone, I could stay faithful to Kim." He looked into her eyes. "And then I met you. I know it doesn't make any sense, but when I fell in love with you I felt like an adulterer."

She shook her head as tears ran down her face. "But we spent four months together. Four months of phone calls and road trips and romantic weekends. Then you just—left." She placed her hand over her heart. "I was so hurt."

He dropped his head, shamefully. "I know that, and I'm sorry, but I was eaten up with guilt. I had to go back and, well . . . fix some things."

"And did you?"

He nodded. "It took a whole year. I moved back to Austin, re-established contact with my in-laws, and started making daily visits to Kim and the baby's grave. I'd talk to her, Angel. I told her everything, all about you and my feelings."

Liam rose from the table to stare out the window over the kitchen sink. "I swear, sometimes I'd see people watching me out there at that grave site, and I knew they thought I'd lost my mind." He faced her again, resting his lean hips against the sink, and took a sip from his mug of coffee. "I didn't give a shit, because the more I did it, the better I felt. A couple of days ago when I made my visit, I somehow knew it would be my last one. I woke up that morning, and for the first time in years, I felt like I could move on. So, I told them goodbye and headed back here."

"To walk back into my life and expect us to pick up where we left off a year ago? It doesn't work that way, Liam."

He shrugged. "I didn't expect it to be that easy; I know how badly I hurt you. But if you can just tell me now that you don't hate my guts—tell me that you'll at least let me try to make it up to you, it would mean a lot to me."

She sighed, allowing her head to fall forward while organizing her thoughts. "I don't hate you." She met his gaze again. "I understand why you left to resolve things. To tell you the honest truth, your leaving made me realize I had my own issues to deal with." Angelique pushed her cup away and leaned back in her chair. "I started seeing a therapist, and at her suggestion, I've been celibate for a year. As difficult as it's been for me, I've learned a lot about myself. I'm trying to like me for who I am, not for the men I attract."

"Are you telling me you haven't done anything for a year?" he asked. "You haven't dated at all?"

She got up to pour herself another cup of coffee. "I needed a breather after you, and I found other men distracting when it came to 'finding myself' so to speak. I'm going to tell you the same thing I've told Mike Harper for the last six months, and Tanner Collins just recently. Right now, all I'm offering is friendship. If that's not good enough for you . . . " She lifted her arm and pointed at her doorway. "See yourself out."

Liam gave her a crooked grin before drawing her in close for a hug. "You won't hear me complain. I'm here to make it up to you, not pressure you. Hell, I'm just thankful you didn't boot my ass to the curb as soon as you saw my scrawny mug." He scratched at his four day old chin scruff, then stopped and cocked his head curiously. "As for those other guys you mentioned, I don't know any Collins, but that Harper sure sounds familiar. Would he happen to be a big old boy? A half-breed American Indian?"

She grinned. "That would be Mike, except he's three quarter Cherokee, not half, and he's six foot seven, so I think that definitely puts him in the 'big old boy' category. He's a detective with the Lafayette P.D."

Nash gave a nod of satisfaction. "We started at the police academy together in San Antonio back when God was a teenager. Damn, but that was way before Kim and I got married. I was twenty-five years old and fresh out of the Navy." He looked at her and grinned. "Mike was even younger than that. Is he still a bean pole, or has he put some bulk on since then?"

She cleared her throat. "He's uh, yeah—he's got some bulk."

Nash snorted. "I'll have to get my game on. From what I can remember of him, he was a good guy."

Angelique nodded. "He still is. If I see him before you do, you want me to keep quiet about your past?"

Nash gave a shrug of indifference. "If you tell him, that's one less person I have to explain myself to, but it's your choice." He reached out to pull her to him for another hug. "God, it's good to see you, Angel. If you don't have lunch plans, I'd like to take you."

She passed a hand through her hair. "I think I'm going to have to pass on that, Liam. I need time to absorb all this."

"What about tonight? I know how much you like to dance—care to go cut a rug, friend?" he asked, feeling hopeful.

She smiled graciously at him. "If you want to show up at Red's club tonight, I'll be there."

"How about if I pick you up?"

"No, thank you. That's one of the rules I set for myself. I go alone, I only have one alcoholic beverage, and I go home alone."

"And you've been doing that for how long now?" he asked, as a slow grin spread across his face.

She let out a long sigh, knowing exactly what he was after. "Since you left, Liam."

"Hmmm. That means I was the last one."

She nodded. "Yes, you were."

"Well hell, I guess I can live with that. Liam kissed her forehead, put on his hat and marched to the door. With one backward glance and a tip of his hat, he gave her sexy, one-sided grin. "See you tonight."

Angelique followed him to the door to watch him walk to his pick-up. "Oh no, you didn't, God," she said, emitting a deep sigh. She watched the sexy swing of long arms connected to that buff, broad torso, and legs covered in jeans that fit him snug enough to accentuate his muscular thighs.

She rolled her eyes upward. "First, it was Mike and now Liam? You really like to stir it up, don't you?"

CHAPTER 3

Mike pushed through the club door just after eight p.m. The pounding rhythm of the house band's music assaulted his senses as he pulled his wallet from his back pocket to pay the entrance fee. He turned at the feel of a heavy hand on his shoulder.

"Hey, man, put that away, your money's no good here," Red McAllister told him.

Mike looked down at his old friend. "If that's the case, I'm shit out of luck. I planned to spend some serious green here tonight." He reached a hand out to Red for a firm shake. "How's it going, Red? How are Tiffany and that baby girl doing?"

Red beamed proudly at the mention of his wife and daughter. "Briana's great, growing like a weed in a field of manure. Tiffany's like me; sleep deprived, but seriously wrapped."

Mike gave a hearty laugh. "Sounds like every new parent I've ever spoken to."

"It kills me to leave them at night to come to the club. I think I've got good people working for me, but after what happened at the other place with Benji Bradford, you never know."

"That was an isolated incident, buddy," Mike said with a slight shake of his head. "There's nobody else who'd lift a finger against you or yours. You're a good man."

Red nodded sheepishly. "Thanks, that means a lot coming from you." He nodded his head toward the VIP section. "Angelique is here already, along with somebody who knows you."

"Oh yeah? Who's that?" Mike asked, craning his neck to see.

Red placed a hand on his shoulder. "Come on, let's go meet them."

It took a couple of minutes to get to the section on the other side of the room. By the time they got to the table, Angelique and her 'mystery person' were back on the dance floor.

Mike gave the waitress his drink order and looked up in time to see the couple waltz by along the perimeter. "Nash!" he said, pointing at her beaming dance partner. "We were in the police academy together." He swung around to face Red. "How does she know him?"

"I hired him as a body guard for my sister, Annie, last year. He and Angelique dated for a few months before he hauled ass back to Texas."

"He's the one who left Angel high and dry a year ago?" Mike asked. "What the hell happened to him? The Nash I remember would never have walked away from a lady like that."

Red shrugged. "All I know is that he saved my sister's life."

Mike watched them make another round on the dance floor before the song ended. "Damn it all. Looks like competition to me."

Red slapped him on the back. "Well, I'll tell you the same thing I told Nash—I'm staying the hell out of this, but good luck. Just don't piss her off. She's got a low tolerance for stupidity and holds a grudge forever," he said, before walking away.

Mike swigged from his beer and grinned at their approach. "Liam Nash, you son of a bitch. It's been forever, man!"

"Damn Chief, you filled out some since I saw you last!" Nash said, before the two men shook hands and slapped each other's backs. "Good to see you, man. Small world, huh?"

Mike grinned as he sent Angel a sly wink. "Seems to be shrinking as we speak."

Angelique took that opportunity to visit the ladies room and the two men settled in at the table.

Mike looked over at his old friend. "You look good, man. So, what have you been doing with your life since we spoke last?"

Nash picked at the label on his beer bottle. "How much do you know?"

Mike shook his head. "Not a thing."

Nash spent the next few minutes bringing Mike up to date. He twirled his beer on the table. "I hadn't dealt with anything yet when I started dating Angel, and that's when it caught up with me. I had to go back and get my shit straight before I could move on to another relationship. But, I did, and that's why I'm here."

"Without going into any details, I can say you've made the last six months pure torture for me," Mike told him, glumly.

Nash grinned at him. "Yeah, she mentioned the celibacy thing. It'd be a damned lie to say it doesn't thrill the shit out of me."

Mike shook his head. "You know, I hear the Navy's looking for older men to train the new batch of youngsters joining. Might be a good chance to jump back in there, Flipper," he said, reverting back to the nickname he'd given the former Navy Seal.

"Not a chance, Chief, but nice try."

Mike gave him a hearty chuckle. "I guess I'd feel the same if I were in your position. But, that's okay. She knows I'm here for her if she needs me."

Nash nodded. "And after today, she knows the same about me. He held up his beer and they clinked bottles. "Let the games begin."

∿

Angelique studied her reflection, wondering what those two men waiting for her at the table could possibly see in her. Between the two of them, they could make their own 'man of the month' calendar, fully clothed or not. She closed her eyes, remembering the feel of her hands sliding over Liam's nude body. During the last two months of their relationship, they had been intimate dozens of times. The memory of some particularly nice nights together caused her face to infuse with heat. His abs had been tightly muscled and smooth, but for the fine feathering of golden brown hair on his chest and stomach area. She'd confided in him once that she was completely turned off by men who waxed, shaved, or used creams to remove their body hair. He'd seem pleased by her statement. Oh, Lord, had he been pleased.

She'd never known that kind of intimacy with Mike, but they'd been to the beach together last summer and he had a great body. She'd seen evidence of his own needs several times, only through the fit of his jeans or swim trunks, of course. She lay in bed nights, trying not to picture him and what it might be like if she broke down and slept with him. Not that they'd get much sleep.

Angelique closed her eyes and groaned aloud in the otherwise empty restroom. "I miss sex. And there are two perfectly good candidates out there." She shook her head. No . . . She would be strong. She had to be strong.

Her resolve reaffirmed, she exited the restroom to stand watching the two men who would, no doubt, pull out all the stops to try to get her to break. Both men were prizes in the looks category—tall, male model material in facial features and physiques—and both of them charming as hell. If she had to choose today...what would she do?

She released a long, slow sigh and began the walk back to the table. Both men stood and reached to pull out a chair for her. She bypassed the chairs and took the one on the end, between the two of them.

∿

An hour later, she let Mike lead her back to the table. Normally, the intimate press of his hand to her lower back would cause a rush of sexual need, but the ache in her feet was over-riding all pleasure. Hoping to join the band as they took their break, she nearly cried when the house DJ kicked in a slow country belly rubber. As she suspected, Liam appeared, ready to steal her for the next dance.

He grinned charmingly down at her. "My turn."

Angelique looked from Liam, to Mike, and then back to Liam. She took Mike's left hand, and placed it in Nash's open palm. "You two can play happy feet with each other the rest of the night. My feet are killing me and I'm going home." She mumbled a few choice words then walked away from both of them. Once at the door, she looked back at the two men who stood staring after her, both no doubt confused at her departure.

"God help me," she groaned. How could she possibly choose between two men who both meant so much to her?

CHAPTER 4

Nash jerked awake, realizing immediately that he wasn't in his own apartment. He looked over at the clock and groaned. Nine o'clock? He let his head fall back against the pillow trying to remember what time he'd come in. He remembered fumbling with the key Annie and Drake had given him to get in through the side door of their new country home. Once they discovered she was pregnant, they'd decided to build about midway between Lake Coburn and Kenton. When he'd called to tell the couple he was relocating to the area permanently, they'd insisted he stay with them until he found his own digs. He was looking forward to spending quality time with his old roomies.

His plans hadn't included waking up with a hangover, but once Angelique left the club, it'd turned into one of those 'What the hell?' nights old men tell their sons and grandsons about when they're too long in the tooth to do anything other than talk.

He remembered Red taking their keys once they'd decided to discover which brand of tequila was the best for shooting. It had taken them the rest of the night to test out the shots of Cuervo Gold and Silver, Patron, 1800, and Sauza Gold – the club's entire line of tequilas. For the life of him, he couldn't remember the outcome. Nash rubbed a hand roughly over his face and swallowed. Hell, from the foul taste in his mouth, he could have been shooting lighter fluid.

He got up, took a quick shower and brushed his teeth. After throwing on a pair of jeans and a long sleeved button down, he slipped on his boots and headed downstairs to see what his host and hostess were up to.

He found them in the nursery putting together a crib for the baby that was due to arrive in one month. Nash stood quietly in the doorway, checking out the room's cheery Noah's Ark theme. His gaze was drawn to the couple, Annie, seated in the glider rocker, so similar to the one he'd last seen Kim seated upon. Drake was on his knees, completely enclosed by the rails of the crib, a cordless screwdriver in one hand and a bag filled with dozens of nuts, bolts, washers, and screws in the other. He was leaning over the crib's schematic, studying the diagram.

"Uh, babe?" Annie spoke hesitantly, frowning over the sheet of instructions.

Drake's head dropped back onto his shoulders. "Oh God, what now?"

"I think you put that last piece on backwards."

"No, it shows Part A on the inside," he replied, tightly.

Nash smiled, as bittersweet memories came rushing back at him. He distinctly remembered being in that same position and using that exact tone of voice with his pregnant wife. It had taken him hours to put that crib together. He hadn't realized at the time that it would never be used. Thanks to a year of therapeutic graveside visits, he could now save his friends a little trouble by offering some guidance.

He walked into the room and cleared his throat. "It's not backwards, Drake, but it is upside down." He leaned over and pointed to a latch. "You see, that part needs to be on top, but it's an easy fix." He looked over at Annie, who mouthed a silent "Thank you".

Drake took a deep breath and exhaled slowly. "It already feels like I've been working on this damn thing forever."

"Unless it's been over four hours, I don't feel sorry for you," Nash told him. He squatted down next to Annie and placed one large hand on her considerable belly. "How's the little LeBlanc doing this morning?"

She grinned up at him. "Very active. I think he's a future kicker for the New Orleans Saints."

"Or maybe she's going to be one of the Saintsations," Drake retorted, speaking of the football team's cheerleading and dance squad.

"Maybe she'll be a field goal kicker for the Saints," Nash interjected.

Annie grinned mischievously at Nash and winked. "Or maybe he'll grow up to be a Saintsation."

Drake frowned at the two. "Y'all are freaking hilarious. We'd know if we were having a boy or a girl, if someone didn't insist on not finding out." He ended the comment by glaring at his wife.

She gave him a huge grin. "You're just pissed because you thought I wouldn't have the patience to last this long."

Drake clenched his jaw noticeably. "Yeah, yeah. Now how about some help over here?"

Nash laughed and walked over to meet him. "A word of advice, pal. When you take that panel off to flip it, step outside of the crib to put the rest of it together. It's not that easy to get out of there if you don't."

Drake grinned sheepishly as his wife bit back a laugh.

"Damn Nash, you ruined all the fun! I was dying to see him try to get out of that one," Annie said, giggling before turning to Nash. "You want some breakfast?" She tried to lift herself up out of her chair.

Nash placed one hand on her shoulder. "Don't get up, Annie. Honestly, I can't eat anything right now, but I could use a cup of coffee, and some aspirin or something."

"Help me up, first. I have to go pee again," Annie said. "I'll bring you something when I come back. Coffee's in the kitchen."

∾ဃ

Mike Harper woke slowly to the sound of a baby crying and a pounding in his head. He reached over to look at his watch and grimaced at the time. He vaguely remembered the bartender dumping him and Nash into a cab and being delivered to Red and Tiffany's place.

After a quick shower he redressed in his same clothes and popped three ibuprofens from a bottle he found in the medicine cabinet. He walked into the couple's kitchen and grabbed the oversized mug next to the automatic coffee maker. After pouring himself a cup of good, strong Cajun coffee, he followed the sound of two adults making absolute fools of themselves over a giggling, cooing baby girl.

Red and Tiffany LeBlanc sat side by side on the couch while baby Briana sat up, supported by her daddy. The child gave an adorable belly laugh as her father made a face and a funny sound with his mouth.

"Oh man, she's a beauty," Mike said of the child who showed the promise of her mama's golden brown hair and big brown eyes. "There's nothing like the sound of a baby's laughter."

Red beamed at Mike as he handed his daughter over to Tiffany. "I have to agree with you there," he told his friend.

"She's got a set of lungs on her, too, from what I heard a little while ago," Mike added.

"This child hates two things—dirty diapers and being hungry. I had to change her dirty diaper before I could feed her," Tiffany explained. She stood up and walked over to meet him, holding the baby on her hip. "How are you, Mike?"

Mike hugged her fondly. "I'm good. Or I will be as soon as the ibuprofen takes effect. Man, I don't know how long it's been since I pulled one like that. Somewhere along the way, I seem to have lost my mind."

Red laughed. "Yeah, I think I heard Angelique saying something along the same lines just before she limped out of the club last night."

Tiffany swung around to face him. "What d'you do, step on her feet?"

"Nah," he said. "We just kept her on the dance floor all night."

"Poor Angie must have been burnt out," Tiffany said.

Mike didn't even have to think about it before he answered. "I don't know why she would be. I barely broke a sweat."

Red exchanged a look with his wife. "Could that possibly be because you sat out every other song?"

Tiffany laughed and shook her head in amazement. "Is that kind of cluelessness a man thing?"

Red snorted. "Don't you lump us all into one. I think it's more likely a law enforcement thing."

Mike groaned. "It's a 'who's gonna get to go home with the prize' thing. Nash only thinks he's as serious as I am about Angel. I plan on marrying that one."

Tiffany clasped her hands in excitement. "You're ready for that kind of commitment?"

Mike nodded. "Yeah, but don't get too excited, she doesn't know it yet. And it may take some time to get her to forget the past she's had with Nash." He looked over at his friends. "I didn't realize he'd lost a wife and child."

Red nodded somberly. "He told you?"

"Yeah. We both kind of spilled our guts last night." He frowned, and placed a hand on his belly.

Red laid his hand on Mike's shoulder. "You look like you're about to spill yours again."

Tiffany turned to her guest. "We have all the ingredients here to fix you up. Trust me, Mike. It doesn't look like much, and tastes awful, but it really works."

Mike covered his mouth as he tried to suppress a belch, then a groan. "Oh, God, please excuse me. I'll take anything if you say it helps. I haven't felt this bad in twenty years."

∾

Angelique curled up on her sofa with a second cup of coffee as she reached over with her free hand to rub her sore feet. The boots she'd worn the night before were of high quality leather, and a great fit. Under normal circumstances, she wouldn't have sore feet this morning, but being the pawn between two extremely competitive males did not fit into the realm of normal circumstances. For a solid two hours she'd volleyed back and forth between the two men, until she'd called it a night and came home early. A soak in her tub and a half bottle of wine had calmed her nerves, but hadn't done much for her old dogs this morning.

It was obviously out of the question to expect the three of them to spend any time together as friends, at least not unless she set down some serious ground rules first. She smiled to herself, thinking the old her would have enjoyed having two men fight over her. It didn't sit well at all with the person she was trying to be today.

Angelique grabbed the notepad and pen from the end table and added coffee to the ever lengthening shopping list. She got up from the sofa, groaning as her feet hit the soft carpet, and padded to her bedroom. The last thing she felt like doing was grocery shopping but she'd already put it off too long. One thing she couldn't face was waking up to a morning with no coffee.

❧

Angelique threw the vacuum sealed pound of Community dark roast in her shopping basket. She scanned her list while heading toward the dairy section for a quart of milk. Still mulling over the events of the night before, she turned the corner at the end of the aisle and collided her basket into another shopper's.

"Oh, I'm so sorry!"

"Excuse me. Angelique?"

She glanced into the familiar face. "Hey Tanner, I was totally distracted and not paying attention."

"I'm sure all of my eggs are intact." He flashed his brilliant smile. "It was worth it to run into someone as lovely as you."

Angelique looked down at her faded jeans, brown leather slides, and basic long-sleeved pull over. She self-consciously put a hand up to her hair before remembering she wasn't trying to impress anyone.

"How do you like my new look? I'm thinking of starting my own line: faded clothing, scuffed shoes, ponytail holders, and make up that replicates that just crawled out of bed look."

❧

Tanner scanned the lovely, smiling face and sensed something he hadn't felt in years. A true fondness for another human being. A woman at that. One with whom he could let down his guard and treat as a friend. All without the mind numbing effort of trying to get her into bed to get in the way. "Angelique, you are truly lovely just as you are." He stood back and shifted his feet to relax. "Besides, somebody already beat you to it. That's called the 'celebrity incognito' line of fashion and they accessorize with thousand dollar sunglasses that cover half their face." His heart warmed at the sound of her soft but sincere laughter. "So, what are you up to today?"

She leaned on the shopping cart handle. "After this, going home to rest my tired dogs from last night's dancing."

Tanner put a hand dramatically to his chest as though to pull out a make believe dagger. "You went out and didn't call me? I'm so hurt."

She put her head back and laughed. "I don't have your number, for one thing."

He pulled his wallet from his back pocket and removed a business card. "Here, my personal cell is on here. You have no more excuses not to call me when you need a dance partner."

She let her head drop back and shifted on her sore feet. "That's one thing I didn't lack last night. So much so, that I called it a night at ten o'clock."

He jerked his head back in surprise. "Tell me more."

She shook her head. "It's too long of a story to tell standing up, Tanner. I'll tell you over a cup of coffee and a comfy chair."

He beamed at his newest friend. "I'd love that. Where to?"

"My place is just around the corner. Let's finish our shopping and you can follow me home."

Thirty minutes later, Tanner was helping her put groceries away while the smell of freshly brewing coffee permeated the air.

"So, start talking," he said, as he placed a quart of milk in her side by side refrigerator.

Angelique placed the last of her canned goods in the small pantry of her apartment and pulled two mugs from the cabinet. "I have two guys fighting over me," she said, exhaling loudly.

"Yet, you're complaining."

"Truthfully, not so long ago I would have been thrilled."

She lifted the carafe and filled the cups with the dark, aromatic coffee, placing one at each end of the table. "Sit," she told Tanner, as she took the chair across from him.

He took a sip and nodded in appreciation. "Now, fill me in." Within minutes, he'd heard all about her situation with Mike Harper and the recently returned Liam Nash.

Tanner leaned back in his chair and crossed his arms. "You've got yourself a genuine lover's triangle there, little lady." He placed his forefinger on his lip in concentration. "Since you like them both, maybe you should turn to the three P's to break the tie."

She raised an eyebrow, obviously clueless as to what he meant, and he grinned at her.

"An old friend of mine used this method to thin down the considerable herd she always had sniffing around her. Prowess, as in sexual, Personality, and Personal Assets. Which one's better in bed, which one do you prefer to spend time with, which one is worth more financially," he explained.

Angelique shook her head in a show of frustration. "It's not that simple, Tanner."

"Sure it is, Ang . . . And don't try to tell me that all women don't think about those things." He suddenly remembered Tiffany. "Well, nearly all women, anyway."

She took a sip of her coffee, seeming to think about it for several seconds. "They both have great personalities, both have backgrounds in law enforcement, both well educated, and intelligent. God knows they're both easy on the eyes. As far as their worth, I have no earthly idea. Not that it matters to me, anyway."

"Money may not be able to make you truly happy, but it sure can make things a hell of a lot easier. Don't think of it as money, think of it as security. Which one has the steadiest income? Which one could more easily put a child through college, or enable the two of you to travel?"

She raised her hands. "Look, they both seem to do well enough in my opinion. Besides, I didn't come from money like you did and their net worth isn't important to me."

"Well," he drawled, "How are they in bed? And if you tell me it isn't important I'll know I've just wasted half my life perfecting my technique."

"You didn't," she laughed. "It's very important, but I've only been intimate with one of them, and he's—extremely accomplished," she said, trying to choose her words carefully.

He grinned. "As in equipment or technique?"

She turned her face away. "I am not having this discussion with you."

"Hey, Ang, I'm only trying to help you narrow it down. Now, is he packing or is he simply adequate, but talented in all other ways?"

She gaped at him. "Oh my God, doesn't it bother you to talk about something like this?"

He shrugged nonchalantly before answering. "Why should it? I'm not in the running. Even if I was, I'd be able to hang with the competition, if you know what I mean."

She snorted in disgust and put her hand up in front of her face. "Come on, Tanner. I didn't need to hear that, and you know it. You just felt the need to brag."

"And why not? It's taken me years to build up to my level of expertise in pleasing the ladies, and if I do say so myself, I'm well gifted. I know you girls talk amongst yourselves. I might need you to pass that information on to someone else one day."

Angelique chuckled softly. "To pass it along, it would have to be on the merits of personal experience rather than hearsay, especially coming from you."

He put his coffee cup down abruptly. "What the hell does that mean?"

She smiled sweetly at him. "It means that sometimes guys think they're doing better than they actually are." She batted her eyelashes.

"Oh, hell no! Trust me, there are no scenarios from When Harry Met Sally going on in my bedroom."

"So, you say, but have you actually seen that movie?"

He nodded. "I'm positive; and yes, Tiffany forced me to sit through it with her after I put it in her stocking for Christmas one year. She requested it," he threw in, at the amused expression she passed him.

Angelique raised an eyebrow. "She forced you to sit through it? Maybe there was a reason why."

"You're so off-track."

"If you say so," she said, smugly.

He gave her a wink. "Now, see, if you'd given me a chance to prove it to you the first night we'd met, we wouldn't be having this conversation."

She laughed loudly. "If I'd done that, you'd be nowhere around and you know it."

"That's not true. I have plenty of repeat performances."

She nodded. "Yeah, Tiffany told me all about your repeat performances with other women."

"When did she do that?"

"When I called her yesterday to tell her I'd met you in person."

"Did she tell you I was good in bed?" he asked, hoping to get verification of his own high opinion of himself.

"Do you honestly care what she thought?" Her face registered slight surprise.

"Of course I care. Feedback is always good."

"Even if it's negative feedback?"

Judging by her sudden outburst of laughter, his expression must have shown his horror at her answer.

"Relax, Tanner. We didn't discuss your abilities. I am a little surprised that the great Tanner Collins has his own insecurities, though."

He wiped a hand over his face. "It's a guy thing, okay? You didn't have to do that."

She giggled. "I know, but it was fun to catch your vulnerable side. Besides, if you want to hang with me, you'll have to loosen up some."

He shook his head, finally able to join in her laughter. "You can be pretty fun to be around when you're not being a pain in the ass. I think I could get used to having you as a friend."

CHAPTER 5

It was Wednesday before she saw either of her suitors again. She got home at six forty-five after running errands and checked the message on her voicemail.

"Angel, it's Nash. I thought I'd take you to supper tonight. I'll be there a little before seven to pick you up unless you call to let me know you can't make it."

She checked her watch, accepting that it had to be better than the frozen pizza she would have eaten tonight.

She had just enough time to hang up her dry cleaning and place the various items she'd purchased throughout her house, before the doorbell rang. She pulled out her compact and dabbed quickly at the shine on her face and nose then snapped it shut and threw it back into her purse.

The smell of roses reached her as soon as she opened the door. Liam stood in her doorway, looking so damn sexy in his black jeans, crisp white shirt, and dark gray blazer with the same color Tony Lamas.

He brought his hands out from behind his back, revealing an arrangement of fragrant red roses, mixed with baby's breath and greenery in a gorgeous hand blown vase.

Angelique smiled and shook her head. "They're beautiful, but you didn't have to do that, you know."

He shrugged and gave her a crooked grin. "I know, but I wanted to. I hope you're hungry for seafood; I have a table reserved at that new restaurant on the lakefront."

"You got reservations to Chez du Lac? It just opened up two weeks ago, and it's nearly impossible to get in right now."

Liam's eyes sparkled with amusement. "That's what happens when you have connections. We have one of the best tables in the house. Speaking of which, are you ready to go?"

She looked down at her tailored suit and sensible pumps. "Do I have time for a quick change of clothes?"

"You're beautiful just like that," he said, giving her outfit serious appraisal.

"Thanks, but I really don't want to wear this to a four star restaurant," she explained.

He looked at his watch. "Can you do it in ten minutes?"

She gave him a nod on her way toward her bedroom. "I can do it in five."

He nodded. "Don't forget your coat. That front will have moved in by the time we leave there."

∾⌣∾

Twenty minutes later, they were seated at their table in front of large windows that made the most of the panoramic view of Lake Coburn.

"This place has great ambiance as well as an excellent view." She stared out at the water.

Liam seated himself across from her and studied her profile. "Yeah, I'm enjoying the view right now."

She met his gaze and sighed. "Please don't look at me like that. I told you I couldn't promise you anything more than friendship right now."

He nodded. "So you did."

A young woman walked up to their table with crystal goblets of water and two menus. She lit the votive inside a delicately cut crystal holder situated at the center of the table, and asked if they'd like a drink.

"What do you say, Angel? White wine?" She nodded and he ordered for them both before sipping from his water before speaking again. "I meant what I said earlier, I won't pressure you. I'm fully prepared to treat you as a close friend. It's been a whole year for you, and I can appreciate how you must be feeling."

She cocked her head to the side. "And how long has it been for you?"

He watched as the fractured candlelight danced, casting flickering shadows over her face and bare neckline. "Not as long as you," he replied, noncommittally, as she shook her head.

"Men . . . " She let the comment trail off.

"Dogs. Each and every one of us, right?" he asked, determined to let her think what she wanted before turning his gaze to the lake view. Just since their arrival, the icy winds had picked up, now thrashing frigid waves over the top of the bulkhead. Due to the elevation of the property, the water receded as quickly as it appeared. Neither the restaurant nor the parking area, were within reach of the icy waves of Lake Coburn.

"Maybe not all of you," she murmured quietly.

Nash kept his silence, thinking he'd give his left nut to know if she was thinking of him or Mike at that moment. She didn't need to know that, apart from a one night stand a week after he'd left her, he'd been without it as long as she had. The interlude had occurred during a particularly heavy night of drinking whiskey. He couldn't deny that he'd enjoyed it at the time, dog that he was. But he could testify to how low he'd felt after waking up with a woman whose name he didn't know, and didn't care to know. He'd made it a point to stay out of the bars from that night on, preferring to spend his nights at home, alone, or with friends, old co-workers, and clients when they extended invitations.

She interrupted his thoughts with her next query. "Have you worked any interesting cases this past year?"

He waited until their wine was poured before answering. "Most of the stints were just a week or two. Inexperienced types stalking little rich girls who wouldn't give them the time of day, or who didn't return their feelings of undying love. Hell, one of the stalkers turned out to be a woman's old college roommate. Another woman."

Angelique looked up from her menu, in surprise. "Really? Did she threaten her?"

Nash raised an eyebrow in amusement. "She was quite creative, actually. Bordering on psychotic, I guess you could say. She had that poor vic terrified to leave her home until I got there."

"Did you know you were looking for a woman?"

Nash shook his head. "Not for the first few days. Then she let something slip; a comment in a note that tipped me off. Once I figured that out, all the pieces fell into place."

"I'm curious. What did she say to tip you off?"

Nash sucked in his breath through his teeth. "I'm not saying. You're bound to use it against me."

"I won't," she drawled, focusing her feminine gaze on him.

He snorted, narrowing his eyes suspiciously. "The hell you won't, but I'll go against my better judgment and tell you, just so you'll know how sincere my intentions are toward you." He took a sip of wine and put his menu aside, after deciding what he wanted to order. "It was something to the effect of her admitting to having the temperament of a pit bull with a toothache."

Angelique let her mouth fall open in shock. "That statement made you think it was a woman?"

He took another sip of wine. "This is an excellent wine, don't you think?"

"Nash," she drawled, still waiting for an answer.

He grinned at her. "Well, she actually added the words 'this month'. I put two and two together and came up with PMS or PMDD or whatever the hell new name doctors have come up to describe man's worst nightmare."

Angelique's eyes sparkled with laughter even as she admonished him. "That's a hell of a sexist remark if I ever heard one."

"It's not sexism talking, it's experience. I was married for over two years to one of the sweetest, best natured women I've ever had the privilege to know. But every month, for two or three days, I avoided Kimberly like she had a head full of poisonous snakes for hair. What was that mythical chick called?"

Angelique did her best not to crack a smile. "That 'chick' was a gorgon, and her name was Medusa."

He gave an enthusiastic nod. "That's it! Medusa! I swear to God, one look from Kim when she was pre-menstrual could turn a mere mortal man to stone."

Angelique laughed, in spite of herself, thinking how relieved he must be to be able to speak of things like this and laugh about them. "Honestly! You should be ashamed of yourse—" She stopped, realizing what she'd nearly said, and blushed with her own shame. "I'm so sorry! I didn't mean that the way it sounded."

Nash smiled and reached out a hand to cover hers. "It's fine, Angel. It was actually Kim who started calling it the 'Snake Lady Syndrome'. She'd actually warn me to stay out of the house when she'd feel it coming on. Of course, when I did, she'd get pissed and give me the third degree about where I'd been, and we'd get into a huge argument." He looked down at his menu, keeping his next thought to himself about the outstanding make up sex they'd have after the smoke cleared.

∾

Angelique smiled wistfully at the man she'd once fantasized about marrying. Here she was, one year later, just hearing about a part of his life she hadn't known existed.

She looked down at the menu as their waitress came back to see if they were ready to order. "I think I'll have the broiled snapper with lemon butter sauce, along with a small spinach salad. House dressing on the side, please."

Nash handed his menu to the woman. "I'll have the twenty four ounce Porter House, medium rare, the steamed asparagus, and a side dish of baby carrots."

Angelique watched the other woman's eyes scan discretely over Liam's face and upper torso in silent appreciation.

The woman reached for Angelique's menu, gave her a barely perceptible nod, and smiled as she spoke. "Enjoy your view."

Angelique returned the smile. "Thank you, I will." As the woman left, she looked over at Liam to see him watching her quizzically.

"What the hell was that?"

She gave a throaty chuckle. "It was about you. She was congratulating me on my 'catch', in a sense."

Nash emitted a sudden laugh. "You've got one hell of an imagination."

She dipped her fingertip in her wine and circled it along the rim of the wine glass. Her wine glass emitted a crystal clear ringing with every revolution of her finger. "Sometimes it's the subtle messages that come across the loudest, Liam. You just have to be in sync with them. Women are better at subtlety than men, obviously."

He watched her finger, thinking how it would feel to have her touch him like that again. "You play that thing like a pro, hon." He finished his wine in one swallow and looked up to meet their waiter's gaze. He lifted his glass an inch and gave a slight nod of his head. Within moments, the man had refilled his wineglass.

Nash met Angelique's amused expression. "You see? Guys can do that, too. But only when it involves alcohol, food, or the check," he added.

She smiled, then sat back in her chair and crossed her long legs. "Where are you staying?"

"Annie and Drake asked me to stay with them in their new place. Have you seen it yet?"

Angelique sipped at her wine then nodded. "I went to the house warming party her family threw for them and got the tour. It's a beautiful home. Annie's due next month, isn't she?"

"Sometime around the end of March," he agreed. "They're putting the finishing touches on their nursery to get ready."

She watched the smile come over his face as he spoke. "Is it difficult for you? Seeing that, I mean?"

He blinked and picked up his wine glass. "Not anymore, Angel. I can remember now, without feeling sad about it." He raised his glass. "Life goes on, you know?"

She nodded and smiled. "They still don't know what they're having, do they?"

"Nope; she insists on them being surprised. Annie told me that Red and Tiffany have a new baby at home."

"They sure do; a beautiful little girl, named Briana. She's almost five months. I take it you haven't seen her."

"No, but I was hoping to sometime soon. I'm not sure how to get to their place, though." He turned his hound dog expression on her. "Maybe you could come along with me."

She sipped her wine, her green eyes twinkling mischievously up at him from above the rim of her crystal glass. "Or I could just give you good directions."

∽∾

An hour and a half later, Angelique let Liam walk her to the door of her apartment and thanked him for the wonderful meal.

He stood fidgeting, tracing the brim of his gray Stetson. Clearing his throat once for good measure, he leaned toward her, hoping to get at least a good night kiss out of the evening. He groaned, when she turned her face at the last second so that his lips brushed the corner of her mouth.

She laughed as his chin dropped dejectedly onto his chest. "I guess you were expecting a little more bang for your buck, huh?"

He met her gaze with his own. "Maybe…just a little."

Angelique gave him a wicked grin. "Sorry, Mr. Nash; if you're looking for a value meal, next time go to Mickey D's." She closed the door softly on him as he struggled for a comeback.

CHAPTER 6

Mike crossed the threshold into the cramped apartment, his gut tightening at the sights and sounds greeting him. Three EMT's worked diligently on two screaming infants as a fourth tried unsuccessfully to coerce a severely beaten woman onto a gurney of her own.

"Please, are they going to be all right?" She pleaded with the medics, pushing away one more set of hands trying to get her to lie down.

"Yes ma'am, your babies are fine—" the older male emergency tech insisted, "—but you need to lie down so I can take care of you now."

"Sarah?" Mike asked at the sudden shock of recognition. "Sarah Richard?"

The woman whipped her head around, locking her wildly panicked gaze onto his.

After twenty years in law enforcement, not many things shocked Mike, but the sight of the woman's battered and bruised face was enough to cause a hitch in his breath.

The last time he'd seen this woman was the hit and run incident with the spoiled rich kid. The cracked ribs and facial scratches she'd sustained in that accident were nothing compared to the injuries she had now. "Can you tell me what happened to you, Mrs. Richard?"

"Don't!" she screeched. "Don't ever call me that again! Sarah—I'm Sarah!" Her tone defiant.

"Sarah…" Mike tried to soothe her with the sound of his voice. "Absolutely. Who did this to you, Sarah?"

Her blackened eyes narrowed, then grew angrier as she seemed to come to a personal revelation.

"You did."

His hand froze on his pocket as he reached for a notepad and pen. "Excuse me?" Several other heads ratcheted in their direction.

"Troy Richard—my husband—he did the physical damage. But your department led him straight to me and my babies."

"Wh...What do you mean?" He couldn't ignore the gnawing pain developing deep in his gut.

Sarah shook off the tech's helping hand as she hobbled closer to Mike. "Two months, Detective Harper. Yeah, I remember you, also. Two months I was able to hide from that monster, until someone from your department notified him because his name was on the registration of the car. The car I paid for with money my dad left me. Was it you?" she demanded.

Mike took a deep breath before tackling the subject. "Honestly, I didn't make the call, but I'm sure I ordered someone to do it. It's stand..."

"Standard procedure!" she spat. "I'm fully aware of the police department and its standard procedures. They've allowed Troy to walk free, while my babies and I have to hide like criminals in the local women's shelter, depending on everyone else to keep us safe, warm, and fed. I can't even work to earn a living because of him."

Mike felt himself nodding, sick that he and the department had played any part in her misery, while simultaneously enraged at the man who'd done this. "Can you tell me what happened since the hit and run accident, Sarah?"

"They called him," she said. "And he showed up at the hospital just in time to bring us here. Then he left us, but not before doing his best to teach me a lesson. It was all for my own good, though. And he did show some mercy," she sneered. "When I told him I thought my ribs were cracked on one side, he kicked me on the opposite side." She grabbed her ribs and leaned forward. "So he wouldn't break them. God forbid I should die when he gets so much satisfaction out of making my life a living hell."

She straightened and lifted one arm slowly to encompass the apartment's tiny bedroom and bathroom. "So this was our home for four days—or was it five? I lost count at some point. Nice view, huh?" She pointed to the window, boarded up from the outside. "It came with a matching door."

Mike turned, seeing the boards and framing nails that had been painstakingly removed from the bedroom door by someone. "Who got you out?"

"Concerned neighbors called the landlord when the babies wouldn't stop crying." She dropped her eyes to the floor. "I ran out of milk."

"Canned formula?" He jotted down some notes on his pad.

"No, I was breasting feeding them, and I-I quit producing."

Mike took in her gaunt appearance and already tiny frame then looked around the room. No signs of any kind of food wrappers, containers, or waste.

"He locked you up in here with no food?"

She shrugged, wincing at the apparent pain it caused. "At least I had water."

∽◡∾

Mike pulled up the number and hit the call button, eagerly anticipating the dulcet tones of Angelique's voice. He wasn't disappointed.

"Hey Mike."

He smiled at the immediate easing of the tension in his shoulders as he took a deep breath to answer. "Hey Angel. How was your day?"

"I had a good day. Et vous? And you?"

"It was—okay," he said, unwilling to talk about what he'd seen. "Tell me about your day, instead." He heard a pause in her voice, and for a moment he expected her to insist on hearing about it, when he only wanted to put it out of his mind for a bit.

"My boss told me about an opening at another office he thought I might be interested in," she said.

"In a different hospital? Your job's not in danger, is it?"

"No, it's nothing like that. I'm not actually employed by the hospital, but by Dr. Maze. He has an office at Memorial and another one in Lafayette at General. He's losing his Office Manager in Lafayette and wondered if I was interested in the position."

Mike clenched his fist in jubilation, barely able to contain his whoop of excitement. "Are you going to take it?" He heard the tell-tale click of her fingernails on the casing of her phone, a sure sign she was struggling with an answer.

"I don't know yet. The OM over there wants to stay home after she has her baby, but she's not due for another two months. She's planning on working up until she delivers—."

"So in two months you could be back here," he interjected, about to explode with joy at the idea.

"Well, if I decide to take the job—I guess I could be. I'll have to think about it, though."

He stood so he could pace the length of his living room. "I thought because of your folks, you know, you'd welcome the chance to be back on this end."

"Well sure, but I just got moved in here. I've signed a lease agreement and I'd lose my deposits if I broke it. I can't afford to pay rent in two cities, and I sure don't want to make that drive every day."

"I could help you out." He prayed she wouldn't refuse him this time. "It'd be a loan, of course, because I know you wouldn't take it as a gift, but I could lend it to you with no interest and no pressure. I'd trust you to pay it back whenever you could."

Her breath released in an exaggerated huff. "Believe me, I appreciate the offer, but I couldn't do that. Besides I don't have to decide for another month or so. If I transfer, I'd have to train someone to take over here at the Lake Coburn office." She stretched out on her comforter and stifled a yawn. "Now tell me about your day."

He pressed his lips together, keeping his silence.

"Are you still there?"

Mike cleared his throat before changing the subject again. "Hey, where'd you go this afternoon, anyway? I called you two hours earlier and you weren't home." He heard the distinct pause before she answered, a sure sign she wasn't fooled by his attempt at diversion.

"I went to dinner with a friend."

"Good, I'm glad you got out of the house. Did you go with anyone I know?"

"Liam Nash took me to dinner. It was kind of last minute."

Mike groaned inwardly but kept his voice even. "Oh, the competition."

"He's not your competition. He's my friend—just as you are," she said.

Mike released a low-volume, but lengthy string of curses, making her laugh.

"Enough hedging, Detective Harper. Tell me what happened today. You'll feel better once you do."

Mike scraped a hand over his two day growth of stubble along his jaw. The sudden recall of the day's images, as well as a particular conversation, sickened him, but he knew she was determined to hear everything.

"Do you remember the hit and run I told you about?"

"The young mother and her twin babies?"

"Yeah, it turned out she'd been staying in a woman's shelter to keep away from her estranged husband. He's a real prize—likes to throw his wife around for shits and giggles. Oh. Sorry, Angel. I forget I'm not talking to one of the guys."

"It's okay," Angelique said. "Keep talking."

Mike related the story—down to every heart-wrenching detail. "We need to catch this guy then keep him away from her and her children."

"Jesus, Mike. She must have been in agony the entire time, and trying to keep her babies fed . . . " Angelique's tortured whisper trailed off. "But, if the neighbors heard the babies crying, it seems like she would have been able to call for help, or bang on the wall or something."

"She was too afraid. The last thing he told her before he left was that his neighbors were drug dealers and pedophiles. She said she knew there was a possibility he was lying, but felt she couldn't take that chance."

"Oh, holy mother," Angelique said. "She would have been far too terrified to call for help. Was he telling the truth about the neighbors?"

"I questioned two spinster school teachers, both retired, in the apartment on one side of her, and two gay men sharing the one on the other side."

"Cochon Pig!" she seethed. "So how close are you to catching him?"

"He went to work on a land drilling rig right after he locked her up. We called the Sheriff's Department from Vermilion Parish to pick him up. By the time they got there he was off-rig. They said he'd gone into the nearest town for cigarettes, but he never came back. They think one of his co-workers gave him the heads up because no one could find him in town afterwards."

"So he's out there somewhere and waiting to get to her. Is she still in the hospital?"

"For now she is, and there's a security guard posted at her door. The hospital is allowing the babies to stay in the nursery they have set up for children of the employees." Mike sighed. "You know, Angel, abuse is never good, and I see all kinds of people with piss poor parenting skills in my business. It burns my ass when I see someone who's obviously trying her damnedest to be a good mother getting abused like this." He cursed under his breath before continuing. "It chaps my ass that I played a part in helping him find her."

"You couldn't have known if she didn't tell you," she said. "Is it okay if I ask her name?"

He knew she was right, but it didn't dispel his feelings of guilt. "Her name is Sarah. Sarah Richard. Spelled like the man's name, but pronounced Ree-shard. I don't know how much longer she'll be using it though. She makes us call her Sarah, just Sarah. Like she doesn't want to be tainted by any part of him, even his last name."

"That could be a challenge when she has two constant reminders in her twin girls."

"I hadn't thought about that, but I'm sure you're right." He released an exhausted sigh. "I should let you get to bed before I bring you down, too."

"You're not bringing me down, but I know something that'll cheer you up. My mom is definitely baking fig tarts tomorrow."

Mike smiled in spite of the cloud of despair that hovered over him. "No kidding. I think it's time I paid a visit to your folks."

CHAPTER 7

Mike pulled his truck onto the concrete drive of a small, but neatly-kept, brick home on St. Louis Avenue. Marceline Baptiste greeted him at the kitchen door, the one reserved for close friends and relatives. The spry seventy-two year old beamed up at him as the wonderful aroma of baked goods and coffee wafted through the opening.

"*Bonjour*, Michael! I had a feeling I'd be seeing you. It's something, how you always manage to show up when I'm baking tarts."

Mike folded his tall frame in order to embrace the petite, but plump woman. He straightened, passing a hand over his flat belly as he smiled into eyes the same shade of green as Angelique's. "It doesn't hurt to have an inside informant." The woman's deep rich laughter put him immediately at ease.

"It also doesn't hurt that I ask her to let you know," she said, plating several of the half circle shaped pastries and placing it on one end of her antique kitchen table. "*Sit tois*."

Mike obeyed, seating himself and within seconds, was savoring a delicious mouthful of spicy sweet dough oozing with delectably sticky fig preserves. "Oh God, manna from heaven." He planted a kiss on the woman's cheek, then settled down with a tart in one hand and a steaming mug of coffee in the other. "I've been dreaming about this all day long."

Angelique's mother was a retired librarian and an avid gardener. The latter revealed itself in the abundance of color in her pampered front yard, even at the end of winter—as well as the nimbleness of her movements around the small, neat kitchen. Her still smooth skin was the color of rich coffee laced with a generous portion of cream, a testimony to her Creole bloodline.

Mike craned his neck to see through the door into the living room. "Is Mr. Rene here?"

A tall, thin man with dark hair, liberally peppered with silver, spoke from the hallway. "*Ici, Monsieur Harper!*"

Mike gave the man a broad smile, extending his arm to shake the big man's hand. "Mr. Rene. It's good to see you."

"*Comment to ye*, Mike?"

"I'm good . . . *C'est bon, merci.*" Mike squinted and scratched is head. "Did I say it right?"

The seventy-six year old man flashed him a brilliant smile, his hazel eyes glinting with approval. "That is correct. *Ca c'est bon.* It's good. Somebody's been practicing."

Mike winced. "No sir. To tell you the truth, I don't have anyone else to practice with anymore. The one guy at the office that spoke French retired a few months ago and Angelique moved, so . . . " He put up his hands in a show of helplessness.

"Ah, *merde.* You'll just have to come visit us more often," Rene commented.

"*Merde?* I'm not sure I know that word," Mike said.

"That's because it's foul and he knows I don't like that kind of language." Marceline shook her finger at her husband, "And for sure not in my kitchen, old man."

Rene winked at Mike as he mouthed the word shit to him. The big man leaned over to wrap his arms around his wife from behind and planted a big kiss on her cheek. "It won't happen again, *mon coeur.*"

"It won't if you know what's good for you," she said. "Sit, old man. You take up too much room in my kitchen." Marceline commanded, as she bustled around, getting two more mugs from the cabinet for her and her husband.

"So, what's going on with you and my daughter?" she asked. "Has she agreed to marry you, yet?"

He smothered a laugh at her bluntness. "No ma'am, but she knows I'm ready to throw my hat in the ring as soon as she's ready."

"*Bon. Bon.* She is *tete dure*-stubborn, my Angel. Just like her *pere.*" She smiled at her husband.

Rene grunted and gave Mike a wink. "Her *mere* is the stubborn one. Don't let this *vieille femme* fool you."

Marceline placed her hands on her formidable hips. "*Vieux verrat! Bouche ta gueule* or I'll send every last fig tart in this kitchen off with this gentleman, here. No sense wasting my good baking on someone who doesn't appreciate me."

Mike cleared his throat and decided to intervene. "Okay, you two, let me see if I got all of that. You," he said, pointing to Rene, "called her an old lady, and you," he said, pointing to Marceline, "called him an old boar and told him to shut his mouth, right?"

The couple stopped their good natured name calling long enough to beam up at him in approval.

"*Bien bon*—very good, *Monsieur* Harper," Marceline gushed.

"*Merci beaucoup*—thank you very much, ma'am," Mike replied.

Rene slapped him on the back and laughed. "You must be practicing somewhere."

Mike shook his head. "I have an excellent memory. Now you two quit the name calling long enough to sit and visit with me. Besides, it's useless . . . ah . . . *inutile* . . . because I know the two of you are crazy in love." He grinned as the couple exchange affectionate glances. "I bet as soon as I walk out that door, you'll be all over each other."

Rene chuckled and sidled up next to his wife. "Only if she lets me, eh Marceline?" He pulled his wife close and nuzzled her neck.

"*Arret ca*. Stop that." She pushed him away, but couldn't stop the blush that crept over her face. She gave in, giggled like a school girl then shook her head at her husband of fifty-three years. "Can't you behave yourself even when we have company?"

Mike swallowed a mouthful of pastry. "Ms. Marceline, just be thankful he's not aiming that charm at all the other ladies in the neighborhood."

Rene winked and wiggled his eyebrows at her. "That's right. You could be married to a 'Creole Casanova'. You'd better be thankful I'm a one woman man."

The old woman snorted with amusement. "I think it's you who should be thankful. At our ages, a woman who's a good cook is a lot more useful than a horny old goat. Besides," she said, holding up a dangerous looking pair of kitchen shears, "I keep these sharp. After I'd finish with you, you wouldn't be much use to anyone, including me."

Mike exploded with laughter as the couple joined in.

After two cups of coffee and three more fig tarts, he sat back and rubbed his belly in satisfaction.

"Ms. Marceline, nobody makes fig tarts like you," he told her.

"Oh, *mais no*." She waved off the compliment. "That recipe came from my grandmother, cher. Everyone in my family makes them just like that, but *merci beaucoup*, anyway. You take some with you to share with your co-workers at the station."

"That'd make their day, ma'am. The last time I brought some of your tarts to the office I had to distribute them to keep some of those guys from hogging them all. When it came down to the last one, the captain pulled rank and claimed it."

Marceline chuckled and got up to wipe down her spotless countertop. "So." She glanced back at Mike. "Angel told me you're acquainted with Liam Nash." She passed a warning glance at her husband, who'd grunted his disapproval at the mention of Liam.

"Yes ma'am, I've known Nash for fifteen years. He's a good man." He played with his coffee mug, sliding it back and forth in his hands. "It looks like I've got my work cut out for me. He wants her back."

"He left her once, he'd do it again," Rene said, the disdain for the man clearly apparent.

"Rene, *fais pas ca*," his wife fussed. "It's not our concern. Besides, there was more going on than we knew about at the time."

Mike nodded. "Nash had a bad time of it and had to get himself straightened out, but he seems okay now. I really believe he'd be a good husband for your daughter."

The two older people turned to him in shock. "You do?" Marceline asked.

He nodded again. "Sure, I do. Liam's a good man." He gave her a wink and a devilish grin. "But I'd be better."

~~

During that night's phone conversation with Angelique, Mike told her about the visit with her parents. He chuckled as she burst into laughter.

"What was she calling him today? An old goat or an old boar hog?"

"Both, I think, but it's easy to see she dotes on him."

"She spoils him rotten, and he does the same to her," Angelique snorted. "They're still crazy about each other even after fifty something years of marriage."

"That's what I want, Angel," Mike said. "I admit I could do without the name calling. It seems like a waste of time to me, when they could be doing something better."

"Like what? They're just bored and too old to do anything else, for God's sake."

"They're not dead, Angel. I'm sure they still get a little action every now and then."

"Ew. Uh uh! Don't you dare make me think of them doing— of having—ugh!"

"Hey, I've been told that old people do it too, just not as often, and with a lot more creativity."

"Stop," she pleaded. "I don't want to hear that."

He laughed and offered to change the subject. "What did you do today?"

"We had one patient finish her radiation therapy and two more begin theirs. And another . . . "

"What happened, babe?"

"You know, they're catching so many cancers at earlier stages these days, and saving so many lives. But every once in a while we have someone who ignores the symptoms until it's too late to save them."

Mike was quiet for a moment as he pictured her, agonizing over the loss of a patient. He knew that she went out of her way to get close to 'her people' as she called the patients who received treatment at their facility. "Did you lose someone?" Her quiet sniffling told him that if she hadn't, she would soon. "You'll feel better if you get it off your chest."

"Ms. Laura's daughter called to tell us she's not doing well."

"Is she in the hospital?" He wished he could be there to hold her while she cried at the hopeless situation.

"Not yet, but she's at home, and Hospice is there every day to make sure she's kept comfortable until—until it's over." She finished in a whisper.

Mike pushed a hand through his hair, still damp from his shower. "I'm sorry, babe. She's the one that brought cookies and sent flowers to the office, right?"

Angelique sniffed loudly. "That's her. I need to go, Mike."

"I know, but I hate the thought of you being miserable over there all by yourself. I can be there in under an hour if you let me." He held his breath, hoping she'd agree.

"It's tempting, but I can't let you do that."

Ten minutes later he stared at the phone once they'd call it a night, wondering what it was going to take to get her to choose him. He dropped his phone on his nightstand with a clatter and stretched out on the bed. He slipped his hands behind his head, both his heart and his body aching for the gentleness of her touch, her words, her mouth on his.

He looked down at his throbbing erection. "Give it a rest, would ya? You'd think you'd be used to this shit by now." As though it understood him, his painfully swollen body part jerked to nearly upright. He rolled out of bed with a groan, hoping a cold shower would give him some relief.

CHAPTER 8

Friday afternoon, Angelique kicked off her shoes at the front door and dropped onto her comfy couch. She and the rest of Dr. Maze's staff had been informed first thing this morning that Ms. Laura had passed on during the night. They could only afford to mourn a few moments before their first patient of the day came in for his treatment. Depressed and exhausted from keeping her emotions in check all day, Angelique was feeling both physically and mentally drained.

She crossed her feet at the ankles and placed her forearm over her closed eyes, wanting to block out the rest of the world for a while. After a good ten minutes of sulking in silence, she was forced to answer her chirping Blackberry. She rolled over and felt around for her purse until she pulled it out of the side compartment to answer it.

"Angelique, it's Tiffany. I was at the hospital last night when they brought Mrs. Laura Guilbeaux in. Are you okay? I know how you can't help but get close to some patients."

Angelique raised herself into a seating position. "Hey, Tiff. It's sweet of you to call. I'm feeling the loss, that's for sure. She was—she was special."

"I know she was, hon. Why don't you come on over here for supper? You haven't been since you came to see Briana just after she was born."

Angelique wiped a tear from the corner of her eye. "I think I'd really like that, as long as you don't go to any trouble for me. You've got your hands full with work and that baby girl."

"It's no trouble. Red's grilling some steaks. He asked if you still liked yours burnt," Tiffany said.

Angelique stood up and gave a snort. "I like them medium-well, and he damn well knows it. Just because he likes his bloody doesn't mean the rest of us are crazy." She heard Tiffany's laughter as she relayed the message to Red. "What did he say?"

"You don't want to know. We'll eat around six, but come over now so we can visit."

"Tell your barbarian husband I'm bringing wine and fig tarts, but if gives me any more flack over my steak, I won't share."

∼⌣

"Oh, give!" Angelique pleaded, as she placed the bag of goodies and wine on Tiffany's table to reach for baby Briana.

"Not yet, Aunt Angel—If I don't nurse this child right now, one, or both of us is going to explode. Neither will be pleasant, trust me. Will you be uncomfortable if I nurse her here?"

"Of course not," Angel said, cooing to the fussy baby.

Briana's first angry squall was cut short as she latched on greedily to her mother's breast.

The nursing mother dropped her head back on the sofa and sighed with immediate relief. "It was time—for both of us."

Angelique watched the scene enviously. "What's it like, Tiff?"

Tiffany gazed up at her through narrowed lids. "Painful, I have so much more empathy for dairy cattle. Throw our schedule off the slightest little bit and I'm leaking all over the place." She looked down at her daughter who was staring up at her with big brown eyes. "Then daddy has to put up with two cranky girls, doesn't he, Bree?"

Baby Briana smiled at the sound of her mother's voice, exhibiting two deep-set dimples in her rosy cheeks. When she discovered that the act of smiling interrupted her supper, she quickly got back to her former activity.

Angelique smiled at her friend. "I meant having a baby in the house. I still can't believe you and Red are parents."

Tiffany smiled as her daughter wrapped the fingers of one tiny hand around her pinkie. "Sometimes I still can't believe it." She looked back at Angelique. "It's the most exasperating, exhausting, inspiring, wonderful thing you can ever imagine. I can't imagine how I lived so long without her in my life."

Angelique gave her a wistful smile as Red walked into the kitchen from the patio and entered the living room.

"Hey, Angel, you got quick." He wrapped her in a hug and peeked inside the bag she carried. "Is that what I think it is?"

She nodded. "Yep, Mama's fig tarts. I also brought my last bottle of wine from your cousin in Gardiner. If you two go anytime soon, could you pick up a few bottles for me?"

"We're going tomorrow. I'll give Jaimie a call and let her know we need some," he said, as he opened the bottle to let it breath. Red leaned over to kiss Tiffany then gently cupped Briana's head in the palm of his hand. "Hello gorgeous," he murmured. "You're looking more like your beautiful mother every day."

Once again, Briana broke the suction on the food source to smile up at her father, flashing her adorable twin dimples. She cooed at him and blinked her her sparkling brown eyes.

Tiffany snorted. "She's going to be rotten as long as she can flash those eyelashes at her daddy. I can see it now, you'll never be able to say no to her, Red."

He beamed down at his daughter. "Naw, you'll be here to remind me to man up. Besides, I don't want her to be one of those kids. You know, the one's that make everyone groan when they show up with their parents."

Tiffany used the distraction to switch Briana to the opposite breast. "We'll do our best, sweetie."

Red poured himself and Angelique each a glass of wine before leaving to check on the steaks. He returned quickly, saying he needed to throw another one on the grill. "Liam Nash just called to see if he could come see the baby. I asked him to join us for supper. You don't mind, do you, Angel?"

"Don't worry about me. Liam and I have an understanding."

Red and Tiffany exchanged glances before Tiffany lowered her head to tend to the baby.

Angelique noticed the look passing between them. "What?"

Red's smug answer of "Nothing," didn't satisfy her curiosity.

"Come on, what's going on?" she begged.

"Well, since you're asking—"

"Red McAllister, don't you say a word," Tiffany warned. "You are to keep your nose out of this, do you hear me?"

"But if she asks—"

"Angel's a grown woman, and can make up her own mind. She doesn't need you clouding her judgment."

. "This must have to do with Mike and Liam. They both know I'm not ready for anything besides friendship, so don't worry."

Liam arrived ten minutes later, looking somewhat surprised to find Angelique there also. He gave her a huge smile before addressing her. "I didn't expect to find you here. That's why you didn't answer your home phone."

"I didn't hear my cell ring. Did you need something?"

He shook his head and gave her a crooked grin. "I didn't call your cell. I just wanted directions here or try to get you to come with me. So, I'm good."

She smiled, soaking in his appearance. Good fitting jeans with just the right amount of fading, a soft blue chambray shirt, with brown boots. He's good, alright. She turned abruptly from him and closed her eyes. When she opened them, her gaze clashed with Tiffany's subtly amused expression.

Once Liam gave appropriate tribute to the new baby, he walked outside with Red to finish up the grilling.

Angelique settled back on the couch with Briana, who was satisfied from her meal and on the brink of falling asleep. "God, she's beautiful, Tiffany, and growing so fast."

Taking a seat on the couch next to Angelique, Tiffany smiled down at her drowsy daughter. "She is, isn't she? Next thing you know, she'll be crawling and walking."

"Are you and Red planning for more than one?"

Tiffany cocked her head to the side. "I'd like at least one more, I think. Red says it's entirely up to me, so I guess I've got a decision to make." She reached out and gently pushed back a wispy curl from her daughter's brow. "I have a husband and a beautiful, healthy, baby girl. Knowing from experience how quickly things can change, sometimes it terrifies me."

Angelique smiled as the infant emitted a sigh before surrendering to her nap. "If anyone knows how quickly things can change, it's us, huh?" She met her friend's gaze again before adding, "..and Liam Nash."

Tiffany's eyes squeezed shut. "God, I heard. I don't know how he lived through it. When he was Annie's body guard last year, nobody even had a clue of how much he'd already been through. Is he okay?"

With a shrug of her shoulders, Angelique tried to answer honestly. "He says he is . . . He seems to be."

"You know," Tiffany said, "I kind of hate to bring this up, but seeing as how you've already confided in me, I can't help myself. Considering how difficult you said it's been for you to keep your hands off Mike Harper the last few months, you must be in absolute agony with two eligible bachelors sniffing around."

An involuntary shiver passed over Angelique. "You cannot imagine, Tiff...I'm crazy about both those guys."

"So how long are you going to have to suffer through this?"

Angelique shook her head in frustration. "When I can look at one of them as a friend and the other as a partner for life, I guess I'll be able to put myself out of this misery. Until then, I owe it to all of us to be strong."

Tiffany placed a hand on her friend's shoulder. "I guess I'm not the only one with a decision to make."

∽

By nine p.m., Angelique had already had phone offers for a night of dancing from Liam and a strong shoulder to cry on from Mike, both of which she passed on. Good and relaxed after a hot shower and a glass of wine, she'd curled up on the sofa and managed to get through three chapters of a romance novel when her phone rang again.

"Hello Tanner," she said, after checking her screen.

"Hey gorgeous, I've got an offer I think you may be interested in," Tanner said, brightly.

Angelique cringed, bracing herself for another invitation to leave her comfortable nest. "What kind of offer?" she asked.

"I have to go to Houston tomorrow, and I was wondering if you wanted to tag along."

"What's in it for you?" she asked suspiciously.

"Hey, I have to go and wanted some friendly company. If you're not up to it, just say so," he said, sounding slightly disgruntled.

Realizing too late that she'd insulted him, she squeezed her eyes shut. "Sorry. I had a bad day and I'm tired, but that's no excuse to take it out on you."

After a moment of silence he cleared his throat. "All right, so what's going on?"

"Liam and Mike are both so damned available, and—" She exhaled noisily, "—and sexy as hell."

"Hold up, now," Tanner exclaimed. "Where the hell is this conversation going? I said I didn't mind being your friend. I don't remember saying anything about being your girlfriend."

Angelique threw back her head in laughter. "Oh, God, Tanner! I didn't think anyone could make me laugh today. So, tell me more about this offer."

"Here's the deal—every so often I have to go visit the parental units. When I do, I try to get in a trip to the Galleria. As much as I enjoy not having to fight the Houston traffic every day, the mall in Lake Coburn is lacking my favorite men's store and it so happens I need a new suit. So, you want to come with me, or not?" he asked.

"Ooh!" she squealed with delight. "Shopping at the Galleria with my new bud-dy!"

Tanner made a clucking noise with his tongue. "Oh God…It's a sad state of affairs when women just want me as a shopping buddy. Next thing you know Tiffany will be asking me to babysit that kid of hers."

"Oh stop it, you jerk. You know you're irresistible to women," she scoffed.

"Not all women, apparently," he snorted.

"Okay, to women who can't see right through your chauvinistic tendencies and playboy ways," she replied. "And I'm afraid we are few and far between."

Tanner grunted. "Not so few, anymore. They must be teaching a class in college these days."

"Maybe there's a blog out there on the internet warning innocent women about you," she teased.

Tanner gave a low groan. "Don't even joke about something like that. And why is that ringing a bell of familiarity?"

"It was an episode of Three and a Half Men."

"Oh yeah. Charlie was my hero before they killed him off," he said, sounding sad.

"You reap what you sow, dude."

"Well I should have a surplus of wild oats then. That's all I've sown for years," he groaned.

"Now might be a good time to think about sowing a different crop, not just switching fields."

"You know, Angel, I was perfectly happy until I called you."

Angelique rewarded him with a deep chuckle. "So, what time will you pick me up tomorrow?"

"It's a three hour drive. Is seven too early?"

"No. Hell no. Not if it'll get me to the Galleria as the doors open," she purred.

"Now why doesn't that surprise me?" he snickered. "I'll pick you up at seven, then. We'll make a day and evening of it. I'll even take you to supper at my favorite restaurant."

"Thanks, Buddy. It'll be nice to get away."

"Oh, do you mind if we swing by my parent's place first? I have to go by and sign some papers for my father. It shouldn't take long, unless my mom insists we stay for lunch."

"Either way is fine. I'd love to meet your parents."

"We'll see how you feel this time tomorrow. My parents are dry as unbuttered toast," he snorted.

"Hmm, think I'm capable of buttering them up?"

"I think if anyone can, it's you."

Angelique ended the call then sent out a single text to Mike and Liam. Hey guys...I'll be shopping with a friend all day in Houston tomorrow. Later!

CHAPTER 9

Mike nodded to the officer he was about to replace at the door of Sarah's hospital room. He wasn't supposed to work today, but he'd volunteered for this watch. With Angel spending the entire day in Houston today, he didn't have a damn thing better to do.

"Hey, Mel, anyone ask to see her?"

Officer Melanie Finley stood and stretched. "Nope," she whispered. "I checked on her fifteen minutes ago and she was still sleeping. The poor thing is as good as a girl can be after her asshole husband beats the crap out of her and locks her up to starve." She stopped suddenly and exhaled. "Sorry, Harper, but this one hits too damn close to home for me." After jabbing a finger at the closed door, Mel spoke with emotion. "That is why I became a cop."

Mike wasn't surprised, knowing she'd grown up seeing an alcoholic step-father abuse his wife on a daily basis, until the woman had finally ended it, for herself anyway, by taking a bottle of sleeping pills. "I know, Mel," he said, with a reassuring smile. "I'll make sure she stays safe. You go on home now." He watched as Mel disappeared around the corner, headed for the elevator.

Mike waited until he heard her moving around before knocking softly on the door of room 522-E. By then it was 8:00 in the morning. A soft voice told him to go in. He pushed open the door and cleared his throat softly. It's Detective Harper. I wanted you to know that I'm taking over Officer Finley's watch. I'll be here until six p.m. Can I get you anything?"

"No, I don't think so," Sarah told him through lips that were still split and bruised. "Thanks for asking though."

He frowned as he watched her clench her teeth through the pain of seating herself on the sofa near the window.

He walked over to help her. "Are you sure you wouldn't be more comfortable in bed?" he asked.

She gave him a solemn look. "Maybe, but I don't want to leave the window." She raised her face, basking in the morning sun. "I wasn't claustrophobic before but the thought of being shut in somewhere now…" She shivered before continuing. "I can't stand to see the sun go down, either."

Mike's chest tightened with fury for the man who'd inflicted this tiny woman with enough pain and misery to scar her for life. He let loose a long, sad sigh. "We'll get him Mrs. Ri . . . "

"Don't! Just . . . Sarah."

He nodded, remembering her request when they found her. "How are your daughters, Sarah?"

She spoke from the couch without looking at him. "They're good . . . I can't nurse anymore, so thank God they've taken to the formula well." She looked longingly at the clock on the bedside table. "I get so lonesome between visits. The nurse was supposed to be here five minutes ago to bring me to them."

Mike eyed the empty wheelchair resting in the corner of the room. "I could wheel you over there, if it's okay with the staff."

She gazed up at him hopefully. "It wouldn't hurt to ask."

Five minutes later he parked her wheelchair inside the daycare and leaned over to lock the wheels. He assisted her in rising then walked with her over to the playpens holding her daughters. As the infants recognized their mother, first one chubby girl, then the other, squealed with delight.

Mike watched as unadulterated joy illuminated the young mother's face, transforming her instantly.

"Hello, my babies! How are my girls this morning? Did you have a good night?" she cooed, as her daughters began kicking and rolling their way to her. She reached a hand inside and both babies began to get frantic for her to pick them up.

"Sit and I'll bring them to you," he suggested.

"I'd appreciate that." She made her way to the softly cushioned sofa and settled herself to accept the first bundle of squealing baby. "Hey Sammie, how's my girl doing?"

Mike picked up the second frantic baby and stood holding her, unsure of how to handle the situation.

"Someone usually sits next to me on the sofa with one because I can't hold them both. I have to take turns."

Seating himself beside her on the sofa, he tried to keep the squirming child from jumping out of his arms and over to her mother. "Whoa there, little lady! Not so fast!" he said, readjusting his hold on the infant. "Who do we have here?" he asked, holding her up in the air.

Sarah leaned over so her daughter could touch her face. "You have Danielle and I've got Samantha. Danni and Sammi."

Even in direct comparison, he couldn't see a difference between the two identical children. Both had the same big brown eyes and the beginnings of what would, no doubt, turn out to be golden brown curls. "How the hell...uh...excuse me...but how do you know which one's which?"

She smiled and kissed both girls' foreheads. "It's a mom thing, I guess. I always could see a difference in them. Failing that, Sammie has a tiny beauty spot on her right leg, and Dannie has one on her neck."

He checked out the birthmarks and shook his head. "Won't do me a bit of good because I'll forget which one had which. They sure are two little beauties, though." Danni turned her brown eyed gaze toward him and gave him a huge toothless grin as she grabbed his nose with both hands. He pulled back, made a funny face, and beamed as she gave him a belly laugh.

"She likes you, Detective. You must have kids of your own."

Mike pulled his gaze away from the drooling, chuckling baby long enough to see Sarah's amused expression. "Nope, no kids, but most all my co-workers have at least one. Their kids come in to the station every now and then, and they love me. It must be the height."

He held the child in a one armed football grip while coaxing her into a belly laugh with his other hand.

"You're a natural with kids, unlike their father," she said, looking on. "I hate that he's out there somewhere, trying to get to us...free to do whatever he wants."

Mike felt his features tighten with anger at the thought of the monster she'd tried so desperately to flee. "We'll keep you safe, Sarah."

She shrugged and emitted a shaky sigh. "While I'm in here, sure, but I know from experience there's not much you can do once they release me. Troy has a way of sliding right out of sticky situations."

He shook his head angrily. "Not this time. Everyone at the station is dedicated to keeping that slimy son of a b . . . uh . . . I mean your ex away from you and these two babies."

She wiped a tear from the corner of her eye. "It's okay—he is a slimy son of a bitch." She hugged her daughter tightly then let her own head fall back on the sofa. "I can't figure out how I got into this mess. I had two loving parents, and my brother and I grew up so close."

"The report says you lost your mother to cancer fifteen years ago, when you were just fourteen and your father to a massive stroke five years later. And if I'm remembering correctly, your only sibling is a brother who's in the military?"

"Yep, Master Sargent Mitchell Hebert," she said, proudly. "He's been a Marine for thirteen years...he's in Fallujah." She cupped her child's head gently. "I never thought I'd be the type to exist in an abusive relationship."

Mike listened attentively, praying he wouldn't have to deal with tears. To his relief, she didn't seem to be extremely emotional, as much as she was curious.

He stretched his leg out and repositioned baby Danni on his thigh. "Look, Sarah, by the time you were nineteen, you'd basically lost your entire family in one way or another. The combination of those events had to be downright devastating for you."

She bit her bottom lip thoughtfully as she pulled her daughter's head closer. "I suppose I was looking to fill the void of my brother and father's absence...or trying to find someone to take care of me. Boy," she said, snorting. "Did I fall short of that mark, or what?"

Mike raised one hand while keeping his hold on Danni with the other. "I'm just a cop, Sarah, not a therapist. I am curious to know how long you were with him before he started abusing you."

"He used to hang around with my brother when they were in high school. He left town, I graduated, went to technical college for office administration, got a job at the local hospital. Four years ago he came back to town and asked me out. I married him a year later. The first year was okay; we got into one shoving match during an argument but nothing serious. He slapped me once just after our first anniversary. I threatened to leave him then, but he knew I had no place to go, and no one around to help me. It gradually got worse and by the time I was ready to walk out for good, I discovered I was pregnant. He begged me to stay, said he wouldn't hit me anymore, and he didn't throughout the pregnancy."

She reached out to touch the daughter Mike was bouncing on his knee. "When the girls were two weeks old he said he had the opportunity to make better money, but we'd have to relocate. It had been so good, and I believed him when he said he'd changed." She shook her head slowly. "I couldn't see it then, Detective Harper. But I see now, how well he planned everything. Once he had me isolated from anyone I knew, he had me where he wanted me...completely dependent on him because of the babies. He controlled everything...turned me into a prisoner in my own home."

"Why didn't you call your brother?"

"Mitchell had enough to worry about over there." She turned her stern gaze toward Mike. "He still does. I don't want him bothered with this. Do you understand?"

Mike nodded, even knowing that they may have to deal with a good and pissed-off Marine if he paid his sister an unexpected visit anytime soon. "I can understand how you wouldn't want him distracted over there."

"That's exactly right. I'd like to hang onto the only family I have left, other than my babies. Speaking of which, let's switch babies now," she said, probably looking to change the subject.

He took Sammi, and handed Danni gently over to her.

Sarah nuzzled her daughter's soft hair and pressed kisses all over her face. Danni giggled and cooed then began to chew her fingers while drooling. "This one is about to cut a tooth."

"How can you tell?"

Sarah placed one finger inside the child's mouth and massaged her gums. "Feel that."

He placed his finger in Danni's mouth and frowned when he felt her swollen gums. "Poor baby, that's got to be painful."

She asked the sitter for a tube of something then handed it to Mike. "It can be, but it's easier for her if you rub this on her gums. It doesn't taste too good but it numbs it so it won't hurt as much."

Mike did as he was told and laughed at the face the infant made. He sobered quickly as a thought crossed his mind. "Has he ever abused the girls?"

She shook her head adamantly. "Never, and I know that for a fact because I've never left them alone with him—not for one solitary second." Her tear-filled gaze flicked back and forth between her daughters. "I'd kill him before I let him hurt my babies. I know it's a sin, but if I had a gun in my hand and he walked through that door, I could do it, just to make damn sure he never lays a hand on them. Of course," she added with a bitter laugh, "I'd get thrown in prison and my children would be without a mother."

Mike swore quietly under his breath. "You don't have to worry about that happening, Sarah. We're going to keep him away from you and the girls."

Sarah turned to face him. "You can't promise that. Can your department watch me twenty-four hours a day for the rest of my life? Even if you catch Troy tomorrow, it's not likely he'd spend much time in jail. The second he's out, he'll be looking for me." She shook her head. "I've got to find a way to relocate—to disappear—or all this protection will be for nothing."

Mike set his jaw in a determined show of stubbornness. "Then I'll help you start a new life in a new area. You said you worked in a hospital before you married Troy?"

"I worked part time in an insurance office while I was in school then in a hospital. I wasn't rolling in the big bucks, but it was respectable enough." She passed her hand softly over her daughter's rosy cheek. "I could provide for them, but I've been out of the loop for a few years. I may have trouble finding a job right away." Suddenly she dropped her head back and groaned. "Who am I kidding? I've got no car, no way to replace the one I lost, and no place to stay. It all seems so unbelievably hopeless."

Mike placed a comforting hand on her shoulder. "Hey, I don't want to see defeat on that face of yours, you hear me, Sarah? I have some connections in Lake Coburn—really good people who may be able to help you. I know it's only two hours from where you were living before, but would you mind if I made some calls on your behalf?"

She looked hopefully up at him. "I can't . . ."

"Think about it before you say no, Sarah. I know people over there that can protect you."

She shook her head. "I wasn't going to say no, Detective Harper. I have two children to think about, and I can't afford the luxury of pride. I'd appreciate any scrap of help you can give me."

He nodded in agreement. "I won't be able to make any phone calls until tonight or Sunday, but you'll be here for another three days, so as soon as I know something, I'll contact you."

Mike walked back outside and went to the nurse's station to ask for a cup of coffee, never losing sight of Sarah's door. After settling in the chair placed outside the door, he wondered if Angelique's employer would be willing to give Sarah a shot at working for him. He couldn't wait for tonight to speak to her about it.

Mike stretched out his long legs and crossed them at his booted ankles. He took a sip of coffee, leaned his head back against the wall, and wondered if Sarah would get the fresh start she and her two babies so desperately needed. Maybe this would turn out to be her singular, life-altering occurrence that would change all of their lives.

What was that old saying his grandmother had repeated dozens of times over the years? Our destiny is shaped around the people we meet in our lifetimes. He sensed his own destiny shifting and reshaping to admit Sarah Richard and her daughters into his circle of friends and acquaintances. He could almost feel the subtle change in the air, as though futures were being remapped before his eyes.

CHAPTER 10

Tanner pulled his Lexus into the driveway of his parents' home. "Here we are. Be it never so humble . . ."

Angelique swung her long legs out of the car and stood up, stretching the kinks out of her back. She pulled her sun glasses off to get a better look at the spacious grounds, sculpted lawn, and landscaped flower beds. She turned to observe the contemporary style of the home inside the ritzy gated community on the outskirts of Houston. "Oh, mais non! How do people live in such squalor?"

Her exaggerated gasp brought a genuine smile to Tanner's lips. "All right smart ass." He walked around to her side of the car to meet her. "I didn't grow up here. They bought this about five years ago. What do you think?"

She paused long enough to put her sunglasses back on then turned his way. "I prefer more classic lines in a home, actually. It seems really new, and . . . spacious," she said, trying her best to sound like she meant it.

Tanner's chest rumbled with laughter. "It's atrocious, isn't it? One day mother decided she'd had enough of living in a home built with classic good taste. I still can't believe she convinced dad to buy this monstrosity." He looked up at the house and shook his head. "At least he had the good sense to hang on to the other house and not sell it. Now that is a truly beautiful home. I guess it's mine if ever I decide to move back to Houston."

Angelique smiled at him before looking down at her casual slacks, blouse, and comfortable leather shoes she'd worn for shopping. "Suddenly, I'm feeling a little underdressed."

"Don't be silly, Angel. It's just a house. Hell, I'm dressed as casually as you are."

"You're wearing Ralph Lauren, Tanner. Not to mention Oakley sunglasses that probably set you back a few hundred bucks," she hissed. "You could have warned me, you know. A person never gets a second chance at making a first impression."

He pushed his shades up into his blond hair and beamed down at her. "You're stunning no matter what you wear."

She grinned. "All that charm going to waste. Just remember, flattery will still get you absolutely nothing but friendship."

He nodded before offering his arm, bent at the elbow. "Understood. Shall we go?"

∾

Celine Collins narrowed her eyes in disapproval as she watched her son from the window of her formal sitting room. "Oh, dear, just look what the cat's drug home this time. He is your son, Justin."

Justin Collins' blue-eyed gaze met his wife's icy countenance. "If not, somebody owes me for college and med school."

Celine released a disgruntled sigh. "Everything's about money to you, isn't it?"

"It replaces many things," he told his wife.

"Well, it can't replace breeding. The creature our son is about to bring into this house obviously has neither. You really must speak to him about this, dear."

∾

Tanner led Angelique into the living room, his hand placed gently on the small of her back. "Anybody home?" he called out.

"Of course we're home, son. You informed us you would be arriving this morning." Celine walked stiff backed up to her son and offered her cheek to him. "However, you neglected to tell me you were bringing a . . . guest."

Tanner stiffened at his mother's tone, gave her a quick kiss on the cheek, anyway. "Mother, I'd like you to meet a friend of mine, Angelique Baptiste. Angelique, this is my mother, Celine Collins."

Angelique had noticed the slight hesitation in the woman's obviously displeased comment. Undaunted, she lifted her chin and pulled her shoulders back to meet the woman's judgmental gaze head on. She reached out her hand. "It's a pleasure to meet you, Mrs. Collins."

Even a head shorter than Angelique, the older woman still managed to look down her aristocratic nose at her guest. She touched Angelique's hand for the barest second then brought her linen handkerchief up to her nose in distaste. "Mmm . . . yes," she said, before turning away abruptly.

Angelique pulled her hand back quickly, knowing better than to feel hurt by the snub. She turned as a tall, silver haired man entered the room.

"Hello, son," he said to Tanner.

"Dad, this is Angelique Baptiste, a very good friend of mine," he said, as though warning him.

"Nice to meet you, Ms. Baptiste. Is that French?"

"You also, sir. Yes, Baptiste is French, as well as my first name," she told him.

"From Louisiana, I'm supposing."

"You supposed correctly," she said, bowing her head slightly. "I was born and raised in Lafayette, but I'm currently living in Lake Coburn for my work."

"Your work? What is it you do?" Justin asked her.

Before Angelique had a chance to answer, Celine interrupted. "Oh dear, don't put the girl on the spot; she may not want to discuss her work with us." She turned away in dismissal.

Angelique stared at the woman in disbelief then spared a look in Tanner's direction. Judging by his horrified expression, he hadn't expected his mother to be quite so ungracious. She cleared her throat and leaned in to whisper something in his ear.

∿

Tanner nodded and pointed Angelique toward the powder room down the hallway. Once she left the room, he turned on his mother.

"What the hell was that?" he demanded angrily. "You just treated a friend of mine like—"

She turned on him and interrupted in a quiet, but cold voice. "Like what, Tanner? Like the trash she is? How dare you bring that creature into our home," she hissed.

Tanner stood there, his mouth gaping, at a complete loss for words. He turned toward his father hoping for a better reaction.

Justin raised his hand to stop him from speaking. "Really, son, what did you expect would happen by bringing her here? I've got to agree with your mother on this one."

Celine turned on her husband. "And you asked about her work."

"I know, dear; thank God you had the foresight to stop me."

Tanner looked from one to the other of them. "Just what is it you think she does for a living?"

"Really son, how do you pay her? By the hour or by the day?" his mother demanded.

Tanner clutched at his head. "She's not a prostitute!" he hissed at his mother. "She's the office manager for a radiation therapist in Lake Coburn. I can't believe you two."

"Well, just look at her," Celine hissed back at him, waving her arm toward the powder room door. "She looks as though she has, as if she's not—"

Tanner's face tightened in anger. "As if she's not what?"

After a moment of searching, Celine finally spit out what she'd been dying to say. "As if she's not Caucasian As if she's a mixed breed. A cur!"

Tanner's left brow lifted as he cocked his head slightly to the side. He gave one good snort of derision and began to laugh.

Celine stared at her son angrily. "I fail to see the humor in this situation."

Tanner calmed himself enough to answer her. "Of course not, mother. You fail to see the humor in any situation."

"The boy has a point, dear," Justin told his wife, earning a glare from her.

"And you know why?" Tanner continued. "It's because you're a cold hearted bitch who thinks she's above everyone else."

Celine's pointed features seemed to draw up even tighter. "You see, hanging around trash like that has you talking as they do. I won't have my own son speak to me in my home that way." Her tone indignant and superior.

"Not a problem, mother. I won't be in your home much longer, I can promise you that," he shot back, furious with her. He turned to his father. "I came here to sign some papers for a will, but on second thought, just forget about it. I don't want a damn thing from either of you."

His father grabbed his arm. "Now just hold on, son. Are you going to put some piece before your mother and I? We'll be your parents long after you've finished with her and have thrown her away. Take it from me, girls like that are fun to have around during a slow week, but you never bring them home to meet your parents."

Before Tanner could reply, Angelique cleared her throat from the doorway of the room.

Tanner spun in her direction, expecting to find her in tears, or at the very least wearing a horrified expression. What he saw was a woman who stood calmly, shoulders back, chin lifted proudly, in as near a regal demeanor as he'd ever seen. At that moment, he could have believed her to be a descendant of royalty.

"My lineage is Creole, Mr. and Mrs. Collins. That would be a mixture of Spanish, Native American, French, and a little Haitian. Tanner, are you about ready to go? I'd really like to get some shopping in at the Galleria. I hear Anne Fontaine calling out to me." She turned to somberly face his parents. "It was lovely to meet both of you." Then she turned and walked toward the door they'd come in through earlier.

Tanner tossed one last look at his parents and spoke in a voice filled with icy angriness. "If you two can't treat a friend of mine

with more respect than this, you can both kiss my lily white ass."
He stormed out, slamming the door behind him.

~

Angelique shot a glance in Tanner's direction as they both buckled
their seat belts. She felt terrible for him as she watched his jaw
clench and unclench furiously.

"It's no big deal, you know, Tanner."

He held up a hand to stop her and shook his head. It took
several moments for him to calm down enough to speak. When he
did, it wasn't pretty.

"Son of a bitch!" He slammed his hand on the steering wheel.
He cursed again—then once more, before finally working up the
nerve to speak to her.

"Angel. I am so damned sorry you had to hear that. I'm sorry I
brought you here." He turned and pointed at her. "And don't you
dare make excuses for those imbeciles!"

She reached out slowly and covered his hand before gently
lowering it to the seat. "When you come from a background like
mine, you get used to hearing people say things like that. It's okay,
though, because thanks to a year of therapy, I know I'm just as good
as they are."

"Just as good?" he scoffed. "Hell, you surpassed them the
millisecond you were conceived." He started the car and threw it
into reverse then backed quickly out to the very end of the driveway
before stopping. He sat in stony silence for a minute before he let
out a huff of laughter.

"You know, I just realized something, Angel."

"What's that?"

He shook his head sadly. "I am truly a product of my parents'
high opinions of themselves. I turned out just as selfish, vain, and
arrogant as they raised me to be."

Angelique reached over and placed a hand on his arm.
"You're not like them."

"I am, in more ways than you know. If you don't believe that,
ask Red and Tiffany," he snorted.

She studied him silently. "Maybe you were, but not anymore. I
overheard what you told them before I spoke up. You're a good
man, and a good friend to me."

Tanner lowered his head shamefully then raised her hand to
his mouth and gave it a soft as silk kiss. He slowly lifted his gaze to
meet hers. "I swear to God, Angel, from this day on, I'll be the best
friend you've ever had. I only ask one thing from you in return."

"What's that?"

"Your help in making me the best man I can be."

A slow smile spread across her face. "Oh hell, Tanner, Is that all? I thought you were going to ask me to save the rain forest or something like that." She leaned over to give him a big hug and whispered in his ear. "This'll be the easiest job I've ever had."

~~~

They spent the rest of the afternoon cruising one store after the other in the huge Galleria shopping center. Tanner went straight to Armani to get fitted for a new suit. Angelique walked over to the Coach boutique, where she hit some excellent sales and purchased a bag and several accessories. Still waiting on Tanner to finish, she looked in at the black and white fashions of Anne Fontaine and didn't see a thing she liked, even if she could have afforded something from there, which she couldn't. She walked over to Bottega Veneta to drool over an eight hundred dollar pair of boots and a three thousand dollar handbag.

Deciding she'd tortured herself enough, she ventured over to Ann Taylor where she spent another three hundred dollars on several mix and match sale items to add to her working wardrobe. The classic business styles with a feminine touch, along with the reasonable prices, were exactly what she was looking for. Loaded down with bags, she left the store and lucked out on another sale at Talbots—a two hundred dollar pair of leather boots for less than fifty bucks. Feeling like she'd hit the veritable jackpot, as well as extremely hungry, she called Tanner's phone and they met up at Ninfa's for lunch.

He walked toward her to relieve her of her bags and gave a low whistle. "Looks like you racked up!"

She beamed up at him. "I got about two thousand dollars of clothes and accessories here for about five hundred. How'd you do?" she asked, noticing his empty arms.

"They're altering the hem on my slacks for me. I'll be able to pick them up in another two hours. Can we wait or do you need to get back sooner?"

"Me, stuck in the middle of a huge mall full of fantastic deals? I may never recover from such a torturous afternoon."

He laughed as the waitress escorted them to a booth.

"So, what else did you plan to buy besides the suits?" She eyed him critically.

He shrugged. "I hadn't planned to buy much of anything else. My casual wardrobe is pretty complete as far as I'm concerned."

She took a sip of water and picked up her menu, trying not to comment, though she felt his gaze on her.

"Okay, what the hell was that about? Spit it out, Angel."

She lowered the menu. "It's just that you come off as a little aristocratic at times. I think a few adjustments to your wardrobe would make you seem less stuffy and arrogant." She gave him a slight shrug. "That's just my opinion, of course."

Tanner relaxed then leaned back against his seat. "Are you saying I just spent two thousand dollars on suits I can't wear?"

"Of course not; every man needs a couple of good suits, and I'm sure you look fantastic in your Giorgio Armani's," she replied. "I'm just saying maybe you should also invest in a truly casual style that makes you seem more—approachable—to people."

He crossed his arms and gave her a crooked grin. "Are you telling me you're intimidated by my Brooks Brothers slacks?"

Her eyes sparkled with laughter. "Do you even own a pair of jeans?" She continued quickly as he opened his mouth to interrupt her. "And I'm not talking about a hundred and fifty dollar a pair Brooks Brother five pocket jeans."

He emitted a huff in defeat. "I guess I don't, then."

"Never underestimate the appeal of a pair of good fitting, faded jeans on a man, along with a pair of high quality boots," she insisted.

Tanner sat up, suddenly looking tense. "You're not going to take me to one of those second hand stores to buy somebody's old jeans that are broken in, are you?"

She burst into laughter. "Of course not."

He relaxed visibly. "Good, because approachable or not, I draw the line at wearing a pair of pants that some other guy's ass has graced."

Angelique giggled again. "You're a trip Tanner." She glanced at her menu and spoke to the waiter who'd arrived to take their order. "I'd like the tortilla soup and a salad."

Tanner handed the man his menu. "Beef fajita's and uno cerveza, pour favour...Dos Equis amber. How about a margarita, Angel?" he suggested.

"I guess I could indulge myself since you're doing the driving," she admitted. "On the rocks and no salt, please."

They exchanged small talk until the waiter appeared with the requested margarita. Angelique thanked him then took a sip. "Mm, that's good."

Tanner sat back and watched her. "So, where do you suggest I buy this casual wardrobe to express the new me?"

She took another sip then set down her drink. "Do you trust me?"

"Absolutely," he answered, giving her a nod. "You seem to have very good taste, even on your limited budget. I know I can count on you to re-dress me to your satisfaction."

"Not just to my satisfaction, Tanner; we have to find clothes that you feel comfortable wearing, as well as a style that will enhance your masculinity without making you seem like such a preppie rich boy."

Tanner winced at her words. "Don't hold back, Angel. Why don't you tell me how you really feel?"

She gave a low chuckle. "Relax, it's not like I'm asking you to get rid of your entire wardrobe. I've seen you in some nice polo shirts and dress shirts you could dress down with a pair of jeans."

"Do you have a specific shop in mind?"

She sent him a mysterious smile along with a wink. "I certainly do."

~~∽~~

Angelique's shoes hit the floorboard of Tanner's Lexus. She stared out the window at the passing landscape of I-10 eastbound and rubbed her feet. "I love shopping, but the older I get, the worse it is on my feet." She reclined the comfortable leather seat of the Lexus and looked over at the driver. "So, how do you feel about the new additions to your wardrobe?"

Tanner signaled to shift lanes then glanced back at the bags filling the rear seat, some of which contained several pairs of something he thought he'd never wear; Wrangler and Levi jeans. "I have to admit, Angel, when we walked into that place I was ready to dislike anything you picked out for me. They are comfortable, but I'm not sure if they're me."

"They're the new you, remember? Trust me."

He looked over at her and grimaced. "I do trust you, but you need to understand what you're dealing with, here. I'm a professional man, and my wardrobe has to portray that."

Angelique laughed. "Jeeze, I'm not asking you to show up at a Mardi Gras ball dressed in overalls and a straw hat, Tanner. Red McAllister is a professional man and he mixes jeans in with his wardrobe."

Tanner rolled his eyes. "Red owns a dance club. I'm a surgeon."

She clasped her hands, affecting a southern belle accent. "And you're a brain surgeon too. Oh my, how could I have forgotten?"

"You really are a shit, you know that?" He shook his head as she dissolved into laughter.

"Red has owned many businesses, Tanner. All of them very profitable. He is a tremendously successful businessman and probably worth twice what you are. Sheesh!" she said. "Not only were you raised to think you were better than everyone else, but you're also suffering from the God syndrome."

He started to say something, but clamped down on his jaw, instead.

Angelique laughed again. "You're not even going to deny it, are you?"

He gave her a shrug. "Tiffany used to accuse me of that all the time. I can't help it if I'm good at what I do."

"So was the heart surgeon I used to date a couple of years ago," she said smugly, "but at least he didn't have a problem wearing jeans."

"And yet you're not with him anymore," he smirked.

She shook her head. "He couldn't accept it when I told him I could only worship one God at a time." She sent him a scathing look. "Besides, Tiffany's the best at what she does, too. People don't come any sweeter than her."

"I can be sweet," he said.

"You can be a pain in the ass," she scoffed before shaking her head. "Hey, if you want to live the rest of your life with the same mind set as your parents, just take all the jeans back to the store. You can continue the way you were and end up marrying some poster girl for the rich and famous." She turned her head toward him. "The two of you can raise yet another generation of pains in the ass who treat us regular people like the trash we are." She turned her head to look out of her window. "The choice is yours."

Tanner broke the ensuing silence after several moments. "I'll wear the jeans, Angel."

She smiled, but remained silent until Tanner, true to form, made one more comment.

"I guess I'll have to trade in my new bottle of Acqu Di Gio Homme for a bottle of Old Spice next time I go shopping for a loaf of bread and some bologna."

Angelique snorted loudly before she could contain it and they burst into laughter. She finally managed to catch her breath, and wiped the tears from her eyes. "You're such a jerk."

He gave one last chuckle. "That's what I hear."

CHAPTER 11

Mike walked in his home around six-thirty, toting a bag of Tex-Mex take out and thinking of Angelique. He wondered if she was back from Houston or at least on her way home. His next thought was for the friend she'd gone with. That door was blown wide with possibilities. Hell she called him a friend and he'd marry her in a skinny minute. His one consolation was that she'd sent Nash the same text.

The thought of his old buddy and his line of work made him think about Sarah Richard. That poor girl had been through hell—was still going through hell. And the worst part was that she was right about them not being able to protect her forever. That son of a bitch would get to her, sooner or later. Assholes like him always did, unless the victims had round the clock protection.

He grabbed his phone and punched in the familiar number. Nash picked up on the third ring.

"Harper, you son of a bitch! What's up, Chief?"

"Nash, how busy are you, as far as clients are concerned?"

"Not at all, obviously, or I wouldn't be here. I'm on vacation, so to speak. Why? You afraid I'm gaining ground with Angel and hopin' I'd have to haul ass?"

Mike's chuckle rumbled deep in his chest. "Angel will decide when she decides and nobody is going to rush her. No, the truth is, I'm working on a case right now that's bugging the hell out of me."

∽∾

Nash sat back in a chair and watched as Annie entered the room, waddling uncomfortably in the way of all end of term pregnant women. He listened intently as Mike opened up to him about a young mother of twin girls, Sarah Richard. By the end of the tale, Nash sat stiff backed in the chair, seething with fury over the situation Sarah and her baby girls were in.

"Son of a bitch," he muttered, wiping his hand over his face. "No idea where the asshole is, I guess."

"You got it," Mike huffed. "That piece of crap could be anywhere in the country, or hiding outside of the hospital, waiting to get his hands on her as soon as she's released." He drew in a deep breath and released it slowly. "Damn, I'm getting tired of cases like this, Nash. It seems like for every one of these bastards we put away there are five more to take his place."

Nash snorted in disgust. "I know what you mean, Harp. I lost my wife and child, and here's this fool throwing his wife around like she's worthless. What can I do?" he asked, thinking he'd like to get a piece of that asshole.

"Well, that's what I was calling about. Once Sarah's released, we'll be able to watch her a day or two longer, but I'm sure the department will have to pull us off the case. We don't have the funds or the manpower for something like that. Mel Finley is begging to be left on it, but as it stands now, nobody knows what's going to happen."

"Who the hell is this Mel?" Nash asked.

"One of our officers who's mom was abused by her husband. This case hits too close to home for that one."

"Well, I tell you what, Harper, you tell Sarah Richard I'll be glad to keep her and her babies safe from her ex-asshole."

Mike passed a hand through his hair as he paused. "She can't pay, Nash, but I'll be glad to pay you something."

"Oh, hell man, I wouldn't take a dime for this. That's what's good about being my own boss. I can do any damn thing I want to. Besides, that last babysitting job was a veritable windfall for me. I could sit on my ass for the rest of the year with what that rich girl's daddy paid me."

"I was praying you'd say that, Nash. I told her I knew good people who could help protect her. Man, I can't wait to give her some good news for a change. When do you want to meet her?"

Nash looked at his watch. "I ain't doing a damn thing right now, how about you?"

"It'll take you about an hour to get to the hospital from Kenton. That'll give me time to eat my take out and do some laundry."

"Sounds good, Chief, now where's that hospital?"

∼◡∽

The two men stepped off the elevator and walked toward Sarah's room. "Remember, call her Sarah," Mike said to Nash. He frowned and put his hand on his gun when he saw there was no one posted at the door. He approached cautiously, relaxing only when he heard the sound of women's voices inside.

Giving Nash a quick nod, he knocked softly on the door. The voices inside came to an immediate halt as he heard shuffling on the other side of the door.

A stern voice demanded, "State your name and business."

Mike nodded, satisfied with the way the officer had responded. "It's Mike Harper. I've got another visitor."

He heard the sound of the lock clicking and the door opened slowly. Officer Finley nodded in his direction then seemed to freeze in her tracks as Nash came into view.

Liam wasn't as nearly surprised at seeing the female officer at the door, as seeing such an attractive one. Not many women could pull off such a shade of vivid red hair paired with green eyes…or were they blue? The look, partnered with a buxom build and fair skin, obviously worked on this particular woman.

He shook himself mentally and used caution to venture into the room. Once inside, he gazed at the tiny woman seated on the sofa. She held one beautiful golden haired infant, while a second child, equally beautiful, occupied an infant seat next to the mother. Both children were drooling and squealing in delight, almost seeming to communicate with each other in their own special twin language.

Nash managed to hold back a wince as he took stock of the young mother's battered face, as well as the brace on her arm. He nodded and gave her a grim smile.

"Hello Sarah, I'm Liam Nash," he said, holding out his hand before realizing she couldn't very well shake his hand with one broken arm while holding her infant in the other. He pulled his hand back nervously.

"It's nice to meet you, Mr. Nash." She turned toward Mike Harper. "Good to see you again, Detective."

He nodded. "Sarah, Nash is about the best body guard in the state of Texas, and he's offered to take over watching out for you once you're released from the hospital."

"Oh . . . " Sarah raised deep brown eyes to Liam's again. "But, I can't pay!"

He shook his head. "No charge, ma'am. It would be my pleasure to keep you and your beautiful daughters safe. Detective Harper has already apprised me of the situation with your husb . . . uh . . . your ex."

Sarah pulled her daughter closer with her one good arm. "But, why would you do this for a stranger?"

Nash gave her a sad smile. "Because it's the right thing to do, ma'am; and since I work for myself, I can tell the boss to kiss my ass anytime I like," he said, giving her a wink. When her frown didn't dissipate, he turned serious. "Look Sarah, I do work for myself and I didn't have anything on the books right now. I just spent two months babysitting a spoiled little rich girl for a major amount of money. Because of that, I can afford to do a pro bono case right now. It would be a real treat for me to do something that'll make me feel good about myself."

Sarah looked to Mike for an answer.

Mike nodded. "He's a good man, Sarah. I've known him for a long time. And you were right about us not being able to watch you all the time once you get out of here. This is the perfect solution."

Sarah closed her eyes and dropped her head forward. "I don't even have a place to stay," she whispered. "My girls and I were staying at the women's shelter."

"I'm working on that," Mike said. "I've still got a few calls to make." He seated himself next to the young mother on the couch. "Sarah, I know you might have trouble trusting after all you've been through, but between Nash and me, we'll take good care of you and the girls. I know good people in Lake Coburn…people who are in the position to help you."

Officer Finley stepped up. "I've already asked the captain to let me work your case if he can spare me."

Sarah looked up at the other three adults in the room. "I haven't felt this—cared for—in a long time." She wiped the tears from her eyes and released a long sigh. "Thank you . . . Thank all of you." She looked at Liam Nash and nodded. "We're in your hands."

∼∽

By the time Liam stepped back out to the hallway, he thought he had a better grip on the situation. He'd asked Sarah dozens of questions and gleaned as much information about her and her ex as he thought was significant. Mike followed him out, closing the door behind him.

"What do you think, Nash?"

"I think I'll kill the bastard if he tries to get to her."

The door opened once more and Mel Finley stepped out to join them in the hallway. "Harper, do you really have some leads on a place for her and the girls to stay?"

Mike nodded. "I have an idea. Like I said, I need to make some calls first." He watched the officer throw a furtive glance toward Nash. "I'm sorry, I forgot to introduce you two, didn't I? Mel, this is Liam Nash, an old friend of mine and an excellent private investigator and bodyguard. Nash, this is one of the department's best officers, Mel Finley."

Nash's gaze landed on those beautiful eyes again, this time long enough to study the color. Her irises weren't green at all but a bluish-green, lined with a ring of dark blue, and flecked with gold throughout. He nodded. "Good to meet you, Officer Finley."

～

Melanie gazed into the face of Liam Nash. "Same here," she said, extending her hand to one of the handsomest men she'd ever seen.

"Your eyes," he murmured, "the color is extraordinary."

She laughed nervously. "Thank you." She fidgeted with her belt buckle. "I think I've seen you before," she commented, knowing that was an out and out lie. She knew she'd seen him before. She'd lusted after the man from afar at Annie McAllister's wedding, but he'd been too wrapped up in a tall brunette to notice her. "I believe it was at a wedding last year."

He nodded. "That would have been Annie and Drake's wedding." He cocked his head to the side marveling that he hadn't noticed her there. "Were you at the reception too?"

She nodded. "I was in the wedding party." She laughed at his frown of concentration. "Relax Mr. Nash, you probably wouldn't recognize me as the same person in that dress she picked out for me."

Nash smiled. "You live here in Lafayette?"

"A little south, in a suburb called Maurice. You've probably never even heard of it."

Nash gave her a crooked grin. "South on one sixty-seven, home of the World Famous City Bar, not to mention Hebert's Specialty Meats, where they sell the best stuffed chickens I've ever tasted." His deep chuckle resonated throughout the hallway. "Oh yeah, I've heard of, as well as have been to Maurice, Officer Finley. Passed through it on the way over here. It's grown a lot even in the year I've been gone."

"We can thank urban sprawl." She turned her attention back to Mike. "So who are you making those phone calls to, Harper? Is it anyone I know?"

"You know Annie's brother, Red McAllister?" he asked.

"Sure, I know Red. I don't know Tiffany that well, but she seems sweet," she said.

"I'm going to ask Red and Tiffany to let them stay in their home, at least until her ex is behind bars. They have a whole wing not being used in their place out in the country."

Melanie nodded her approval. "The McAllister's are good people, and I imagine Red will help any way he can."

Mike nodded. "Glad you approve."

Melanie started at the sound of Nash clearing his throat and addressing her.

"Excuse me Officer Finley, but you seem to be particularly interested in this case. Is the vic also someone you knew previously?"

"No, sir, it's just that I was there when we got the call from the neighbors about Sarah and the babies. I saw what kind of shape she was in. You can probably tell from the still visible cuts and bruises that her husband worked her over pretty good." She paused to get a grip on the too vivid memories that came flooding back. "I know Sarah still seems thin, but, believe me, you're seeing the fattened up version of her."

Mike grunted in agreement. "She's right, Nash. That poor girl had easily dropped ten pounds because she nursed her two babies until her body shut down on her."

Nash nodded. "Now that I see that little lady and her two daughters—" He also paused, seeming to have to deal with the image, "I can well understand that the sight of those three in that situation would have tugged at even the most hardened officer's heart strings." To Melanie's shock, he sent her a direct gaze. "And although you seem well-trained and thorough, you don't seem all that hardened."

"I was raised in an abusive household, Mr. Nash. It's made me harder than you might think. Regardless, once they leave here, if there's anything at all I can do, or i-if you need any help," she stammered. "I guess what I'm saying is, I'm available. To assist you in any way. With Sarah and the girls, I mean," she finished in a flustered voice. She shifted her gaze up to Mike's curious expression. "I mean on my days off, Harper."

Mike's expression was smug. "Didn't doubt it for a moment."

She nodded. "You're not relieving me early, are you?"

"No, I'll be back at six in the morning to take over," he said.

Melanie pointed to the door. "Then I'll go back inside with them." She ducked quickly back into the room, thankful to escape the presence of the two men, and mortified at her school girl crush behavior.

She locked the door from the inside and turned to lean against it, fanning her face. When she noticed Sarah eyeing her warily, she pulled herself together.

"Okay, it's Sammi's turn now, right?" she said, as Sarah agreed. Melanie had just settled herself beside her to get the baby placement situation under control when she realized Sarah was crying. "Oh God, are you in pain? Do you need me to call the nurse?"

Sarah sniffed noisily and grabbed for a tissue. "I'm just so relieved." She lowered her face into her daughter's golden curls and sobbed. "I didn't know what we were going to do, Mel. People at the shelter are very nice, but it's hard not having any family or friends around, you know?"

Melanie placed a gentle hand on her arm. "I know you didn't want to contact your brother, but maybe it's time."

Sarah closed her eyes and shook her head. "No! I don't want Mitch bothered with this."

Melanie sighed and passed her fingers through Sammi's curls. "Even if you don't tell him what's going on? Maybe it'll make you feel better to hear his voice."

"If I hear his voice, I'll break down. I know I will." Sarah wiped her eyes and lifted her chin. "Besides, I'm over it, and I want a change of subject," she said, narrowing her eyes suspiciously. "What's the deal with that Liam Nash guy? You're obviously attracted to him."

Melanie stared, dumbfound at the other woman. "Of course I'm attracted to him. You saw him! Who wouldn't be?"

Sarah raised her shoulders in a shrug. "I'm not."

"Are you serious?"

"As a heart attack. He does nothing for me."

"Yeah, but you're medicated, and probably leery of all men right now, which is totally understandable."

"Well, yeah," Sarah admitted. "I can't deny any of that, but when I look at him . . . Nothing. Now when you look at him, I can almost feel the air crackle with electricity," she said.

Melanie rolled her eyes. "Oh please."

∾

Liam held the door opened to the elevator so an older woman could exit before he stepped inside. He pushed the button that said LOBBY, and stepped back with his arms crossed. "You know, every time you spoke about Officer Finley, I pictured a guy."

Mike's head jerked in mild surprise. "Really? Why would you think that?"

Nash looked over at the other man. "You never mentioned anything other than the name Mel, and I took it to be a man's name. I was shocked as hell when I met her."

"Why wouldn't you take it to be short for Melanie, or Melody? You know, like that actress, Mel Harris," Mike suggested.

"Or it could have been a guy's name; you know, like Mel Gibson, Mel Torme, Mel Brooks, or Mel's Diner," Nash added. "It may have even helped if you had uttered, even once, the words her or she."

"I guess you're right," Mike snorted. "Huh, all of those sexism and sexual harassment classes paid off. I don't even think of Mel as a woman; I think of her as a damn good cop."

"You're joking, right?" Nash exclaimed.

Mike shrugged. "Mel came to the department as a rookie five years ago and proved early on to be an asset. She's a hell of a shot, a master at hand to hand, and a magician with a computer."

Nash nodded as he mentally filed away that information. In his job, it was beneficial to have friends with abilities.

∾⌣∿

Troy pulled his baseball cap lower on his head and stood staring at the closed hospital door. He'd seen the female cop come out of the room and slide her security card in the automatic locking mechanism. After hearing the tell-tale click of the lock, she'd walked away. He watched as she spoke quietly to the nurse, who then escorted her toward the centralized station at the intersection of hallways.

Knowing she wouldn't be gone long enough for him to attempt to disengage the lock, he satisfied himself with staring at the door that kept the room's occupants away from him. When he heard the sharp clip of the lady cop's footsteps just moments later, he walked to the supply closet he'd hidden in for the past two hours and stepped inside.

Once it was safe, he left the closet and slipped out of the hospital the same way he'd slipped inside earlier, completely unobserved. He'd hoped to get his hands on her . . . Force her to leave town with him. He could see now that was impossible. He'd have to disappear for a while; possibly a long while, until he could relocate and get on his feet again.

He walked back to the truck he'd borrowed, smiling smugly to himself. He had friends who could help him disappear; the kind of friends who would make that wife of his wish she'd never been born—if he asked them to.

CHAPTER 12

"Hold on, Mom," Angelique said, as the distinctive beep signaled an incoming call. Checking her caller ID, she smiled. "I'm gonna let you go now, Mama. I love you." She took a deep breath and accepted the call. "Hey, Mike."

"Hey Angel, how was the shopping?"

"I hit some great sales on accessories and business clothes. I had a good day, and met some rather interesting people." Bypassing the sour disappointment of meeting Tanner's parents, she got up to pour herself a cup of freshly steeped tea before pushing on. "How was your day, and how are the young mother and her daughters?"

Mike gave a grunt of satisfaction as he recalled today's events. "Things are finally looking up for her, thanks to Liam and some good friends of ours," he boasted. "Liam has volunteered to give her and the girls free bodyguard protection."

She settled herself comfortably on the couch. "That's fabulous! He certainly seems to have the free time on his hands."

"He also has the funds, thanks to his wealthy clients."

His prolonged pause followed by a loud sigh caught her attention. "What's wrong?"

"Aw, hell...maybe I should leave the department to do something more lucrative."

"But, I thought you loved your job," she said.

"I do, and the majority of us are like family. But I see myself in another thirty, or forty years with the same pitiful amount in my personal savings account, a pension plan that won't provide, and relying on some form of crappy government health care." He passed a hand over his face. "It doesn't seem like it's enough . . . "

"Enough for what, Mike?"

"For anyone else. I can't imagine my salary being enough to take care of a family."

Angelique sensed the hesitation in his reply and wished she could give this wonderful man the answer he wanted. "It'll be more than enough for the lucky woman who ends up with you, Michael Harper, whoever that may be." She changed the subject quickly.

"Now which good friends of ours, other than Liam, are helping Sarah and her girls?"

"Red and Tiffany McAllister offered to let her and the girls stay at their place for as long as she needed."

Angelique laughed. "That should be an interesting household for a while with three infants under the same roof."

"It would be, but Red's father-in-law came up with an even better suggestion. Sarah and her daughters will be staying with them. They live just down the road from Red and Tiff's place."

"I've been there! That's where Tiffany's baby shower was held. They even have a nursery set up already with two cribs…one for Briana and one for Annie and Drake's baby when it comes."

"That's what Daniel said. They have plenty of room for them and Liam, too. Plus, he's retired, so he's home more to help keep watch over them. His wife, Leah, trains horses on the ranch, and she claims horses make excellent burglar alarms."

"The two of them are going to adore having those babies underfoot. They're already doting grandparents to Briana." Angelique placed her cup on the end table then sat back to put her feet up. "I'm glad things are working out for her. Do her spirits seem to be up?"

"She's so grateful, Angel. I don't think Sarah's the type of person who's ever relied on others for help. Can you imagine how difficult it must be for her to trust virtual strangers, especially considering what she's been through? Mel Finley wants to stick particularly close to this case."

"It's a woman thing," she replied. "We can't look at another woman in that horrible situation and resist the urge to give some kind of comfort."

"Hey, did you always know that Mel was a woman?"

Angelique tapped her teeth with her fingernail. "Maybe not the first couple of times, but I figured it out eventually."

"Can you tell me what gave it away?" he asked her.

Angelique concentrated, trying to remember the situation. "You must have finally let a 'her' or 'she' slip, somewhere in there. You're not much for using pronouns, though. You generally just say Mel, which I assume is short for Melanie. Why?" she asked, as his deep rumble of laughter carried over the phone.

"After Nash met her today, he said he'd been surprised, because he assumed Mel was a guy from what I'd told him."

"That really doesn't surprise me, because when you talk about Mel, she's just another cop." She smiled at his grunt of acceptance. "Well, I sure hope things work out for them. Please tell her I'd like to help in any way I can."

"She needs to relocate and she'll need a job once she's recovered and we've caught her ex. She's trained in office administration and worked three years previously at a hospital. Think you could keep your eyes and ears open for leads?"

"I may be able to do better than that," she said. "I'll get back to you." Mike couldn't possibly know that the previous call from her mother already had her considering taking the job in Lafayette her boss had offered. Her mom would need hip surgery and her dad needed a knee replacement. Angelique had pictured the endless driving back and forth from Lake Coburn to Lafayette while looking for someone to take her place. She was dreading it with a passion.

"I'm going to see my parents tomorrow. You want to come for lunch?" she asked.

"Can I bring something?"

"Mama said just yourself, but daddy said if you had any of that homemade blackberry wine of yours, he'd sure like a bottle."

◦᷍◦

The next afternoon, Mike, Angelique, and her parents all sat inside the old couple's glassed in back porch, enjoying the bright sunshine of the clear, cloudless sky—a rarity for a late winter afternoon in south Louisiana.

Angelique watched as a pair of squirrels frolicked on the branch of the old oak tree in the back yard. She smiled at the memory of her father climbing that tree to attach a rope for the tire swing she'd spent countless hours on. She shifted her gaze to him, thinking it was difficult to imagine, knowing the trouble his knees gave him these days.

If only she could go back and apologize for all the hell she'd given them during her late teens, sneaking out of the house, breaking curfew, sometimes drinking, smoking, and using the occasional drugs.

She remembered thinking her mother was a slave driver because she expected her daughter to help with the cleaning and cooking if she wanted the privilege of going out on the weekends. She thought her father was an ogre for not letting her sleep past ten o'clock on weekends.

She hated that they both expected better grades than B's and C's on her report cards, and also for her to be in mass every Sunday morning if she hadn't made it on Saturday afternoon. They pushed her to excel, and although she had initially fought it tooth and nail, she'd eventually buckled down just so they'd stop their nagging. Thank God they'd nagged.

Her mind drifted to some of those other, so called privileged kids she'd hung around so she'd be considered cool. Bobby, whose politician father had pulled strings all his life to get him out of one scrape after another, was serving a twenty year stint in the state pen. While drunk, he'd run a red light and caused a serious accident involving a young a mother and her six year old son. The mother, whose husband happened to be a state senator, had been paralyzed from the waist down. The judge had ignored Bobby's and his attorney's pleas for leniency.

She thought of her best friend, Janice, the A-student, who had ended up in Vegas, prostituting to keep herself supplied with the heroin she craved. The summer after their senior year, Janice had begged Angelique to accompany her to Las Vegas so they could find jobs together and share the rent.

But of course, her parents, strict and un-cool beasts that they were, had refused to let her go. They hadn't let her have one dime of her graduation and college fund money. She'd railed and pouted at how unfair they were being, and insisted she was old enough to do whatever she wanted. Her parents had won out, and Janice had gone without her. By the time Angelique had started a technical college two months later, her old friend was already prostituting.

Every time she thought of her old friend, a famous quote came to mind. There but for the grace of God, go I. Yes, the grace of God, and the persistence of her parents. She owed them both so much. She thought of the pain they were in now and the surgeries that would give them some relief. They would both need serious help and no way could she turn her back on them now that they needed her.

Her dad and Mike were deep in conversation about the New Orleans Saints and when they'd make it to the Super Bowl again.

Seated at her left, Marceline stared silently out through the clear glass separating them from the flora and fauna of early spring. Angelique leaned slightly toward her mother before speaking in a low tone.

"Mom, I want you to know that I'm going to transfer to the Lafayette office as soon as I've trained my replacement."

Her mom gazed at her in obvious confusion. "But you'll be spending all your paycheck on gas from driving back and forth, Angel. That won't be worth it."

"I'll move back to Lafayette, of course," Angel replied, simultaneously wondering if her old place was still vacant.

The mother paused as she studied her daughter's face. "Honey, I know you're worried about us, but our insurance pays for homecare after surgeries. Don't do this because of your dad and me."

Angelique set her empty coffee mug on the table next to her chair then faced her mom. She reached out and gently took hold of her mother's hands. Those gentle but aged hands had comforted and cared for, as well as disciplined her throughout the years. She caressed them with soft strokes then raised them to her own face. "I'd do anything for you and pop, just like you both did everything you could for me."

Marceline's eyes filled with tears. "Angel, it's not necessary."

"I want to be here for you and pop, not just once or twice a week, but every day. Not another word about this, Mom."

Her mother seemed to study her in that quiet way she'd perfected. "Have you come to any other decisions about your life yet, my Angel?"

Knowing her mother spoke of her unresolved love life, Angelique let her own gaze travel past her mother to Mike, who sat talking animatedly with her dad, three chairs over. She thought of her therapist speaking the words that had become her mantra over the past year. "You should learn to love yourself before you can love others, Angelique. If there's something about you that you're not happy with, change it, then move on."

She watched Mike, knowing he wanted marriage and a family. She knew she could easily love him as a wife should love a husband. She closed her eyes and pictured Liam, finally healed from a devastating personal loss and ready to begin a new life with her. She could easily love him as well. Nope…still no resolution.

She smiled at her mother and tapped her own head with one forefinger. "It's still up for debate."

∿∽

Angelique turned her gaze from the window to Mike, seated behind the wheel of his truck, as he drove them both back to his place. "I told mom I'd be moving back to Lafayette as soon as I trained my replacement for the Lake Coburn office."

He shifted to face her, obviously taken off guard by her statement. "As much as that pleases me, I didn't realize you'd found a replacement already."

She gave him a sly smile. "I haven't yet, but I'm hoping to meet her today. Do you think it's too soon to meet Sarah Richard?"

Mike gave her an ear splitting grin. "I think she'd be thrilled to meet you today." He reached out to take hold of her hand. "Thanks, Angel, this is going to mean so much to her." He turned back to face the front but the grin stayed on his face.

Angelique stole furtive glances at Mike until the smile eventually faded from his face. Even then, his eyes reflected the joy he obviously felt as he maneuvered his truck through the moderate Sunday traffic toward the hospital.

As much as she hated to admit it, it bothered her that he could feel this intensely about the welfare of Sarah Richard. Could he be developing feelings for the young mother of twins? She felt uncomfortable even thinking it. What if his feelings for Sarah surpassed his feelings for her?

For the past six months, Mike had been steadfast in his attempts to win her heart. Maybe she had grown too complacent by thinking he'd wait for her no matter how long it took her to decide. Heat crept up her face and neck as the thought took shape in her mind. She turned to look out her side window until the uncomfortable heat faded. By then they were pulling into the hospital parking lot.

CHAPTER 13

Melanie had just brought Sarah back to her room after a visit to the nursery when someone knocked on her door. She reached for the handle, demanding the usual "State your name and business."

"Mel, it's Mike Harper and I have someone with me who needs to speak to Sarah."

Mel stepped aside to let him use his pass key to open the door. For the second time, she stared in surprise at the visitor Harper had brought by the hospital. It was the same woman Liam Nash had been all over at Annie's wedding last year. What the hell was she doing with Harper?

Mike gave Mel a quick introduction then led Angelique over to the bed where Sarah was seated. "Sarah, this is a good friend of mine, Angelique Baptiste. Angel, this is Sarah Richard."

∿

Angelique struggled to catch her breath as she got her first good luck at the woman that Mike was so concerned about. Now that she saw the poor girl, she could understand his concern. There wasn't a spot on this woman's face that wasn't covered with a bruise or a nasty looking cut, and she was far too thin. Even through all of that, she could see the stubborn determination in the gaze Sarah fixed on her as Angel extended her hand.

"Sarah, it's very nice to meet you. I hope you're feeling better."

"I am, thank you. I'm over the worst of it. Trust me when I say it looks worse than it feels," she said, pointing to the bruises on her face. "It's nice to meet you too, Angelique. What a beautiful name."

Angel smiled and thanked her before taking her seat in a chair Mike placed next to the bed. "Sarah, Mike tells me you have experience in office management and you're looking to relocate to another city. It happens that I'm looking for a replacement in our Lake Coburn office so I can relocate to our Lafayette location as soon as possible." She spent the next ten minutes telling her about the workings of the medical facility, as well as her employer, Dr.

Maze. She spent another ten minutes gleaning information about Sarah's work experience and training.

Once Angelique was satisfied, she stood up and smiled down at the other woman. "It seems you've got the experience, even though you haven't worked in a while. I'm certain you'll have no difficulty learning the system. When you get out of here do you think you could get a resume ready?"

Sarah beamed up at her. "I already have one, but it's at the women's shelter where the twins and I were staying. They were going to help me find a job. When I leave here, I can go and pick it up. I don't have a vehicle right now, and truthfully I don't know how I'll manage getting one. I'm not sure how the insurance company will settle since Troy's name was on the title, but if I have to use the public transit system to get to work, I'll do it. I only hope this Dr. Maze is willing to give me a chance."

Angelique extended her hand again. "Sarah, I'm responsible for hiring my replacement, and as far as I'm concerned, you're hired. The resume is just to put in your file. When you're ready, give me a call." She reached into her purse and handed Sarah a business card with her contact information. After answering a few more questions, she left the room.

∽

Melanie watched as Mike followed the tall brunette out of the room. Angelique Baptiste. She'd heard Mike mention 'Angel' dozens of times, but she had no idea it was a shortened version of her real name. Everyone in the office knew he was crazy about her. They even had a pool going as to when he'd pop the question. She looked toward the door as he re-entered a minute later.

"Your company left?" she asked.

He shook his head. "No, she went to speak to a friend of hers who works on this floor. When she's through, we'll leave."

Melanie tried not to broach the subject, but her curiosity finally got the better of her. "I think I've seen her before."

"She was involved in the Benjamin Bradford case a little over a year ago. He'd earmarked her as a potential victim."

"I wasn't talking about that, but I do remember it now. I think she was with that Nash guy at Annie McAllister's wedding."

Mike gave a shrug of indifference. "Could be," he mumbled. "That's around the time they got together for a few months."

"I mean, they were only dancing and talking, but it seemed as if they were close," she quickly explained.

He stared at her for a moment then grinned in understanding. "It's okay, Mel. Angelique and I only started . . . " He paused here for a moment, as if he weren't certain how to finish, turning his gaze to his size fourteens. He lifted his right hand to rub the back of his neck and groaned. "Hell, I'm not sure what we're doing, and that's the damn truth of it." His eyes glazed over for several seconds as though he forgot there were two other people in the room.

He chose that moment to snap out of his pondering and glanced up in time to catch them attempting to wipe all expression from their faces. His chest rumbled with laughter. "Am I that transparent?"

"Only a little," Melanie admitted.

Sarah released a snort of laughter then wrapped her arms around her tightly wrapped ribs. "Oh, crap. That hurts."

Mel and Mike burst into laughter and Sarah joined in. After they'd finally slacked off, Mike turned to his co-worker. "Don't worry, Mel, I'm doing my damnedest to make sure Nash stays a free agent, in case you're wondering."

"Oh hell," she groaned. "Am I that transparent?"

Mike grinned as he held up two fingers. "Only a little."

A soft knock at the door interrupted them.

Mike opened the door to Angelique. "Are you ready to go?"

"Yes, but I wanted to let Sarah know that Dr. Maze is all for trying her out."

Mike nodded, giving Sarah a big thumbs-up signal before he and Angel headed out the door.

Melanie locked the door after their departure and turned to see Sarah rubbing her sore ribs. "I guess we shouldn't make you laugh for a while."

Sarah smiled up at her. "It feels good to laugh. Especially since I didn't think I'd ever get a chance to do that again."

Mel shook her head. "It must have been torture for you, thinking he'd come back any time to . . . "

"Finish what he started," Sarah continued, when Mel didn't want to. "It was. I've never prayed so hard in my life, Mel. I couldn't stand the thought of my babies growing up without me, but better that than them not getting a chance to grow up at all. And I kept wondering what his horrible neighbors would do if they found us." She let her head fall back against the pillow. "He used our children to control me."

"Cowards like him use anything they can to control a situation," Melanie explained.

"You don't have to tell me," Sarah added before changing the subject. "So you've met Liam Nash before," she said, wearing a smug expression.

Melanie raised her eyebrows. "We weren't introduced the one and only time I'd ever seen him."

"When he was with Angelique," Sarah added.

"Yes . . . or Angel, as Mike calls her."

Sarah lifted up her glass of juice in a toast. "Well here's hoping Angel is out of Liam Nash's picture very, very soon . . . And that you're in it."

∽∾

Angelique stole another look at Mike, slightly bothered that the smile was still on his face. Knowing what kept it there didn't help her mood.

Mike caught her looking at him and flashed a full frontal grin at her.

She gave him a half smile and turned to look out the window once more.

His smile faded as he mistakenly assumed the reason for her quietness. "Hey, don't worry, Sarah and the girls will be fine now. You did a good thing today, Angel. Thank you."

She turned abruptly and spoke to his profile. "Mike, I didn't hire her because you asked me to, or because I felt sorry for her. I questioned her first; that was an interview. If she hadn't told me what I wanted to hear, I wouldn't have told her she had the job."

"Oh . . . I thought," he murmured, then stopped.

Feeling waspish for snapping at him, she reached out a hand to cover his as she tried to explain. "Look, it's Dr. Maze's business, not mine. I'm responsible for my replacement because I'm backing out of an agreement to work in the Lake Coburn office for two years. The truth is, I'll give her a two week trial period, but if she can't cut it, I'll have to find someone else. I owe it to Dr. Maze and the other employees of the clinic."

"I understand, Angel. I'm impressed as hell that you're even willing to give her a chance. If you could see her with her girls—I should have taken you to see them; if I had, you'd feel like I do."

She bit at her lower lip worriedly before turning to face him. "Mike, are you beginning to care for Sarah Richard?"

Mike's jaw clenched as what she'd been thinking suddenly came to him. He pulled inside the nearest parking lot and threw the truck into park before turning to her.

"Yeah, Angel, I care for Sarah. I care because she's an abused woman, I feel compassion for another human being, and I really hope she can turn her crappy life into a good one for her and her girls. I'd hoped you would feel the same way after meeting her." He turned his head away from her and stared out the front windshield of the truck. "I guess I hoped for too much."

"That's not fair, and it's a crappy thing to say to me," she said, her irritation rising to a dangerous level, especially when he still didn't look at her. "You know, I only met her for the first time thirty minutes ago, and I hired her, without seeing her adorable twin girls. Shouldn't that count for something?"

He continued to stare straight ahead.

Angelique tossed her clutch irritably onto the truck's dashboard. "Enough, Michael," she said in a tight voice. "Take me to my car."

Her irritated tone seemed to jerk him out of his daze. He leveled a stern gaze on her, his brow furrowed with deep lines. After a few uncomfortable moments, he grinned smugly at her. "Be careful. Your skin tone's beginning to match the color of your eyes."

She swung around to face him. "What?"

"You're jealous."

"I am not," she snapped, far too quickly. "But I do want you to take me to my car, please."

∾∾

Halfway to Lake Coburn, Angelique pried her aching fingers from her steering wheel and tried to ease the tension from her stiff shoulders. She'd left Mike's place in the midst of an unusually icy silence, neither of them willing to concede to the other. She groaned loudly as she pictured his smug, satisfied expression as he'd given her one curt wave before turning his back to walk away from her car.

Angelique adjusted her rearview mirror and stared at her reflection. The color of her eyes seemed deeper, brighter than usual. Was it a result of the green eyed monster revealing itself? Was she jealous? Could she be possibly be so horrible a person to resent a woman who'd been through such an awful experience? An image of Mike hovering over the tiny figure of Sarah Richard flashed in her mind. She closed her eyes and turned from the mirror in annoyance as the truth slammed home.

She stared at the roadway ahead of her, half blinded by tears of shame and humiliation. Shame for feeling this way, and humiliated because Mike had seen through her pitiful attempts to feel justified before she'd realized it herself.

She wiped hastily at her eyes and tried to pay closer attention to her driving. After a torturous trip home, she finally entered her apartment. Exhausted from her feelings of turmoil, she threw her purse on the floor and dropped belly down onto her living room couch.

Tears made a trail down her face as she admitted the truth. She had taken Mike for granted—that he'd always be there, he'd never concede to Liam, and he'd never look at another woman. What would she do if he suddenly stopped being there for her? She'd asked herself that question before, but it had never bothered her . . . until now. Would she feel the same way if Liam walked away from her? She strongly suspected she would.

"God help me. I'm so confused," she said, covering her eyes. She closed her eyes, hoping to clear the fog of futility from her mind for just a little while.

∿

Mike came in from his run and waited for his breathing to steady before pouring himself a glass of water. He drank deeply then walked around his kitchen, trying to keep his leg muscles loose. When he thought he could participate in a conversation without sounding like a heavy breather, he called the one person who must have been put on this earth to drive him crazy.

It had been over two hours since she'd left him and he hadn't heard a peep from her. After the third ring, he told himself that surely he'd given her long enough to cool off. He looked at the phone as her voice mail picked up after the sixth ring—or maybe he hadn't.

∿

Angelique reached for her chirping cell phone and cracked her lids enough to see Mike's name flash across the screen. No way could she talk to him yet. She set the phone carefully on the end table to let her voice mail pick it up. She glanced at her watch and groaned as she realized she'd slept for two hours.

Raising herself from the sofa, she waited for the fogginess to clear from her mind. What would she say to that man when she spoke to him again? She got up to fix a cup of chamomile tea, knowing the coffee she craved would keep her up all night. Just as she sat down with the cup palmed between her hands, her phone rang again. This time she answered without checking the caller ID.

"Hello."

"Hey Angel, how are you today?" Liam's voice boomed from the other end.

"I'm good." She sat back against the cushioned arm of the sofa and curled her feet under her. "I just woke from a nap and I'm trying to snap myself out of it with a cup of hot tea."

"You need me to call back later?"

"Nope," she said. "I've been gone all day and I have some laundry to do. I went to visit my parents today."

After a slight pause, Liam spoke up. "Alone?"

Angelique took a sip of tea. "No."

Liam grunted. "I bet your folks are crazy about Harper."

Angelique pictured the earlier scene as her parents had spoken French with Mike. Her dad had enjoyed teaching him several more words and phrases from the Creole French language. "They like him."

"I guess they were pissed at me for taking off like I did," he added.

"At first they were upset with you, but now they know what you've gone through. They both admire you for doing what you had to do to get your life back."

"They know about the fire?" he asked solemnly.

"I told mama; I hope that's okay." She listened as Liam took a deep breath and released it.

"Yeah, it's fine," he said. After an uncomfortable silence, he continued. "I almost forgot; I acquired a new client yesterday."

"Mike told me about her," she answered. "It's good of you to take Sarah's case on pro bono. I met with her this afternoon, and hired her as my replacement in the Lake Coburn office."

"Your replacement?" he asked. "You're leaving the clinic?"

"I'm transferring back so that I can be closer to my parents."

"To the Lafayette office," he stated dryly.

"Yes."

"Lafayette . . . Where Mike Harper happens to live."

"It's also where my parents happen to live." Dead silence. "This has nothing to do with Mike," she added, when she could no longer bear Liam's stony silence.

More silence followed. Finally he spoke. "So you say."

Anger started as a slow burn in her belly, and quickly built to a fiery rage, and still she remained silent.

After several agonizing moments he finally broke the icy silence.

"Are you still there?"

"Yes…" Her voice low and controlled.

"Angel?" he said, after another prolonged silence.

"I'm trying to get my head around the fact that you just called me a liar."

"I'm not calling you a liar, but I do think you're in denial when you say your transfer isn't about Harper," he replied.

Angelique managed to respond in a tight voice. "My mother will be having hip replacement surgery, and my father needs both knees replaced. Not that I owe you or anyone an explanation."

After several icily silent seconds, Liam tried owning up to his mistake. "I screwed up, huh?"

"In a big way," she returned.

"I'm sor . . . "

She cut off his reply with a push of the power button. "Men," she muttered, dropping the phone on the couch on her way to the bathroom for a hot shower.

CHAPTER 14

On the day of Sarah's release from the hospital, she was accompanied by two off duty cops and her personal bodyguard, with her daughters in tow.

Mel pushed Sarah's wheelchair up to the opened door of her personal car. She helped to seat her comfortably, while Liam and Mike each secured a child into their car seats in the back seat.

Leery of taking another uncertain step into her future, Sarah closed her eyes and recited a silent prayer. Needing a familiar face around, she had asked Melanie to drive her to her new temporary home on the outskirts of Lake Coburn. She felt safe having her at the wheel, and the fact that Liam and Mike followed in Nash's vehicle also comforted her.

Melanie pulled slowly out to the roadway. "It'll be alright Sarah. I know the McAllister family and anyone associated with them is bound to be good people."

Sarah opened her eyes to look at her new friend. "I know that, Mel. I was just praying that all of this mess is straightened out while my girls are still babies. I don't want them to have any memories of this."

Melanie reached over to lay a comforting hand on Sarah's. "It will be."

"Eventually, maybe. But it's more than just the situation with Troy. I want my girls to remember me as a good provider, not as someone who had to survive on handouts from total strangers. What kind of example am I setting for them?"

Melanie nodded as she maneuvered the car through the Lafayette traffic. "The fact that you're concerned about it is proof enough that you're setting an excellent example. Every now and then, people need a helping hand. You'll be strong enough to stand on your own two feet soon."

Sarah dropped her head back onto the seat and wiped a tear from the corner of her eye. "I hope you're right, Mel."

Mike buckled his seat belt as Nash pulled out behind Mel's car. Once they knew for certain they weren't being followed, both men relaxed back into their seats.

Nash glanced over at the other man. "How's Angel doing?"

Somewhat surprised at the question, Mike turned his head to face him. "I figured you could tell me. I haven't heard from her since Sunday."

"Neither have I," Nash said. "She's not returning any of my calls."

Mike grinned. "Mine either. What'd you do to piss her off?"

"You first," Nash replied.

"I'll pass."

"Me too."

The two men looked at each other and laughed.

"She's something, isn't she?" Nash murmured.

Mike grinned and nodded. "She certainly is."

"She's the second woman I've ever loved," Nash commented.

Mike turned toward his old friend. "She's the only woman I've ever loved. I expect she's it for me."

"Yeah, well. I've thought that before, but I was wrong. You could be, too, Injun Joe."

A deep chuckle rumbled through Mike's chest. "Nobody's had the balls to call me that in years. It must be that crazy English blood of yours, you son of a bitch."

"Irish, man . . . I'm Irish!" Nash said, letting the r's roll off his tongue. "Me great, great grandfather came over in the eighteen hundreds as just a wee lad," he added, his voice thick with the Irish brogue.

"Aye, and bringing a bit of the old Blarney Stone with him as well, I'd wager," Mike volunteered in his own passable Irish accent.

After the laughter slowly died down, Mike turned serious again. "I love her so damn much."

Nash gave him a sympathetic look. "I know you do, man, and if I thought I loved her any less, I'd walk away. But I don't—so I can't. I guess it'll be up to her to choose."

Mike snorted. "If that's the case, she could tell us both to kiss her ass. As it stands now, we're both as cold as a brass witch's tit in a blizzard." He turned to watch the scenery as it passed quickly outside the truck's window. "How'd you do it, Nash? How'd you live through that?" He shook his head slowly. "Knowing how I feel about Angel, if I lost her that way, I'd want to die."

"Who says I didn't?" Nash drove through the next green light in silence. "I wished I'd died instead of her. Hell, I wished I'd died right along with her . . . or them, rather." He paused, visualizing something from a past that he sometimes wished to forget. "When I saw Kim holding our son in her arms—I cursed God for making me miss out on the chance to hold him myself. But, now I realize how merciful he was by taking Nicholas before I got a chance to bond with him. If I had, I think I would have drunk myself into an early grave, instead of stopping when I did."

Mike groaned at Nash's words. "And here I am, praying Angel will pick me over you. I feel like an egg-sucking dog."

Mike's heartfelt confession gave Nash the chance to crack a grin at his old friend. "Don't worry about it, buddy. It's not your fault I screwed up and walked away from her. I've already survived the worst thing that could happen to me. If she chooses you over me, I'll live."

~~

Sarah and her entourage arrived at Daniel and Leah's home around ten a.m. on a bright Tuesday morning. Melanie turned off the ignition and popped open the trunk of her car. As she circled around to help Sarah out of the passenger's side, Red and Tiffany McAllister walked outside to meet them. She smiled broadly at the tall, good looking, auburn haired man and his pretty wife.

"God, it's good to see you again, Red," Mel said.

"You too, Melanie. Have you met Tiffany?" he asked, as his wife walked forward.

"Only once; how are you?" she asked, opening Sarah's door.

"I'm good, thanks. I'm dying to meet Dad and Leah's house guest and those gorgeous twins I keep hearing about." Tiffany leaned in to help Sarah out of the car. "Hi Sarah. I'm Tiffany McAllister and this is my husband Red. It is so good to finally meet you."

Sarah smiled and nodded. "Thank you," she murmured. "It's beautiful out here," she said, gazing at the well-tended yard and fenced in pastures surrounding the ranch style structure. "Are the LeBlanc's here?"

"They're putting the final touches to the nursery. They already had one crib up for our daughter, so they went out and bought two more for the twin's use."

Sarah's eyes widened as she stammered. "Oh they didn't have to do that."

"Don't worry, honey—they'll get used. Annie's will be here soon, so they were going to get another one anyway. The nursery is huge." She leaned over and spoke quietly to Sarah. "Leah couldn't have children of her own so she dotes on any baby that's around. Believe me when I tell you this is no imposition on them at all.

They begged us to let you stay with them." Tiffany helped her inside and got her settled on the overstuffed couch.

Melanie and Red brought the twins in just as Leah entered the room, followed by Daniel carrying a baby girl.

"You're finally here!" Leah gushed as she sat beside Sarah and took her hand. "I'm Leah and that's my husband Daniel holding our granddaughter, Briana. Welcome to our home."

Sarah studied the lovely woman sporting a tan and freckles, she assumed from spending time outside training her horses. Her gaze travelled to Daniel LeBlanc, a large man who towered over his wife. He smiled down at her while gently cuddling his granddaughter.

"Thank you both for this. You can't possibly know how much this means to me." Overcome by her emotions as well as physically exhausted from the trip, Sarah wiped frantically at the escaping tears. Daniel sat in the chair beside the couch and rested the infant on his knee.

"Sarah, we want you to feel safe here. This place is as well protected as Fort Knox, and either Leah or I will be here with you at all times. You and your girls are safe," Daniel told her. "We want you to relax and concentrate on getting better."

"That's right, and speaking of your girls, let's get a good look at these little beauties," Leah said.

Red and Melanie placed the car seats on the floor in front of her. As soon as the twin gazes focused on their mother, their chubby legs kicked as they emitted similar squeals of delight.

"Oh, how adorable," Leah exclaimed. "They are identical, aren't they?" She looked over at Sarah. "Any identifiable markings?"

"Sammi has a birthmark on her right leg," she told her.

"Good, now I know who I'm talking to, don't I, Sammi?" Leah said, finding the mark on her leg. She picked up Danni and placed her on her hip.

"Someone hand me Sammi so I can see what this poor woman has been going through," she said.

Red picked up the other infant from her seat and held her in midair. "Hello beautiful." The child rewarded him with an earsplitting grin as she cooed endearingly. "Aw, I bet you say that to all the guys," he murmured, before handing her to his mother in law.

Leah took a spin around the room carrying a baby on each hip then turned toward Sarah. "I am so going to enjoy having the three of you here," she gushed.

Suddenly overwhelmed with all the kindness, Sarah got teary-eyed again. "I don't know how to thank you all."

Leah gave her a reassuring smile. "You must be exhausted, hon. How about if we show you the guest room and nursery now?"

Tiffany helped her up from the couch and gave her a tour of the large nursery and her luxurious suite just next door. After Leah caught her in a yawn, Sarah agreed to lay down for a nap while they took the babies back to the living room.

The plush bed enveloped her like a warm hug, making her feel safe and secure. Even then, it took some time for the pain meds to kick in, numbing her mind as well as her body enough to succumb to a deep, restful sleep.

CHAPTER 15

Sarah stirred the pot of spaghetti sauce, stopping to inhale the aromatic ribbons of steam drifting up from the pot. Herbs simmered with onions, bell pepper, and fresh Portobello mushrooms, while chunky tomato sauce merged with lean ground beef to a create a delectable array of taste bud tempting bliss.

She turned off the burner and covered the pot before heading out to the huge back deck overlooking the picturesque horse pastures. After two weeks of being here, the beauty of this place still overwhelmed her. Taking the steps slowly, she reached ground level and made her way to where Leah and Daniel stood by the fence, each holding a baby in their arms.

"The spaghetti's done if anyone's ready to eat," she said, reaching out to brush her daughter's stray lock into place.

Daniel faced her. "Good, because that trip to Houston about did me in; I didn't even have time to stop for lunch." He held Danni up in front of him and kissed her cheek. "And I missed these munchkins like the dickens," he said.

Leah grinned at her husband. "I knew it was only a matter of time before I'd be replaced by someone younger and prettier."

Daniel rewarded her with a kiss. "You're irreplaceable, babe. I know where my bread's buttered, don't you worry about that."

Sarah watched the older couple enviously. In the two weeks she and her girls had been there, Leah and Daniel had only had one disagreement. It had been a minor one, with no name calling or attempts at humiliation, no bullying by Daniel, who towered over his wife, and no slaps or punches involved. Seeing them together had given her hope that maybe relationships could be good, after all.

She still feared that Troy would return and try to get to her and the girls, but Daniel hadn't exaggerated when he'd said this ranch was as safe as Fort Knox. When she lay her head down at night, with the LeBlanc's just down the hall from her and her children, it was with a peace of mind she hadn't felt in years. Not only that, but both sides of their families seemed to be involved in making her feel safe and secure. She'd never in her life been treated with such kindness from virtual strangers.

At the sound of a vehicle crunching along the gravel drive, the group walked to the front of the huge ranch house. Tiffany and Red drove up in his truck, followed by two people in a Lexus SUV.

Recognizing the tall brunette from the hospital, Sarah broke into a wide grin. "That's Angelique, the lady who's responsible for hiring me to work for Dr. Maze." Her face suddenly turned serious. "I hope she's not here to take back the job offer."

Leah draped an arm over her shoulder affectionately. "You can borrow trouble like nobody I've ever seen, Sarah. What did I tell you about losing the pessimism?"

"You're right," she agreed. "I'm sure she's just here to let me know when I can start."

"That's more like it," Daniel said, sounding pleased. He walked over to his daughter and gave her a hug. "Hello, baby girl."

Tiffany beamed up at him. "Hey Daddy, how's everything going over here?"

"Wonderful! Where's my gorgeous granddaughter?" he asked, bending low to look into the back seat of the truck. Briana kicked her feet and squealed loudly at the sight of her grandfather. "There's Paw Paw's big girl!" he said, handing off Danni to Tiffany, who immediately began loving up on the baby, causing the twin to erupt in giggles.

Daniel bent over the car seat and straightened, bringing Briana with him as she cooed and tugged at his face lovingly.

Leah approached, nuzzling the baby's neck. "Hello sweet girl," she purred to her granddaughter, before turning her attention to Tiffany and Red. "Hey, you two, Sarah just told us supper is ready."

Tiffany smiled at her step mother. "We brought guests, I hope y'all don't mind."

Leah hugged her step-daughter. "Of course not; Sarah just cooked a huge pot of spaghetti."

"Along with garlic bread and a salad," Sarah added. She turned as Angelique walked up with a tall, blonde man she'd never seen before. "Hello, Angelique, it's good to see you again."

Angelique took Sarah's hand and squeezed it. "My God, you look fantastic. The LeBlanc's must be taking good care of you."

Sarah beamed at her host and hostess. "They've been wonderful."

Angelique turned toward the driver of the Lexus. "This is a good friend of mine, Tanner Collins. We finally decided we had to see these gorgeous twins everyone's been talking about."

Sarah narrowed her gaze toward Tiffany at the mention of Tanner's name. Tiffany's nod and laughter told her she was on the right track.

"Yes, that's the same Tanner I was engaged to," Tiffany admitted.

Sarah turned back toward the man to study him. Tall, built, good looking, blonde, and blue eyed . . . dressed casually in jeans, un-tucked polo shirt, and a leather jacket. Definite hunk possibilities, despite the fact that there was something off about the way he carried himself. He moved as though he weren't quite comfortable in his skin. Whatever his reason, it initially made her feel as uncomfortable as he acted. Rather than be rude, she ignored the spidey-sense that urged her to retreat from him, and instead, extended her hand.

Tanner grimaced, seeming put-off at the wary expression on her face. "It seems that, once more, my reputation has preceded me," he said before offering her a bright smile. "Relax, Sarah, I'm not the ogre you may have heard I was."

"Not anymore, anyway," Tiffany and Angelique stated in unison, resulting in an all-around burst of laughter at his expense.

Tanner gave a good-natured chuckle. "You'd think they'd at least cut me some slack for making the effort." He gave her hand a gentle squeeze. "Everyone has been saying how strong and courageous you've been through this ordeal. Given my history, I guess I shouldn't be surprised that no one mentioned how drop dead gorgeous you are."

"Probably not," Daniel said in clear warning to the former womanizer.

Tanner nodded in agreement as everyone laughed, and gave her a gracious smile. "I really have heard wonderful things about you."

Initially uneasy at the way he focused his gaze on her, she calmed at the sound of sincerity in his tone and the way he was willing to poke fun at his previous bad boy reputation. "Thank you so much, Tanner. It's nice to meet you, too," she said, offering a cautious smile. A slight pause had her grinning up at him, trying not to laugh. "And it's too bad I can't say the same," she added.

Tanner seemed to pay no heed to the laughter around them, as he gave her a reluctant nod. "I wish you could too."

Sarah gave the kitchen counter one last polish as Leah pushed the button on the dishwasher to begin its cycle.

"That was a good visit," Daniel said, with satisfaction. "My granddaughter is growing so fast. I think she's definitely going to have some height to her."

Sarah looked at her diminutive twin girls and groaned. "My poor kids don't have a chance."

Daniel's chest rumbled as he laughed. "That's to be expected when you've got a midget for a mother." His face grew solemn as he dared to ask the next question. "What about their father?"

Sarah shrugged. "I used to think he was tall, but now that I've lived in the valley of the jolly green giants, I'm guessing five foot, ten inches isn't that tall for a guy."

"Not in my family, it isn't," Daniel snorted. "My two older brothers had a good three inches on me and I'm six foot three in my socks."

Sarah groaned as she leaned over to embrace her daughters. "Yep, they're doomed to munchkin land, just like their mama." Sammi and Danni took time out from gnawing on their teething biscuits to grin adorably up at their mother. She passed her fingers over their gums to feel the teeth just breaking through the skin. "I can't believe they both got their first tooth on the same day."

"I can't believe it was Tanner who found them," Daniel growled in disappointment. "I've been checking four times a day for the last week, damned determined I would find them first."

Leah laughed at her husband. "Babe, there's still Briana—she hasn't cut a tooth yet."

"Red told me that McAllister babies don't cut their teeth for nearly a year," he grumbled. "That's a long time to wait to buy her a new outfit."

"For God's sake, Daniel," Leah huffed. "You don't need an excuse to buy any of these kids a new outfit—just do it."

Daniel frowned down at his wife. "It's not the same, hon. Angelique said it's supposed to give them good luck if the person who finds the tooth buys the outfit. I wanted to be the one to give them good luck."

Sarah smiled at the giant of a man in front of her. "You two have given them more than luck, Daniel. You've given us all hope and opportunity, don't you know that? We were in a women's shelter before you took us in. I will always be grateful to you and Leah. You've made the difference for us."

Daniel embraced Sarah in a warm, fatherly hug. "We're glad to hear that. You've become like another daughter to us, Sarah. Leah and I talked about it last night, and we want you to know that you can call this place home as long as you need to."

"You're stuck with us now," Leah said. "We couldn't love these two babies more if they were grandchildren by blood."

"I never thought I could fall in love with an entire group of people I've only known for two weeks," she said, giving Leah a hug.

Daniel leaned over to stick his face in front of the two high chairs holding the twin girls. They giggled and both began jabbering to him as they reached out with their sticky fingers. He laughed as he looked up at their mother. "Listen to 'em go." He lifted one out of her chair and turned to Leah. "Grab the other one, Maw Leah. Let's wash off all this rice cereal and applesauce and see what we find."

∽◡∾

Thanks to Leah and Daniel, Sarah got to take a leisurely shower in the guest bathroom. By the time her hair dried, it was time to put the babies down for the night. Sarah smoothed their curls and patted their freshly diapered bottoms while they yawned and rubbed their eyes sleepily. Within a few short minutes they settled into their sleep positions, their movements executed in perfect synchronization, as usual. With one adjustment to their comforters, she turned on the night light and pulled the door closed behind her.

Back in her own room, one over from her daughters, Sarah powered on the baby monitor and stretched out on her bed. After two weeks in the LeBlanc's care she only felt an occasional twinge in one side from her nearly healed ribs. She still wore a brace on one arm, but with Leah and Daniel's help, she could manage caring for her daughters.

Burrowed into the warmth of the thick, down comforter, she thought about the new job she'd start tomorrow with an anticipation that made her insides feel like a plateful of Jell-O. Leah had told her not to worry about finding a daycare or sitter for the girls, of course. Daniel insisted that she stay with them long enough to put a good amount of money aside to start up another household.

As of yet, Liam Nash had only stayed with them part time, switching off with Daniel to have some days to himself. Starting tomorrow, he'd be Sarah's full time body guard, both at the LeBlanc home and during work hours as well as anytime in between.

She smiled to herself, remembering Leah's subtle hints about the benefits of Sarah having a man like that around, permanently. But what she'd told Mel two weeks earlier still held true. She'd never consider him as anything other than a good friend. Besides, after the nightmare called Troy, she couldn't say she'd ever be ready to forfeit, or even share, control over her own life by committing to another man.

~~~

In another part of town, someone else lay alone in his bed thinking of warm brown eyes bearing a hint of laughter, a gorgeous pair of dimpled cheeks, and two of the prettiest baby girls he'd ever seen.

As soon as her image formed in his mind, Tanner pushed it aside. No way would she ever be his type. Not now. Not ever. And who the hell needs kids, especially when they come in pairs? She seemed like a nice girl, someone wanting to get out of a bad situation in the worst way. She sure as hell didn't need the likes of him sniffing after her. His mind suddenly overflowed with Angel's comments from that afternoon. "You're not the same man you used to be, Tanner. You're evolving—growing. You've told me you want to change and I believe you."

"Yeah," he whispered to the dark bedroom. "And the road to hell is paved with good intentions. Do the lady a favor, and put her out of your mind."

He rolled over on his side and punched his pillow, determined to get some sleep. After another hour of tossing and turning, he got up for a glass of water before walking to the windows that overlooked the apartment complex courtyard. For the first time he noticed it wasn't child friendly.

It brought to mind the conversation that had taken place between him and the manager when he'd looked at this place. The woman had told him they were looking for young, successful, professionals as tenants. "No pets or children," she'd told him. The memory of his response to her statement caused him to cringe inwardly. "Is there a difference?"

Had there ever been a time when he wasn't a first class asshole?

His thoughts travelled once more to Sarah and her daughters. Sarah, the girl who'd survived a car accident, only to have her abusive husband beat the bloody hell out of her then lock her up with her babies for days with no food. What he wouldn't do to have a chance at that sadistic son of a bitch.

How'd she end up with a maniac like that, anyway? As soon as he'd met her he'd experienced an unfamiliar disturbance. Who the hell was he trying to kid? It had been more like channeling a freaking Doberman, set on protecting its owner. He could well remember the tension, the tightness at the back of his neck, a perfect pairing with his fisted hands.

Maybe he had changed in small ways, no doubt due to Angelique's undying eagerness to put him in his place. That woman got off on berating him for the slightest snobbish comment, while forcing him to examine his own self from a different perspective.

Despite that, he knew a meaningful relationship was miles away. As much as he aspired to change himself, no way in hell would it happen overnight. His one night hook-up earlier that evening was proof of that. Tanner groaned while adjusting himself at the memory of the busty new nurse just recently back from a stint in the Army. But then he smiled, remembering the momentary pleasure in an evening of hot, meaningless sex.

"Well, hell," he murmured, trying not to be so disappointed in his fall from grace. "Rome wasn't built in a day…"

CHAPTER 16

By noon the next day, Angelique had congratulated herself several times over for hiring Sarah as her replacement. She used all the software proficiently and knew nearly as much about the computers as their IT team. She'd shown up early, with Liam in tow, looking professional, but chic, and had proceeded to make friends with everyone in the office. Angelique had told her about Dr. Maze's weakness for sweets, so Sarah arrived with a batch of homemade macadamia and white chocolate cookies, an instant crowd pleaser.

Angelique passed Sarah's purse to her while walking out of the office for lunch. "They're not going to miss me at all around here, honey. You've even got Dr. Maze eating out of your hand like a pet monkey."

Sarah blushed. "It's just the cookies and your advice."

Angelique stopped midstride to face Sarah, placing her hands on her shoulders. "Stop that, do you hear me? You have done absolutely everything right today, and this place is damn fortunate to have you."

∿∽

"Did someone have a good morning?" Liam asked from just behind Angelique.

Sarah, who'd caught his gaze as he approached, smiled shyly, but managed a nod. "Someone did."

Angelique spun around to face him. "I forgot you were here."

"Nice. Just what every guy wants to hear."

"Oh, grow up," she barked. "We were busy."

He nodded, wondering how long she would keep up the cold shoulder routine she'd given him for two weeks. At least he knew Mike wasn't any better off. They'd spent the last two Friday and Saturday nights drinking beer and having the southern man's version of a pity party. He turned to Sarah. "How's the new job going?"

"Good, if my new boss is to be believed," she answered. "My Excel skills are a little rusty, but I'll get it back."

Angelique snorted. "Don't listen to her, she's an expert user in any software we have. She can already run that place with her eyes closed. Where are we going for lunch?"

"My treat, ladies," Liam added.

"I don't know about you two, but I'm hungry for a big juicy hamburger. Any good places around here?" Sarah asked.

Angelique nodded as she pulled her keys from her purse. "There's a real nice mom and pop restaurant just down the street that makes great burgers and sandwiches. I'll drive."

"I call shot gun," Liam called out.

Angelique shot him a look that would freeze molten lava. "The hell you do. You're riding in the back."

～～

The door jangled again and Nash glanced up at the thirty-something year old man entering the diner. Though the man looked nothing like Sarah's ex, he couldn't rule out the possibility of Troy sending someone to do the job for him. In all likelihood, the asshole probably hung out with people who'd do it for little incentive.

"Does that guy look familiar, Sarah?"

"Nope, never saw him before," she said, wiping her mouth with her napkin before dropping it on the table. "That was the best burger I've ever eaten. I'll definitely be coming back to this place." She scooted her chair back and pointed to a hallway. "Restrooms?"

Angelique nodded. "I'll go too."

Liam placed his hand on her forearm. "A word, please?"

Angel signaled Sarah to go ahead before she sat back down. As soon as she was out of ear shot she turned to Liam. "Have you ever noticed that she will not drink anything unless it's bottled or canned and she's broken the seal herself?"

"I have. Mike said one of the nurses in the hospital said she was obsessive about it. She's even that way at the ranch where she knows she's safe. That's a good damn indication of one thing."

"Date rape?" Angelique said, getting a sick feeling in her stomach at his nod. "Men can be such pigs."

"Not all of us, Angel, although some of us can be pretty damn stupid at times. Are you ever going to forgive me?"

"I forgive you," she said sternly.

"That had all the feeling of a root canal."

Her eyebrow crooked ominously. "I could take it back."

"You're still pissed at me," he commented.

She gave a long, drawn out sigh. "I'm not pissed, I'm disappointed. I shouldn't have to justify myself to you or Mike. We're all friends."

"Not just friends, Angel." At her stony silence, Liam leaned forward. "You know, any normal woman would be jumping up and down to have two guys chasing after her. But not you," he snorted.

"Chasing after me?" she hissed. "Kids in grade school chase each other. Adults strive for something more meaningful, and that involves trust." She turned her head to watch a young mother pick up her crying newborn. "It sure as hell doesn't include questioning my motive to move back to Lafayette."

"I'm sorry, dammit!" he said, loud enough to cause more than a few heads to turn in their direction.

"Wonderful," she groaned, turning a bright shade of crimson. "I just love being part of the main attraction."

Liam sat back and clenched his jaw. When the waitress chose that moment to bring the check to the table, he grabbed it from her. He stood up, pulled out his wallet, and threw a five on the table for the tip. "I'll go pay the check," he said, stalking angrily off toward the cashier.

~~

Angelique grabbed her purse and escaped to the women's restroom. She opened the door, seeing Sarah resting one hip against the wall.

Sarah grinned crookedly up at her. "Was trying to give you two some privacy."

Angelique fanned her flushed face in silence as her co-worker sucked in her breath.

"Oh oh, What happened?"

"It's called a face-off; we're both stubborn." She washed her hands, reapplied her lipstick and threw the tube back into her purse. "I think Liam's under the impression that it's easy for me to be around him and Mike without wanting more."

"You want more?" Sarah asked.

"Of course I want more. God, you've seen those two. They each deserve a spot on the Hunk of the Month calendar. I know from experience that throwing sex into the mix would only complicate things." She blew out an exasperated breath. "Things are complicated enough as it is."

"And now you have to see Liam five days out of the week, all day long, because of me," Sarah added.

Angelique slipped her purse strap over her shoulder and faced her. "Under normal circumstances, I'd be fine with it, but he's not happy that I'm moving back to Lafayette."

"Too close to Detective Harper?"

"Yes, but close to my parents, which is where I need to be." She checked her watch and sighed. "It's time to get back to work."

~◡◠

Angelique placed the last of her dishes in the cabinet and poured herself a half glass of wine before relaxing on the couch with a book. She'd only read three pages before her phone rang. She glanced at the caller ID and made a face.

"I'm sorry," she said immediately into the phone, before she lost her nerve.

"Angel?" the caller asked, sounding surprised.

"Yeah, Mike, it's me; and I owe you an apology," she said.

"I've been trying to call you for two weeks to apologize for the other day," Mike insisted.

"I know, and I should have returned your calls. I'm sorry for that, also."

"Well now I'm confused all to hell."

"You were right, I was jealous, even though I knew I didn't have reason to be." She chewed on her lower lip while waiting for him to reply. "Are you still there?" she asked after a lengthy silence.

"Still here," he mumbled, "just terrified to put my big foot in my mouth again."

"I am sorry, Mike. Sarah is a wonderful lady, and her twins are darling. We're already great friends and I never should have asked if you had feelings for her."

"I don't, you know, but can't I gloat just a little that you were jealous?"

"Go ahead. I guess I have it coming."

"I'll save it for the next time I see you. Now, how was your day?"

"It was good. Sarah is going to be a wonderful addition to the Lake Coburn clinic."

"Great news, but does this mean there won't be any delay in you moving back to God's country?"

"Lafayette doesn't exactly spit out affordable rent homes, Mike. It may take me awhile to find a place."

"You like the neighborhood I live in, don't . . . ?"

"I'm not moving in with you," she cut in.

"I'm not asking you to. There's a house on the next block that's up for rent. The owner asked if I could help her find someone reliable. She's not advertising, because she wants to be selective."

"Is it livable?" she asked. "I'm not sure I can afford a house in that neighborhood."

"It's spacious, and in great shape. Nan is going to Paris for two years and just wants someone in it. She doesn't want to go through the bother of switching all the utilities off; she wants everything left in her name."

"No deposits?" Angelique asked.

"That's right . . . Now you know why she asked me to help her find a reliable renter. She inherited the place and is only asking the loan note for her renovation."

Angelique made the sign of the cross and asked the important question. "How much?"

"Four hundred and you pay for all the utilities. She said the satellite is optional, because she's already fulfilled her contract agreement. She can cancel it or leave it on for you if you want to pay the bill; either way is fine."

"That's less than half what I was paying in Lake Coburn. When can I see it?"

"As soon as possible, because she said if there's any furniture you want her to leave in the house, it'll save her from putting it in storage...especially her antiques...she'd rather have them being used and taken care of. I told her you may be interested, and that I could personally vouch for you."

"So what's this woman's name, and how well do you know her?" she asked, fighting back yet another bout of unexpected jealousy.

"Her name is Nan Miller, and she's head of our neighborhood watch program. She's absolutely gorgeous, inside and out," he added for effect.

"Two years in Paris, huh?" she said, flatly. "How nice."

∾

"What do you think, dear?" The diminutive woman had to step back to look all the way up at Angelique. A curly cap of snow white hair framed the face that was still relatively wrinkle-free, despite her seventy something years. Blue eyes sparkled with delight as she waited for her to answer.

Angelique walked around the beautifully landscaped backyard, to where Nan stood, surrounded by fragrant blossoms of early blooming tulips and daffodils. "It's absolutely perfect, and I'll take it, if you'll have me."

Nan smiled broadly, finally displaying a few well-earned laugh lines. "Of course, dear, I know Michael would never suggest anyone who wasn't completely trustworthy. He's such a good boy. I don't want my wonderful place to sit here empty and lonely for two years. Houses die a little each day when they're alone, did you know that?"

Angelique smiled at her charming, if a little quirky, prospective landlady. "No, ma'am . . . I hadn't heard that, but it makes perfect sense to me."

"Of course it does. A house isn't a home until it's filled with love. Houses aspire to be homes from the second they're created, just as humans aspire to be loved from the second they're born. A home and its human have a symbiotic relationship, you know, each beneficial to the other. It pleases me immensely to know that someone who understands that will be keeping my 'Sonny' company for the next two years."

"Sonny?" Angelique looked around warily, suddenly expecting to see either a pet of some kind, a grave, or even an urn filled with a dead husband's ashes.

Nan smiled at her. "Sonny is the name I gave my home when I moved in. He wasn't a happy home until he got a name." She looked at her with wide set, serious eyes. "You must call him by his name, you know, or he won't be happy."

"And...um . . . what happens he's not happy?" Angelique asked, trying not to laugh.

"Oh, things will go wrong. For instance, the door on the hall closet will stick and you won't be able to get to your things. Or you won't be able to get the windows open, or the front door won't lock or unlock. Lots of little things like that. But—" she said, pointing to Angelique with an arthritic finger, "—If you call him by his name and treat him right, he'll do the same for you."

"I'm assuming you mean he'll treat me right, but not call me by name...correct?" she said, ready to call it quits if she was wrong. Nothing says deal-breaker quite like a talking house.

"Of course, dear . . . Whoever heard of a talking house? What a bunch of malarkey. No, no, what I'm talking about is symbiosis at its finest. Can you do that for him?"

Angelique nodded slowly. "I think so." She turned and looked back at the house. "This place isn't haunted or anything, is it?" Because ghosts would definitely fit in there as deal-breakers also.

Nan put her head back and laughed jovially. "Oh dear, you're not one of those crazies who believe in ghosts, are you?"

Angelique shook her head. "No ma'am! I just thought maybe that's what you . . . What Sonny . . . Oh . . . No, ma'am," she stammered. "I certainly do not believe in ghosts, and I will definitely be sure to call . . . Sonny . . . By his name . . . Occasionally." She sneaked a peek at Mike, who stood behind Nan with his hand planted tightly over his mouth in a gargantuan effort to keep from laughing.

"I'm afraid occasionally won't cut the mustard when it comes to Sonny, dear. You see, I've got him quite spoiled to hearing it several times a day," Nan pressed.

Tight lipped and feeling the desperate need to curse out loud, Angelique finally spoke. "I'll do my best, ma'am."

"But what if your best and mine don't comp . . . "

"I'll do it!" Angelique interjected loudly. "I will! I'll call him Sonny every day, all day long, if that's what it takes to keep him happy. I promise!" The last she threw in as a desperate plea.

The old woman gave her a strange look. "Oh, I believe you dear, but saying it won't help unless you truly mean it."

Angelique stared at the old woman then let her head fall forward in dejection.

Nan placed a fragile hand on her arm and giggled girlishly. "I'm joking, dear."

"You are?" Angel asked, wondering what part of it she was joking about.

"How could I expect you to feel as deeply for my old friend as I do when you've only just met him? That would be absurd!" She turned and walked to the kitchen door, chuckling the entire way. Once she got inside, she called out. "I'll set out coffee and fig cake."

Angelique stared at the door until Nan had disappeared from sight. She wheeled to face Mike. "You might have warned me!" she hissed.

Mike held up his hands in self-defense. "I had no idea, I'll swear to it on the bible! Our neighborhood watch meetings are never here."

"Hasn't she ever mentioned Sonny?"

He shrugged. "Every once in a while she'd say she had to get home to him. I always thought he was a pet of some sort. A few people suggested she had a man waiting for her at home. I guarantee that no one thought she was talking about her house."

Angelique buried her face in Mike's broad chest to smother her laughter as he enfolded her in his arms. "Oh, Lord, what am I getting myself into?"

His chest rumbled with deep laughter. "To tell you the truth, Angel, I'm still not convinced she won't call you from Paris once you've settled in to tell you she was only kidding. She's got a hell of a sense of humor."

"That's what I'd call a twisted sense of humor. And seriously...I don't know what would be worse," Angelique groaned. "Joke or no joke."

CHAPTER 17

By the next Friday, things were nearly back to normal between Liam and Angelique. After a pleasant lunch at a local Mexican restaurant, they waited in their booth for Sarah to return from the ladies room.

"So, do you have plans for tonight?" he asked.

She threw back the last of her water and nodded. "I have to go pay my first month's rent and pick up the keys from my landlady. She's leaving for Paris tomorrow morning."

"What's she going to be doing in Paris?"

Angelique cleared her throat and met his gaze. "To quote Nan, 'Whatever the hell she wants to!'"

Liam threw back his head and laughed. "She sounds like a character."

"You have no idea," she chuckled. "You know, I called her last night for some information, and I finally got the nerve to ask why she gave her house a guy's name. I swear, her answer made me blush."

"What'd she say?"

She looked through the large plate glass window out onto Ryan Street. "She said she'd loved each and every one of her male partners in life, whether they were husbands, fiancés, or just boyfriends . . . That the one thing she missed in life was the sexual satisfaction her men had always given her. She thought that if she gave her home a man's name, she would feel comforted by being surrounded by a masculine presence."

"Wow . . . Did she say if it worked for her?" he asked, leaning back to finish off his iced tea.

"It did not." She blushed slightly and cleared her throat again. "So, she went out and bought the biggest, baddest vibrator she could find, and keeps it in her nightstand."

Liam coughed and sputtered as tea shot out of his nose, cutting off his breath.

She laughed and handed him a napkin. "Her words, not mine."

"She admitted that to you?" he asked, as soon as he'd caught his breath.

"I think Nan would admit it to anyone," she said, nodding.

"How old is she, again?"

"Seventy-six . . . She was big into feminism and free love and all that, but she looks like every typical grandmotherly type you've ever seen. She's tiny, maybe five foot, with white hair, beautiful complexion, beautiful smile, and crystal blue eyes, just sparkling with laughter."

Nash raised one hand. "Oh my God. You just described my paternal great-grandmother. That image, along with what you've told me about her is enough to traumatize me for life. I think I'd rather forget everything you said, and I sure as hell don't want to meet her."

Once they'd controlled their laughter, he managed to ask when she would be making the move.

Angelique shot a look at Sarah, just returning from her ladies room break. "That depends on this young lady."

"What does?" Sarah reseated herself.

"When I move back to Lafayette depends on when you think you don't need me around, anymore. To tell you the truth, I think I could leave tomorrow, she's such a quick learner."

Sarah made a face. "I'm still a little hesitant with the payroll process. Would you mind staying one more week to make sure I can handle it next Friday?"

"That's not a problem. I plan on moving a few things in this weekend, and doing some decorating. I don't think Sonny will die in five days," Angelique threw in.

Liam allowed himself a quick sigh of relief. That meant he had a little less than a week to work on his lady until she was back on Mike's turf. A one week temporary reprieve was better than an immediate move, and he'd take it any day of the week.

∽৹

"Well, honey, wish me luck for tonight," Nan told Angelique as she looped her purse over her shoulder.

Angelique walked her out to a local taxi service's van, where the driver was loading the last suitcase. "Good luck, Nan. Do you plan on doing some gambling tonight in New Orleans?"

Nan gave her an incredulous look. "Hell no. Mabel and I are hitting the male strip clubs tonight on Bourbon Street. Maybe one of us will get lucky."

Already used to her wise cracking sense of humor, Angel barely flinched. "Only one of you?"

Nan made a face. "Mabel isn't all that much to look at, and she's got the bedside manner of a GD pit bull. Those combined traits don't make for a very good roll in the hay," she said with a cackle. "It's my sex-capades that'll keep her imagination going long after I leave this world."

Angelique dropped her jaw in astonishment. "Seriously?"

Nan gave her a sly wink. "Never underestimate the power of a hefty tip, honey."

"Well, all right!" Angelique said, giving her a hug. "Just don't overdo it and miss your flight tomorrow. Oh, and make sure your guy is really a guy. Sometimes it's difficult to tell in some of those clubs."

Nan chuckled. "Not if you check in the right spot."

Angelique laughed as she waved off the cab then turned to look up at her new digs. "Well, Sonny, it's just you and me for the next two years." She walked through the front door and stood gazing at the lovely house that Nan's care and quirky sense of style had transformed into a place to be proud of. Angelique pulled a pad, pen, and measuring tape out of her purse, and carried the step ladder to the living room windows. No sense in wasting a trip when she could be gathering information she needed to put her personal touch into this place.

∿∾

Mike knocked on the door once then cautiously stepped inside at the mumbled answer. His eyes were drawn immediately to Angelique, standing on a stepladder and reaching up toward the existing hardware on the windows. He paused to admire the shapely curve of her calves, clad in dark stockings that complimented her short, black skirt. Her blouse, normally tucked neatly inside, had pulled loose from the waistband and rode up, giving him a tantalizing view of smooth, bare skin.

He walked quietly up to her and cleared his throat.

Apparently startled by the sound, Angelique tried to turn too quickly and lost her balance. She overcompensated, and the step ladder tilted precariously, taking her with it. Before she plummeted to the floor, Mike caught her gallantly in his arms.

Her breath released in a startled gasp as the tape and tablet flew off in two different directions. She instinctively threw her arms around his neck and huddled closer to him.

"I've got you! Sorry, Angel, I thought you knew I was here."

∿∾

The rumble of Mike's laughter pulsed through his shirt and undershirt, making her want to bury her nose in his massive chest and breathe him into her. She lay her cheek against his neck and let his clean, spicy scent tease her senses. Waves of heat and sexual energy travelled between their bodies, separated only by two thin layers of material. Eyes closed, she paused to savor the moment of being surrounded by the feel and smell of him.

Suddenly aware of his silence, she opened her eyes and encountered his surprisingly intense gaze. Without warning, he leaned in and kissed her, softly at first, then deepened the kiss. Her lips parted and his tongue probed tentatively at the soft interior. The kiss ended too soon for her tastes, leaving her wanting for more.

"Can you stand?"

"What?" One corner of his mouth lifted as she focused on the tiny scar just above his upper lip—caused by a fish hook during a Boy Scout Dad and Me camping trip. Feeling the oddest need to touch it, she placed a gentle kiss upon the scar then flicked it with her tongue, tasting the saltiness of his skin. His arms tightened, pulling her closer as she lifted her head to watch him.

Mike opened his eyes to meet her gaze, and slowly released the breath he'd been holding. "Angel." The word came out in a tortured whisper.

"Hmmm?"

"I want you."

"I want you too," she breathed.

He gave her another kiss. The kind that lingered, ended slowly, with him gently pulling on her lower lip before he finally released her.

She gave a low, throaty moan as the need pulled throughout her lower body. Wanting to make him feel as vulnerable as she did, Angelique placed a soft kiss on the side of his neck then tasted him with her tongue. His pulse quickened, and she could feel him tremble, struggling to maintain control. The fact that he was failing miserably, just as she was, pleased her immensely.

"I'm dying here, baby." He groaned, shuddering under her touch.

"I am too, Mike," she gasped.

"Please Angel. Please let me make love to you, Angel. I promise to make it worth your while," he said, his voice deep with need.

"Oh, God, yes."

He carried her to the living room, and stopped. "Where?"

"The sofa," she croaked, sounding desperate.

"There is no sofa."

She looked around, realizing where they were. "Oh, damn."

"Did she leave a bed?" he asked, hopefully.

She shook her head. "The only thing I asked her to leave were the china hutch and buffet, and a couple of armoires."

Mike looked around and carried her over to the peninsula style kitchen cabinet. He placed her gently on the counter top then pulled her to him. She wrapped her legs around his hips and pulled him closer. His mouth settled on hers as their hands frantically found each other, teasing, tickling, and taunting until they were both on the brink.

Suddenly he stepped away from her. "I've got a king sized bed in my place and it's just down the block."

The question seemed to pull Angelique out of the fog of sexual need and back to the present. She covered her face with both hands and groaned loudly. "I shouldn't. I'm sorry, Mike. I can't," she said, regretfully.

He pulled her legs apart and stepped in between them. "Are you sure, Angel?" He pressed himself firmly against her.

"Oh…My…" she said, dry mouthed with need, and wishing like hell she'd never met her friggin' therapist. She hung her head, shamefully. "I'm sorry, but yes, I'm sure." She closed her eyes, waiting for him to protest. To cuss. To try to persuade her again. He remained silent and still. When she finally got the nerve to look up at him, his gaze was so intense, for a moment she thought he was angry with her. "I shouldn't have let it go that far, I'm sorry." To her amazement, he took a step back from her, and smiled.

"It's not your fault, Angel. I knew the rules of the game before I started. But you just looked so damned good up there on that ladder." He shook his head and flashed her a broad smile before helping her down from the counter top. "And damn, I'm glad to have you back in my town."

She smiled up at him sheepishly. "Thank you, Mike."

He reached out and traced her swollen lips with his large, smooth thumb. "Anytime, Angel."

She took his large hand between her own. "You're such a good man—one of a kind."

He laughed. "There are plenty of good men out there, but I guarantee that I'm the only one who loves you this much."

Taken completely off guard by his spur of the moment confession, Angelique stared up into his dark mocha eyes and believed him. The thought had her tearing up immediately. If that realization hadn't done it for her, his next admission would have.

"You're it for me, Angel. I love every blessed thing about you. From your need to curl up on the couch with a quart of rocky road ice cream and a bag of special dark chocolates once a month, to your penchant for destroying your cell phone." He looked down at the floor. "I've never loved before, and I'll never love like this again, whether you choose me, Nash, or some other yahoo. I won't go hang myself if you don't love me back, but I sure would be a miserable son of a bitch if you didn't."

"Aw, Mike."

He met her gaze. "I love you, Angelique."

His four simple words nearly imploded her wall of defenses, making her weak kneed with wanting him. When her legs buckled, he reached out to pull her up against his hard body.

"Hey, are you alright?" he asked, the look of adoration temporarily replaced by one of concern.

"I'm okay," she murmured. "Mike . . ."

∿৩

His heart plummeted at the sadness in her voice and he braced himself for her reply. He'd said he wouldn't hang himself, but faced with the possibility that she didn't love him, he wasn't so sure he wouldn't go out and do just that. Unwilling to hear the words come from her lips he said them for her.

"You don't love me. It's okay, Angel; I only wish the best for you and Nash." He released her and turned quickly so that she wouldn't have to witness a grown man cry.

She grabbed his arm with a strength he didn't know she possessed and pulled him around.

"Look at me, Michael Harper," she said forcefully.

He did and held his breath, waiting to hear the handful of words that would either break his heart or send his soul soaring.

"I love you, too, Mike."

He stared at her for several seconds before the message sank in. "You love me," he repeated, hoping he hadn't heard incorrectly. "You love me?"

She nodded.

"Angel, I was afraid that when Nash came back. You and him, well, you have a history together," he stammered. "And now that you know he had a reason for leaving the way he did . . . "

"But I love Liam, too," she said, sounding desperate.

"What?" He stared into her eyes and saw her dilemma. Suddenly it was clear as a bell. She did love them both, and was terrified to choose and hurt one of them.

"Try to understand. I'd just fallen hard for Liam when he left. It hurt, but didn't alter my feelings for him. Then you came into my life." She closed the distance between them and met his gaze. "How could I not fall in love with you?" She reached up to brush her hand gently along his face.

He closed his eyes and leaned his face into her hand. "Angel," he murmured, reaching out to pull her close. "God I love you so much."

"I know you do," she groaned, burying her face in his shirt. "That's not the issue, here. You and Liam want me to choose, and I can't right now."

Wanting to lighten the mood, he lifted her chin to look into her eyes. "You know, any smart buyer would insist on doing some comparison shopping." His mouth twisted in a teasing grin. "But how can you compare something you've never experienced?"

"What do you mean?"

"Well, if you're going to list the pros and cons of both Nash and me, don't you think we should be playing on an even field?"

"You're talking about sex," she said, flatly.

He nodded then leaned forward to nuzzle her neck, spoke in a low murmur. "I don't want you making a choice until you and I have had a chance to see how compatible we are together."

"I see." Her eyelids fluttered closed. "Take you for a test drive, so to speak."

He grinned—glad to see she was getting into the spirit of things. "Exactly." He nipped at her earlobe and found the sensitive spot at the back of her neck. Her head dropped forward as he used his mouth to drive her closer to the edge, eventually achieving the reaction he wanted from her.

"Oh God," she moaned.

"Let me?" he whispered seductively into her ear.

"Oh, yes . . ."

He scooped her up into his arms, grabbed her house key and carried her to the door before she had a chance to change her mind. He locked the door quickly. "Is your car locked?" he asked, his voice husky with need, as she buried her face in his neck.

"Mm hmmm." She opened her mouth and sampled the lobe of his ear.

He groaned and opened his truck door. Mike seated himself and somehow arranged her across his lap while he drove the block and a half to his own home. Determined not to relinquish his hold on her, he broke several laws during the short drive home. Within a couple of minutes, he'd made it to his front door and unlocked it without loosening his grip on her. He kicked the door shut behind them and strode down the hallway.

Angelique gasped as they both dropped to his massive, king sized mattress. He stretched out alongside her, his booted feet hanging off the foot of the bed. She turned towards him, curling her left leg up around his thighs, groaned in what he could only hope was appreciation as she felt his hardness.

He rolled over on his back to unzip his jeans, partly to get some relief, and partly to give her a glimpse of what she had to look forward to. He rolled back toward her, determined not to hide a damn thing.

"Oh my God," she croaked, staring down at him. "I keep thinking of that movie line, release the Kraken…"

He laughed nervously. "Is that fear or anticipation I hear in your voice?"

She raised an eyebrow. "A little of both, if you want to know the truth. I've never seen-I've never been with-um-s-someone so . . . You're very well endowed," she finally finished.

He lifted himself on one elbow and shrugged. "I'm six foot seven, Angel. I think it's just in proportion to the rest of me."

"That so?" Her voice revealed a slight tremble.

He growled at her reply, anxious to prove that he had the skills as well as the equipment to make this the most memorable encounter of her lifetime.

Her eyes travelled the length of him, eventually ending at his boots hanging off the end of the bed. "You ready to shed those size fourteens, or are we going to do it with your boots on?"

"I'm ready to shed a lot more than that." He pulled her close to nip at her lower lip with his teeth. He slipped his hands under her blouse and splayed his fingers across the flat of her belly, eliciting a gasp from her as his warm hand touched her cool skin. She moaned when he placed a gentle kiss on her flesh and slowly began to unbutton her shirt. Suddenly, he froze.

"What's wrong?"

"I'm trying to remember if I have any condoms."

Her eyes widened and she sat up quickly. "Where do you keep them?"

He rolled over and began to rummage through his night stand. When that didn't produce anything, he checked the other one, then the bathroom cabinet. He walked out, muttering under his breath. "I'll have to go get some."

She fell back on the mattress and groaned. "Mike, maybe we shouldn't—"

"No! Don't say it!" He pointed at her. "I'll be right back. Please don't leave." He grabbed his truck keys, went to the bed and gave her a long, lingering kiss. "Remember, there's more where that came from. Be back in a minute."

～↻

Angelique curled up on her side and buried her face in Mike's pillow, breathing in the scent of him. She smiled to herself, and wondered what her therapist would think if she knew what her patient was considering.

Suddenly determined not to make another costly mistake, she sat up and reached for the phone on the nightstand. She'd never called the clinic before a scheduled session before, but it was understood that she could if she ever felt the need, and mama did she feel the need. In under a minute, she had been patched through to Dr. Carter's private number, and had explained the situation to her.

"Hmmm. You say you love both of these men, Angelique."

"I do," she admitted.

"That's understandable, but have you made a choice?"

"Well, no, but, this will help me make that decision, won't it?"

"Will it?" Dr. Carter asked quietly. "Why do you feel the need to do this today?"

"Well, I know what kind of lover Liam is, but Mike and I have never been together. They should be on an even playing field, don't you think?"

"Playing field? Did you come up with that concept?"

"Well, no. Mike suggested it, but I have to tell you, I totally agree with him."

"Were you both already sexually stimulated when he made this suggestion?"

"Y-yes."

"So, the whole basis for your celibacy is to learn not to make relationship decisions based purely on sexual attraction."

"Yes, but this is different. Isn't it?" Angelique sounded unconvinced, even to her own ears.

"Not unless you've already made your choice," Dr. Carter insisted. "I'll ask you again. Have you chosen which one of these men you want to spend the rest of your life with?"

Angelique hung her head, feeling so ashamed of what she'd nearly done. Again. "No, I haven't." She released a deep sigh. "You're right, of course. This is a mistake. Thanks, Dr. Carter. I knew I could count on you to keep me focused."

~⌒~

Mike pulled his truck into the driveway and barely had time to throw it in park before he had the key out of the ignition. By the time he made it to the bedroom, he had the box of condoms open and his boots off. He came to a screeching halt in the doorway and stared at the empty bed, along with the slip of paper placed dead center of it.

He walked over and picked up the note, knowing exactly what it would say. He unfolded it slowly.

Mike,
I'm sorry about this, but the time isn't right. Please forgive me and believe me when I say that I'm doing this for us! I love you,
Angelique

He groaned loudly before he planted himself face first onto his big, empty mattress.

CHAPTER 18

Angelique had just enough time to run back to her new rent home, grab her things and get to her car. By the time she slipped her key into the ignition, Dustin Lynch was belting Cowboys and Angels from her cell phone, both Mike's and Liam's ringtone. She didn't need to check the name flashing across the screen to know which one of her cowboys was calling. She swiped the screen to answer.

"I can explain." She waited for his response. Pictured him leaned up against the door jamb, running his hand through that thick, board straight, coal black hair.

"You don't have to, Angel. I know I pushed you into it."

Relief rushed over her at the soothing sound of his voice. "You're not angry?" She slipped on her sunglasses and slowly backed out of her drive.

"Of course not. A little sexually frustrated, maybe, but I'll get over it," he assured her.

"While you were gone, I called my therapist, Dr. Carter. She made me understand that going through with it would have been falling back into my old pattern. I don't want that for us, Mike." She bit her lower lip then mumbled, "No matter how fantastic it would have been." She heard the unmistakable rumble of his laughter on the phone.

"It would have been, too. I'd have turned it into twenty-four hours you'd have remembered for the rest of your life."

She closed her eyes, groaning at another image of him—shirtless, tanned, buff, and ready for her. "I know, babe. There's not a doubt in my mind."

"Maybe one day?"

"One day. When my head's on straight."

"You got anything else to do at the house today?"

"You mean Sonny? Oh, hell, that reminds me. I forgot to tell him goodbye when I left."

"Is that important?"

Angelique stopped at a red light to wait it out. "Nan said it was. I guess if my key won't seem to fit the front door tomorrow morning, I'll know why."

"When do you want to move in?"

"Next weekend, but I may have to hire some help. My girlfriends and I can't handle some of those pieces of furniture."

"Don't you dare waste money on movers. I'll get some guys together and we'll knock it out in no time."

His generous offer had her beaming at herself in her rearview mirror. "Thanks, Mike. I didn't want to ask, under the circumstances. I'm so sorry about that."

"There's nothing to apologize for, Angel. Your therapist is probably right."

"Probably right?" She heard the distinct sound of a beer bottle being cracked open. She waited for Mike to take his first drink.

"There's always a slim chance she's a sadistic, man-hater who enjoys having you leave me worked up and wanting more."

Angelique burst into laughter as the light turned. "Certainly not, and I assure you, you couldn't have been any more 'worked up' than I was. If you'd had condoms in the house the deed would have been done already." She smiled again at his low, pain-filled groan.

"Don't remind me."

"Hmmm . . ." Angelique grunted, chewing at her lip thoughtfully.

"What are you thinking?"

"I'm wondering why you didn't have any condoms. A single man like you usually has at least a few on hand." She paused at his silence. "Am I allowed to ask?"

"Sure. I did come across a few in that night stand last week, but I threw them out."

"Why?" She flipped her visor down as she hit I-10 westbound towards Lake Coburn.

"They, uh . . . The uh . . . Expiration dates had passed."

She snickered. "That could mean one of two things. You either don't use protection—"

"I always use protection."

"Or you're as hard up as I am." His silence confirmed her suspicions. "That's priceless."

∽∾

Angelique stepped inside her apartment and dropped her keys next to the phone. She picked it up to retrieve her voice mail, shrinking a little on the inside from guilt at the sound of Liam's voice.

"Hey, beautiful. How about we go dancing? Red's has Country Rhodes tonight and I feel like kicking it up a little. How about you? I'll call you later."

She shook her head. "No dancing tonight, Nash. I need to get an early start tomorrow morning." She hit the button to hear the next message.

"Angel, Tanner here. Just wanted to find out how your week went. How's that new employee. Is she working out for you? Does it look like she'll be sticking around for a while? What's the news on her ex? Did they catch him yet? How about that body guard? Is he keeping a close watch on her?" He paused here and seemed to rein himself in. "I-uh-I'll call you later."

Angelique stared at the phone in amazement. "I'll be damned! I think Tanner's genuinely concerned about another human being. There's hope for my boy, yet."

She dialed Liam's cell number first.

"Hello beautiful, did you get my message?"

"I did, but I'm going to have to pass. I want to get to my new place early tomorrow morning and I have to start packing some things tonight."

"Need some help?"

Images of Liam came to mind as she'd known him a year ago—bare-chested, at the beach, in bed. She thought of the effort he'd, no doubt, be making to sway her opinion before she moved back to Lafayette. She closed her eyes and sighed, thinking she was feeling far too vulnerable to face it tonight. "No thanks, Liam. I want to relax tonight—take my time packing and do some online shopping, now that I have a better idea of what I need."

"Are you sure?"

"I'm positive, but maybe tomorrow night."

"I'll count on it, beautiful. Good night, Angel. I love you."

She hesitated for a moment. "I do love you, too, Liam. Honestly, I do."

He was quiet for several seconds then swallowed audibly. "Thanks, babe. I needed to hear that tonight."

"Goodnight." She disconnected and stood there, feeling a little overwhelmed, and a lot like crying. Determined not to feel sorry for herself, she turned toward her kitchen just as the doorbell rang. She opened the door to reveal a beaming Tanner.

"I come bearing gifts." He lifted a large gift bag in one hand, and a bottle of wine in the other before casting a curious glance around her place. "Are you alone?"

"Yes. Who else were you expecting to see?" As he struggled to find an answer, she waved her hand again and opened the door wider. "Sarah's not here and I understand how disappointed you must be, considering how you feel about the lady."

"I'm just a concerned citizen, that's all," he insisted. "You damn well know ladies with babies aren't my preference."

"Yeah, whatever."

"Okay, then what the hell's wrong with you?" he asked, leaning in to get a better look at her. "Did either of those two bozo's you're in love with say or do something to hurt you? Say the word, Angel, and I'll kick their ass for you."

She placed a hand over her heart. "You'd do that for me?" she fawned, trying to hold back her laughter while batting her eyelashes.

He nodded. "I'd try, anyway. The ex-Navy Seal would probably humiliate me good, but I might have a penny's worth of luck with Tonto."

Angelique grinned at him. "He's six foot seven, you know."

Tanner shrugged it off. "The bigger they are, the harder they fall, hon. He doesn't scare me. And just what the hell's so funny?" he asked, as she snorted and choked on her laughter.

"I'm sorry, but I just can't see you fighting."

"Just because I don't normally choose to go around picking fights doesn't mean I can't hold my own. I've got skills. Besides," he said, sticking out one western boot. "I have a feeling these would come in pretty handy in a street brawl." He smiled down at her. "Are you going to tell me what's wrong now?"

She closed the door and ran both hands through her thick hair. "I don't know what the hell to do, Tanner. I don't want to hurt either of them but I'll have to if I choose. And before you ask—no, I haven't decided."

"Well, before you give yourself ulcers, open this." He thrust the large bag in her face.

"What did you do?" She peeked inside the bag, moved the layers of tissue and gasped in delight. "Oh, it's perfect! How did you know?" She held up a large bronze, antique finished fleur de lis.

"The lady at the gift shop told me they're all the rage since the Saints won the Super Bowl."

"I love it, and I know just where this is going in my new place." She leaned over and gave him a hug. "Thanks, buddy."

He gave her a slight bow. "It's the least I could do, since you're helping me out." He lifted the wine bottle. "Where's your opener?"

She scrunched up her face. "I have to load my car with some things to bring to the house tomorrow morning."

"Let's start with a glass of wine and then I'll help you. How about tomorrow? Will you need help then?"

"I might. Sarah offered to help, so of course that means Liam will be with her."

"I won't be there, then."

"He's her bodyguard, Tanner."

He shook his head. "It has nothing to do with him. I'm not ready."

"What do you mean?"

"I'm not—done—yet." He spoke hesitantly.

She opened a drawer and pulled out the wine opener. "Done with what?"

"With me. I don't want her to get to know me until my metamorphosis is complete." He shrugged as their gazes clashed. "I want to be better."

"For her. You want to be better for her," she added.

"I want to be better for me. I don't want to stick my big foot in my mouth before I've finished, that's all there is to it."

Angelique studied him for a moment, feeling her heart soften toward him. She put her hands together and bowed. "You have travelled far in such a short time, young grasshopper." She laughed as Tanner looked down and shook his head. "I am so seriously proud of you."

He pulled the opener from her hand and began working on the bottle of wine. "Don't be just yet. I've been known to pussy out before the job is completed. Or at the very least, take the easy way out."

Angelique took two glasses out of the cabinet and handed him one. "Why don't you come with me tomorrow and give your new persona a dry run? I think you're ready to at least break the ice between you two."

"You don't think it's too soon? I mean, you and the others know I've changed, but she didn't know how bad of a shit I was before."

Angelique's laughter bubbled out before she could stop it. "I wouldn't worry about that. She knows enough."

❤️

Angelique and Tanner had nearly finished hanging the living room curtains when Sarah and Liam arrived.

"What a great place," Sarah exclaimed, getting her first glimpse of the house. "Liam, isn't this place fantastic?"

His frown gave visible evidence of his displeasure. "It's okay, I guess," he grumbled. "Her other place is better."

"Shhh. You'll hurt Sonny's feelings," Angelique hissed. "I forgot to say goodbye to him yesterday, and we had a hell of a time getting the front door opened this morning."

Liam rolled his eyes. "I still like your other place better."

"You've got to be kidding?" Sarah asked, incredibly. "This place is gorgeous, twice the size, and half the price. What's not to like?"

Liam spoke through clenched teeth. "Location, location, location."

"Fortunately for you, his opinion doesn't matter," Tanner muttered from the top of the step ladder.

Sarah's gaze sought him out. "Oh, hello," she said, timidly. "I didn't see you up there."

Tanner nodded in her direction as he began to climb down the ladder. He missed the last step and landed somewhat awkwardly, nearly tripping over a bag of sheer curtains and some hardware. He recovered, and attempted to act like he was unaffected, without quite pulling it off. "Hello, Sarah."

"I'm sorry, I know we met the other day, but I can't remember your name," Sarah told him.

He passed a hand along the back of his neck. "Tanner Collins."

She pointed at him, grinning. "Tiffany's ex, right?"

He leaned over to pick up his bottle of water, shaking his head. "I guess I won't live down that identity anytime soon."

Sarah looked up at the curtains he'd just hung. "Are you an interior designer?"

Tanner coughed on the sip of water he'd just taken. "Hell no. I'm a doctor," he sputtered.

"Oh. Sorry about that. I don't remember anyone mentioning that before. Or if they did, I was too out of it to remember."

Liam placed his hand familiarly on Sarah's shoulder and leaned close to whisper loudly into her ear. "It's quite an understandable error, Sarah. Especially since he did such a fabulous job on the drapes," he said, with a slight lisp to the letter s.

Tanner sent him a seething glare. "What do you plan on doing here today?"

"Heavy lifting," Liam answered, as he flexed his muscular arms.

Tanner snorted. "She's not moving in, Nash. She's just doing some decorating to get it out of the way before she does."

"I guess I'll have to sit here and be bored, then, because I'm obviously not as talented as you are at decorating."

Tanner picked up a hammer and a portable drill that doubled as a screw driver. "She needed my tools."

"I bet that's not the only tools you offered," Liam growled.

Tanner walked up, and stood nose to nose with the man. "What the fu—" He stopped, casting a glance in Sarah's direction. "What's your problem, Nash?"

Angelique cleared her throat. "Gentlemen, excuse me." Neither man seemed to hear her.

"You're my problem," Liam said, poking at Tanner's chest. "I know what kind of an asshole you are."

"You might know what kind of asshole I used to be." Tanner pushed Liam's hand roughly aside.

"Hey!" Angelique yelled, stepping between the two men. They both looked at her, finally hearing her speak. "Are you two finished with your pissing contest?"

"This pussy—" Liam began.

"That prick—" Tanner chimed in, pointing an accusing finger at Liam.

Angelique raised her hands and lowered her voice to an ominous hiss. "Have either of you fools noticed what this is doing to Sarah?"

Liam lowered his head, but Tanner's head whipped around toward Sarah, who'd pressed herself into a corner as far as she could get. Their loud confrontation had obviously brought back some disturbing memories for the woman who looked like she was trying to vanish into the woodwork.

Tanner took two steps toward her. "Oh God, I'm sorry, Sarah." She squeezed her eyes shut as he took another step and reached out to touch her arm. "Are you all right?" He winced visibly as she jerked away from him.

"Please don't," she hissed.

"Jesus. I won't. I'm so sorry." Tanner backed off immediately.

∽∾

Sarah's eyes flew open at the man's hoarsely whispered apology. She turned slowly toward the source, surprised at first, not to see her husband's eyes glaring at her accusingly, darkening with anger without a moment's notice. These eyes weren't the same shade of blue and actually showed concern for her. This mouth wasn't sneering at her with pure disdain.

Of course this wasn't Troy. Her husband had never apologized for a single black eye, busted lip, or broken rib, much less for upsetting her. That was her role. *I'm sorry for forcing you to beat the hell out of me, Troy. I know I gave you no choice.* Because she knew from experience that the bastard wouldn't stop until she said the words, and sometimes not even then.

This man staring back at her, this handsome, seriously hunky Dr. Collins, seemed crushed, horrified even, that he'd been the cause of her discomfort. She stared up at him, unable to speak, or put into words how touched she was by his concern.

Tanner stared down at her, clearly upset over her state. "I-I won't. Please, forgive me," he stammered, before turning to make a quick exit through the front door.

Sarah blinked several times, mumbled something unintelligible. Then she exited through the back door, closing it softly behind her.

Angelique spun around to send a glare in Liam's direction. "Somebody better tell me what the hell is going on here—and he'd better do it right now."

Liam stared shamefaced at his shoes, reluctant to meet her gaze. "I don't know, Angel. I don't know what the hell to tell you." He lifted his hands. "I have no excuse."

"No excuse, for acting like a complete asshole?" Her voice shook with contempt.

Liam looked up, shocked at her tone. "Collins started it with that remark about my opinion not mattering," he said, defensively.

"It doesn't matter. You're not living here." She shook her head when he lowered his eyes toward the floor once again. "Neither of you showed a bit of concern for either Sarah or me. You just went after each other like two pit bulls while we had to stand by and witness the entire thing."

Liam walked to the window over the sink until he could see Sarah on the back deck, sitting quietly on one of the built-in benches that lined the perimeter. "You're right. I'm sorry." He turned to her again. "It's just that when I see any other guy with you—"

"Tanner's crazy about Sarah."

"What?"

"Sarah, and her twins. He's crazy about all of them. The first time he met her, she was all he talked about for hours. He asks me about her every chance he gets." She tramped over to the bag of curtains to yank out another sage green sheer. "And besides, it's not Tanner you should be worrying about." She cringed at the hurtful words, immediately regretting them.

"What the hell does that mean? That you and Harper have been going at it like rabbits while you give me the cold shoulder?"

"Of course not. But I love Mike, too, Liam – every bit as much as I love you."

He cocked his head slightly. "Maybe even more?"

She looked at him and sighed. "I don't know, yet. But . . ." Angelique let her voice trail off.

"But, I sure as hell didn't score any points here today, did I?" he finished for her.

Tired of the conversation, she walked out back without another word.

She settled herself beside Sarah on the bench. "Hey, are you okay?"

"Other than feeling foolish by freaking out that way, I guess so." She wiped a tear from the corner of her eye. "Maybe I need therapy."

Angelique snorted. "I can give you the name of a good one."

Sarah gave her a half smile. "Seriously, I don't want to cower every time I hear loud voices. I don't want to be this weak person that no one will respect."

"What are you talking about? Everyone respects you! You're a survivor."

Sarah twisted her hands nervously. "I'm a coward. As soon as Troy would begin to yell, I'd start trembling like a terrified puppy. I know I've said I'd kill him if he ever turned that rage onto my girls, but the honest truth is I would have been helpless to stop him."

"You don't know that. People often find hidden strength when they need it."

"I've needed it, trust me," Sarah replied, running her hands through her hair. "Oh hell, enough is enough." She stood up and wiped her eyes. "Come on, you've got Sonny to decorate and I've got babies to get back to. You didn't disable my bodyguard, did you?"

Angelique released a huff of laughter. "I don't know what that was about. Tanner and I are just friends, so there was no reason for Liam to get all defensive."

"Are you sure Tanner is only interested in you as a friend? There seemed to be something else going on there."

"If there was, it wasn't about me," Angelique replied, knowing Tanner would want her to keep quiet.

"Tanner's a kinder man than people think he is, isn't he?"

Angelique couldn't help but smile. "I believe so, but he thinks he needs to be better."

Sarah fidgeted with her hands again. "When you see him again, please tell him that his apology meant a lot to me. It's just that I'm not used to getting one, and I didn't know how to respond."

Angelique nodded. "I'll tell him."

CHAPTER 19

Liam watched from the gate as Sarah worked one of Leah's horses in the paddock. Nearly a week had passed since the fiasco at Angel's, and she seemed to be flourishing. She worked the gelding hard, cutting first to the right, stopping and cutting hard to the left, then making the quarter horse back up. Liam gave a low whistle then broke into applause as she rode up to the fence.

"That's fantastic! Where'd you learn to do all that?"

"Leah taught me how to work him but she trains them, and she's damn good at what she does."

"Is he being trained for rodeos?"

Sarah leaned over to pat the horse's neck affectionately. "The owner originally wanted this guy for cutting cattle, but if his daughter decides to compete like he wants her to, he's plenty fast enough for pole and barrel racing."

Liam nodded and climbed over the wooden fence rails to meet her. "I rode quite a bit when I was younger. Think I could give it a shot?"

"I don't see why not." She climbed off the horse and handed him the reins. "His name is Cutter."

He spoke to the horse in soothing tones, allowing him to get used to his scent and the feel of his hand. Liam waited until Cutter had relaxed before adjusting the stirrups for his long legs. He mounted easily and walked the horse around the paddock then made a round in an easy trot. He made a few more passes and led the horse along the back fence line toward Sarah.

The horse snorted loudly, startling a cottonmouth snake that lay curled around a fence post sunning itself. The snake struck out at the horse's foreleg, its fangs coming within a fraction of an inch. Cutter reared violently, flipping an unsuspecting Liam off his back in an awkward spill onto the ground.

Sarah watched in horror, as Liam flew off the back of the horse and landed hard, head first, onto the compacted soil. She yelled for Daniel and took off at a dead run for her bodyguard.

Kneeling next to his unconscious body, she checked for a pulse, breathing a sigh of relief when she found it good and strong.

"What happened?" Daniel asked, out of breath from running to meet them.

"Cutter got spooked by a snake and reared. He's breathing but he hit hard, Daniel. We need to get an ambulance out here."

He nodded, pulled out his phone and called Tiffany to come over, then called Air Med for immediate transport as his daughter had requested.

"Oh God, I never should have let him ride," Sarah groaned when Tiffany pulled up a few short minutes later.

"No Sarah, I watched him from the window and he handled himself fine," Daniel told her. "That could have happened to anyone." He turned to his daughter. "Think it's a concussion?"

She nodded. "For him to be out this long—at least a mild one, I'd say. No broken bones that I can see, but we may also be dealing with a possible neck or back injury. There's no way to tell until we get him in for x-rays and an MRI."

The air ambulance arrived within minutes to secure a still unconscious Liam and loaded him up, as Tiffany climbed in with the paramedics. Torn between leaving her babies behind or following the ambulance with Daniel, Sarah finally let Red convince her that the twins would be safe with him and Leah.

∾◡∾

Angelique sealed the last box, labeled it, and pushed it against the wall. That did it; everything but the bathroom was packed up and ready for the 'moving men' first thing in the morning. Mike had asked some of his buddies, as well as Red and Liam to help with the loading and unloading. She and Tanner had made several smaller loads during the week, and as a result, there were only a few boxes to deal with, as well as her large items of furniture.

She poured herself a glass of water and took the time to rest her feet while she sipped at it. She was tired and ready to get moved into her new place as quickly as possible. If she worked hard at it Saturday, which was tomorrow, she knew she would have it licked by Sunday. She took a big swig of water before answering her ringing phone.

"Hello."

"Angel, it's Red. Liam was thrown from a horse and knocked unconscious. He's on his way by air med to St. Luke's."

The sound of her cordless phone hitting the floor rang in her ears as she grabbed her purse and rushed out the door.

~

Nearly twenty hours had passed, and still Liam slept, deathly still, except for the steady rise and fall of his chest. He breathed on his own, and tests had shown no sign of brain swelling, bleeding, or fractured vertebras.

Sick with worry, Angelique stayed by his side—waiting, praying for him to wake up and be his normal, irritating self. She said rosaries, cried countless tears, afraid she'd lost him forever— terrified that she'd never be able to tell him how sorry she was for the last hurtful words she'd spoken to him. How much she loved him.

Eight o'clock Sunday morning found her dozing in the hospital room's only chair. She started at a soft knock on the door. Mike stepped inside, carrying a bag with a local café's logo on it.

"Hey, Angel. I brought you some breakfast."

"Thanks, but I'm not hungry." She passed her hands over her hair to smooth the tangles she hoped weren't too noticeable.

His gaze found hers as he dug into the bag, releasing the aroma of bacon into the small space. "It wasn't a request, and don't you roll those eyes at me. You're gonna eat something, and while I'm here to see it."

"I have been eating," she fibbed, while trying to remember the last time she had. The fact was, she had been too damned worried to eat. She still was. An aroma that should have had her stomach growling with hunger, did nothing more than make her queasy.

"Mm hmm, I bet." He sounded unconvinced. "Babe, you'll be no good to anyone if you pass out. You need sustenance." Mike partially unwrapped a crescent roll bursting with bacon, egg, and cheese and held it out to her. "Now mange—eat!" he said, forcefully, "Then you can go home for a while and I'll take over the watch."

Her mouth watered with nausea at the unappetizing smell and she pushed his handful of sandwich roughly away from her face. "Get that away from me before I barf all over you." She stood and faced him angrily. "Do I look like the kind of girl who can't think for herself? I don't need anyone to take care of me, dammit. When I feel like eating, I'll eat."

"Look, Angel, I'm just trying to hel—"

"You're not. I don't want to eat, and I'm not leaving because Liam needs me here. And if you're going to keep up this foolishness, you can just leave."

Mike froze, looking heartbroken at her suggestion. Seconds passed, making the uncomfortable silence between them seem downright unbearable. He re-wrapped the sandwich and put it back in the bag. Folding the top tightly he placed it on the hospital tray stand. "I'll just leave it. Maybe you'll get hungry later."

"Mike, I'm sor—"

"Don't." He raised a hand to stop her. "You've made your choice, about a lot of things, it seems. I'll leave you to it."

"Mike, don't." He walked out, letting the door close heavily behind him. She groaned and sunk her face into both hands, giving into another round of tears. What the hell was wrong with her? Now she'd hurt two men. She finished her tears several minutes later, sniffling into the rough tissues provided by the hospital.

"I smell bacon."

Angelique stopped sniffling long enough to wonder what she'd heard. She swung around to see Liam, who lay there with his eyes closed. No change. She must be hearing things.

"I'm starving," he said, barely moving his parched lips.

"Liam!" She rushed to his side. "Oh God, you're awake."

He gave several heavy lidded blinks before managing to open his eyes. "What the hell happened?"

"That horse threw you off. Don't you remember?"

"Horse?" His brow furrowed. "What's a horse? What's this place?" He gave her a quizzical look. "Am I supposed to know you?"

Stunned at the questions, Angelique straightened and covered her mouth with one hand. "Oh God! They said there was a slim chance this could happen. Let me get somebody in here." She turned toward the door so he wouldn't witness her heartbroken burst into tears.

"Angel, stop."

She froze, releasing the door handle to spin slowly around. He wouldn't. He couldn't do that to her. Could he? The trace of shit-eating grin plastered on his face had her fuming, even as Nash murmured a weak apology confirming her suspicions.

"I'm kidding, babe. I remember everything." He yawned, wiped a hand over his face. "Why all the tears? What's it been, an hour or so?"

She felt the involuntary lift of her left eyebrow, a sure sign the devilish side of her conscience was taking over. Liam's mistake was in not taking notice of it.

"Oh Liam. Years, sweetie," she said, adding a note of sadness, as she walked slowly toward the bed. "It's been so many years. We'd all about given up hope you'd ever wake. Mike and I…" She nearly choked on the effort it took not to smile at his sudden look of horror, yet she somehow managed to press on. "We waited an entire year, Liam. Mike so wanted you as his best man at the wedding." She began digging in her wallet and going through pictures. "Here, let me show you pics of the kids. We even named our son after you."

"What!" Liam bolted upright, before pressing one hand to his head. "That's not possible. I feel fine." He leveled a disbelieving glare in her direction. "You married Harper?"

Angelique leaned in to lock her gaze onto his. "Gotcha."

His brows furrowed. "What?"

"Nearly a whole day, jerk. You've been out for about twenty hours now, and I've been here the entire time, terrified you'd never wake up, or if you did, you wouldn't remember me."

"Angel—"

She waved him off as she turned for the door. "I'll tell them you're awake."

Angelique lingered at the front desk long enough to hear there would be no ill effects from the concussion. Still hovering somewhere between anger and relief, she got the hell out of there before saying something else she'd live to regret.

CHAPTER 20

Sarah began the silent repetition of prayers as soon as she heard the distinct sound of the bedroom door's locking mechanism fall away. Oh God, please not again. Dear God, please, please, not again. Please don't let him hurt my girls. Please, God, if he kills me, protect my babies.

She dared not make a sound to let him know she was awake, even though she knew from experience that if he wanted her awake, he'd find an immediate and painful way to accomplish that. She lay there in the bed, both eyes blackened, at least one rib broken, one hand wrapped in Ace bandages in the absence of a brace or cast. She knew she could use several stitches; the cut over her left eyebrow was ugly and jagged, and her mouth was split and swollen. Too hurt and sore to jump when he spoke crudely to her, she simply opened the one eye that wasn't swollen completely shut.

"Hey, you ungrateful Bitch!" he snarled, giving her a shove. "I'm going to work now. You mind your manners and keep your ass in these two rooms. And just remember what I said about the neighbors. Two child molesters and an ex-con who spent time for raping a pretty little thing like you." He gave a huff of sadistic laughter. "At least you used to be. You're not so pretty any more, are you?"

She winced as he grabbed a handful of her hair and jerked her head painfully so he could see the damages to her face.

"Yeah, that one's gonna leave a nice scar; no stitches for you, babe." He chuckled evilly. "You remember what I said, Sarah. If you and those girls of mine aren't here when I get back, I'll find you, I swear to God I will. I'll slit their throats and make you watch. Then I'll cut your tongue out and give you to the ex-con to finish you off. I hear he likes his women quiet." He pushed her head back onto the bed giving her hair one last painful jerk before he walked out and locked the door behind him. She breathed a painful sigh of relief and dozed off again.

～～

Sarah awakened once more with that same feeling of dread. Only she wasn't in the awful bedroom she'd suffered inside for five long days. She was in her bedroom suite in Daniel and Leah's house. She sat up, feeling her face and mouth. No soreness, no stitches. Just a dream, thank God. She held the monitor close to her ear, but didn't hear anything. The twins were sound asleep.

Sarah sat up and wrapped herself in a thick terry cloth robe to ward off the chill of the early spring morning. Unable to help herself, she exited her bedroom and quietly made her way down the hallway to the nursery. She opened the door and tiptoed over to the cribs. Smiling as she saw both their blankets pulled over their heads. She'd bet her life savings that she'd find them in identical sleeping positions, as usual. It must be one of those uncanny twin things, like inventing their own language.

She reached out with both hands to lower the blankets, but her hands froze in mid-air as something caught her attention. Sarah's right hand cautiously moved to the dark red spot on Sammi's bed rail. She touched the sticky substance and brought her fingers closer to her nose, detecting a faint metallic odor. Her entire body tensed, immobilized by a stark dread as her eyes widened involuntarily. She forced herself to move, reached trembling hands out toward the blankets and pulled them slowly off of her daughter's golden curls. She lowered them to reveal their faces to just below their mouths. The absence of rosiness in their cheeks filled her with a panicky dread.

She pulled the blankets back quickly and had to swallow the bile that rose up in her throat to choke her. Shaking uncontrollably now, she reached out and touched her daughters, searching for some sign of life. She raised her trembling hands, now covered with the dark stickiness, too sick inside to utter a sound at the sight of her daughters' blood.

She heard the laugh, low and menacing, coming from behind her. Sarah turned slowly and stared in shocked horror as Troy leered evilly at her. He held a knife in one hand—A wickedly sharp knife covered in blood; the blood of her innocent babies.

"I told you what I'd do, didn't I, Sarah? This is your fault—all your fault."

He started with a throaty chuckle that turned into deep, rumbling laughter. Within a few short seconds, his laughter turned into full blown, soul wrenching screams.

∾

Daniel was halfway down the hall with a glass of warm milk, when a blood curdling scream scared him so badly he dropped the glass on the thickly carpeted floor.

"Sweet Jesus! Sarah!" He ran to her room and flung open the door, then froze, uncertain of what to do next. Sarah was sitting up in bed, staring at her hands, her face twisted with heartbreaking anguish, and screaming loudly enough to wake the dead.

"Dear God! What's wrong?" Leah cried, running into the room. "She's having a nightmare, Daniel!" She ran over and placed her hands firmly on Sarah's shoulders. "Sarah, wake up. It's a dream, sweetie, it's only a dream."

At the first touch Sarah wakened, her screams reduced to gasps and violent quakes. She sat there, trembling, gasping for breath, her face streaked with tears. "The babies," she moaned.

Daniel approached slowly. "They're fine—the babies are fine, Sarah. I'd just checked on them a minute ago."

"I-I need to see them. I have to make sure that Troy—that he-didn't h-hu-hurt them," she stammered, between hitches of breath.

Leah took a gentle hold of her arm to help her out of bed. "Calm down, Sarah. Come on, let's go see them right now so you'll know they're okay."

Daniel trailed the two women as they walked arm in arm to the nursery. Sarah approached the cribs, reaching in to place both hands on her daughters' chubby pink faces, ran her fingers through their golden brown curls. Seeming to accept they were fine, she covered her face and sobbed quietly into her hands.

Daniel's gaze clashed with his wife's as they gathered Sarah into a comforting embrace. Leah spoke in soothing tones. "Honey, we're gonna keep you and your girls safe, right Daniel?"

"You're damn right we will," he whispered, his voice tight with fury for the man who'd caused this kind of terror in a woman.

"Are you okay now?" Leah asked.

Sarah breathed in shakily, and released it in a rush before nodding. "I'm fine."

Leah placed an arm across her shoulders to lead her out of the nursery. "Would you like a cup of hot cocoa, or some chamomile tea, maybe?"

Sarah nodded as the two women left the nursery.

Daniel stayed behind, watching over the sleeping babies. The two of them slept soundly, unbothered by their mother's episode of night terror. He contemplated the girls, arranged in identical sleeping poses, as they were prone to do, and placed his large hands on their tiny, warm backs.

Sarah's screams came back to him, as well as her words. I have to make sure Troy didn't hurt them. He didn't know what horrors Sarah had witnessed in her nightmare, and he didn't want to. He'd known men like Troy Richard all too well in his lifetime; men who treated their family members with less feeling and respect than they would a stray dog or wild animal.

Daniel had grown to love these two little angels, sound asleep in their cribs. The thought of anyone trying to hurt them or their mother made his skin crawl. He clasped his hands tightly together over the cribs, asking God to help him keep his promise to Sarah.

~∽

She gripped her mug of cocoa until the blood drained from her fingers. Blood. Just thinking the word caused an uncontrollable shiver to run up Sarah's spine.

"Do you want to talk about it?"

She jerked her head violently at Leah. "God, no! I wish I could forget about it. And I wish Liam were here," she added. "I guess I got used to having him around. I just…I feel safer when he is."

Leah patted her arm. "He'll be pleased to hear that. Tiffany told us they only wanted to observe him one more night. He'll be released later this morning."

Sarah gazed out at the darkened windows. "What time is it, anyway?"

"Four a.m. You want to try to get in another couple hours of sleep?"

Sarah shook her head. "I don't think I'll sleep again until Liam's back, or Troy's behind bars—whichever comes first."

Daniel walked in at the tail end of her statement. "Even after he's back, Liam may need to stay off his feet for a while, but Melanie Finley called to say she'd like to stay here to pick up the slack until he's up again.

Sarah nodded, thinking it'd be nice to see Mel again, while also wondering how Officer Finley would handle being under the same roof with Liam.

~∽

Melanie pulled up under the canopy of St. Luke's Hospital, spotting Liam immediately, wheelchair and all. She lowered the passenger window in time to hear him tell the nurse behind him his ride was there as he pointed to her car. When he attempted to leave the confines of the chair, she saw his nurse grip his shoulder tightly and tell him to stay put until she wheeled him to the car.

As soon as he was safely ensconced behind the closed car door, he waved to his nurse. "Adios, Nurse Ratched!" he yelled, earning a glare from his care-giver. "You wretched woman," he growled, as he raised the window. "Wretched Ratched," he said, with a low chuckle.

"Ratched? I've never heard of that name before."

Nash shook his head. "Her tag says B. DeVille. I heard someone call her Betty."

"Then why do you call her Nurse Ratched?"

Liam stared at her, seeming disappointed. "Nurse Ratched from 'One Flew Over the Cuckoo's Nest'?"

"I've never heard of it. Is it out on DVD or pay per view yet?" She never took her eyes off the road.

Liam's jaw dropped in shock. "It's classic Jack Nicholson. I can't believe you've never heard of it. It swept the Oscars in 1975—Best actor, best picture, best damned near everything."

"And just how old were you in seventy-five, Nash? Because I wasn't born yet," she said, in her own defense. And by the time I was old enough to watch television mom had already sold the set to keep the electricity from being cut off.

"I was only three years old," he said, scowling at her. "I just like to educate myself about things like that."

"Yeah? Well I used to read the dictionary to 'educate' myself in my spare time." A snort from her passenger had her looking in his direction.

"So, you were one of those kids."

"What kids?"

"Brainiacs…nerds…" he said.

"My mother never had any money to entertain us so I found my own ways to fight boredom. And stop being obnoxious." She shook her head impatiently. "Jesus, you must have been a horrible patient."

"You don't have to call me Jesus—"

"You're not funny," she shot back.

"You have a lousy sense of humor."

She put the car in drive and eased away from the canopy. "Even if that were true, it wouldn't change the fact that you are so not funny. Now what did you do to the nurse to piss her off?"

He touched the tender spot on his head. "I was told she's the only grumpy old nurse in that hospital, and I had to deal with her the entire time I was there. Crappy luck, Finley—I've always had damned crappy luck."

Mel shook her head as she braked at the edge of the parking lot. "I don't believe in luck, now buckle your seat belt and quit all that bitchin', Prince Charming." She stared straight ahead, heat infusing her body as she felt his glare on her even as he did what she asked.

"I need you to swing by someplace for me before we go back to the ranch," he said.

She stole a glance in his direction. "Where are we going?"

"Just south of I-10 toward the lake. I'll direct you."

~~

Angelique nearly tripped over a packing box trying to get to her door to answer it. She muttered under her breath, but at least managed to keep from spilling her glass of wine. She pulled the door open to see Liam standing there, looking hot as ever, despite the fact that he'd been thrown from a horse two days ago. Under normal circumstances, she'd have slammed the door in his face. A long, luxurious bath, however, as well as a half bottle of wine had mellowed her enough to throw him a morsel of forgiveness.

"Hell-ooo . . ." she said, drawing out the word as she hung on the door handle. As expected, Liam's apologies came pouring out like hot syrup over a fresh stack of pancakes.

"I'm so sorry, Angel. I swear I thought I'd been out for maybe a few minutes to an hour. You have to believe I'd never have done that had I known." He sounded sincere, as well as extremely disappointed in his own self.

She took another sip of wine as she contemplated the man before her. Just looking at Liam made her juices flow. Had it really been over a year since she'd made love to this man? Sometimes it felt like yesterday. But sometimes. like right now—it seemed like she'd been without it far too long.

"I know that, but I stared at your deathly still body all night long, knowing how empty I'd feel if I never got to see that handsome smile again. If I had any damn sense, I'd stay angry." She emptied her wine glass and pulled him in by the belt loop, kicking the door closed behind them. "Lucky for you, I'm feeling generous. Besides," she said, sidling up to him. "I know exactly what you can do to make it up to me."

Liam's low groan let her know he was willing, but as she pushed him gently up against the wall, he grabbed her hands. In a second, she was the one pinned and he'd planted a kiss on her that made her melt from the inside out. He pulled back to take a breath, running the back of his hand softly down her face. "I know I don't deserve it, but please forgive me."

"Oh . . ." she said, in as seductive tone as she could muster...and she wasn't mustering much. "All right."

"Really?" He kissed her again, lightly this time. "You're not going to drag me over broken glass or anything?"

She hiccupped once and giggled. "I don't have any broken glass on hand, but if I find some," she gave him a wink and placed her finger on his chin, "I'll give you a call, how's that?"

He nodded slowly, giving her that sexy smile of his.

"That'll do. You're-ah-sounding a little more relaxed than usual, Babe. What's up with you today?" he whispered, his voice low, quietly seductive.

"Nothing's up," she said. "But something is down, like the half bottle of wine I drank since I opened it up an hour ago. Wine makes me loose, in more ways than one...lucky you," she added, before giggling again.

"Uh huh, I remember. Harper's not coming over here, is he?"

"Nooo, of course not," she drawled. "Am I starting to schlur a little?" Liam's deep laughter tickled her senses, stirring something deep within her. She thought of the many nights they'd spent making love, the way he looked with no shirt on...with no clothes on. She groaned low in her throat, wanting to see him like that again.

"Just a little slur, but not too bad," he said. "God, I love you so much, Angel. I'm so grateful that you were with me in the hospital. The nurses told me you never left my side. I just wanted to thank you, babe."

His words touched her and soon she was sniffing back tears. "I love you too, Liam. I really do. That's why I'm having such a hard time knowing I'll eventually have to choose between you and Mike. I love you both the same." Soon she was blubbering into her shirt sleeve.

"Please don't. You know it tears me up when you cry," he said, sounding tortured.

"I can't help it. I don't want to hurt either of you," she said, sobbing now.

"It'll be fine, sweet girl. Mike and I are big boys. We can handle it, I promise. Now you go on to bed. You must be exhausted after everything I put you through plus trying to pack. I love you, Angel."

She smiled crookedly up at him before starting up a fresh round of tears. "I do love you too, Liam...so...so very much. Are you coming in?"

"Unfortunately," he said, giving her another soul melting kiss before backing away from her. "My police escort is outside waiting for me. We have to get back to Sarah and her girls at the LeBlanc's place, remember? My physician seems to think I could use some assistance in doing my job for a day or two." He stepped forward and placed his hands on either side of her face in a tender gesture. "Are we good, love?"

She nodded, and dropped her head against his chest as he pulled her close for a hug. "Yes, Liam. We're good." She lifted her gaze up to his with a smile. "Now go take care of Sarah and the twins."

∿

Melanie tapped the steering wheel in time to the song on the radio as Nash exited the house looking pretty full of himself. He got into the car and buckled his seatbelt, a huge grin plastered on his face.

"One more stop before we get to the ranch," he said. "I want you to find a video rental place so I can rent Cuckoo's Nest. You've got to see it."

"Why don't I just rent it online?"

"You can do that?"

She looked at him curiously. "Are you that old or have you lived under a rock for the last few years?"

"I'll be forty-one on April first and I've been busy."

"April Fool's Day?" she snickered. "That explains a lot."

"Yeah, yeah, I know. When's your birthday?"

"On May tenth I'll be thirty," she said.

"Hmph, I remember when I turned thirty."

"Over a decade ago," she snorted.

"Shut up, Finley."

She smiled and turned up the volume to her favorite country station. "Oh, I love this guy. He's going to be in Baton Rouge next month. The show's already sold out, but I've been trying to win tickets on the radio." She began humming to his snappy older tune about a guy telling a girl to hold on tight for an eight second ride.

"Do you sing?" he asked.

"I can carry a tune," she returned. "You?"

"Some, but I play guitar better."

"Hmmm. Did you bring it? I'd like to hear that."

"It's at the ranch," he answered. "I'll pick, if you sing."

"Sure, why not," she said, thinking this would definitely be an interesting three days.

Within minutes of arriving at the ranch, Mel had settled into her temporary home easily enough, thanks to the kindness and generosity of Daniel and Leah LeBlanc. Sarah's twins, now seven months old, were crawling all over and getting into everything. Another hour had Mel seated on the floor playing with them.

"You're good with kids," Liam stated, after watching her with Sammi and Danni for several minutes.

"I babysat all through junior high and high school," she explained. "I guess I still got it." She picked up Sammi and kissed her belly, causing the child to erupt into an adorable giggle.

∼◠

Liam laughed softly as he watched them together. Melanie Finley was an enigma, that's for sure. Maybe it's just that he was still reeling from the fact that she was a she. His gaze travelled across the room to where Sarah sat alone, looking significantly more withdrawn than she had in the past week or two. "Sarah, are you okay?"

She gave him a distracted nod. "I'm fine. I'm just glad you two are here."

"Anything happen while I was gone?"

Sarah shook her head. "Nope—everything was fine."

He studied her face. "Why don't I believe you?"

"I don't know, Nash. There's nothing to tell," she said, irritably, before leaving the room.

At the sound of her door closing, he met Leah's gaze. "Talk to me."

Leah sat next to him and spoke just loudly enough for both he and Mel to hear. "She had a nightmare but she won't talk about it. She sat there in her bed, staring at her hands while this God awful, blood curdling scream came from her." Leah's eyes closed as she shivered. "I'll never forget it as long as I live. It scared ten years off of me."

Liam leaned forward "What'd she say when she woke up?"

"Only that she had to see the girls, to make sure Troy hadn't hurt them."

Melanie groaned as she pulled the twin she held closer, while Liam swore under his breath.

"If that son of a bitch is smart, his worthless ass won't show up over here," he muttered.

"He doesn't seem like the smart type to me, Nash," Mel replied. "We'll have to stay sharp and keep our eyes open."

∼◠

Sarah lay face down on her bed, trying to block thoughts of that awful dream. She rolled over and pressed both palms to her burning eyes. The sudden vibration in her pocket made her jump and she pulled out the cell phone Liam had purchased for her. Her heart thundered in her chest as the word 'Anonymous' flashed across the screen. She'd emailed the number to her brother in the Marines last week, but she had no idea if he'd been in any position to retrieve it.

"Hello," she spoke timidly, praying Troy hadn't tracked her down, somehow.

Her brother's deep bass was a joyous sound to her ears. "Sis, is that you?"

"Mitch! Oh God, it's so good to hear your voice." She struggled to get a handle on her emotions.

"Aw hell, what's wrong, Sarah Beth? What did that dick-head brother in law of mine do now?"

"He…" she paused, not wanting to upset him when he couldn't do a thing about it. "He tried to get at me, but I'm fine now," she answered, shakily.

"Now? You're fine now?" He swore loudly into the phone. "Talk to me, Sis!"

"Mitch," she sobbed, suddenly too overcome with emotion to speak.

Within seconds Nash was knocking on her door, asking if she was okay.

"Sarah, is everything alright?" he said, cautiously stepping inside. He tensed immediately. "Who are you talking to?"

"What's going on? Who is that?" Mitch demanded. "Is that Troy? If it is, put him on the phone. I want to talk to shit for brains."

"No, Mitch, it's not Troy. It's-it's Liam Nash, my bodyguard," she sobbed. Her brother's violent reaction had her pulling the phone away from her ear.

"Bodyguard! What the hell happened for you to need a bodyguard?"

Thankfully, Liam took control of the situation. He reached out for the phone. "Sarah, let me speak to your brother while you go calm down."

Practically throwing the phone at him, she locked herself inside her bathroom to pull herself together.

～✍

On the way to his room, Nash introduced himself to Sarah's brother.

"Is she alright? Are she and the twins safe?" Mitch asked.

"They're fine, no thanks to your brother in law."

"What did that son of a bitch do to them, Mr. Nash?"

"Just call me Nash." Liam spent the next five minutes explaining things to Master Sergeant Mitchell Hebert of the United

States Marine Corp. How they'd found his little sister and her twin girls, as well as their current living arrangements.

"Five days, beat up, and with no food," Mitch hissed in a low voice. "When I get my hands on that little bastard he'll wish he'd never been born."

"That's how everyone on this case feels, Master Sergeant." He heard the man exhale slowly, as though to calm himself.

"Call me Mitch, please. I appreciate what you and everyone involved is doing to keep her safe. Whatever it's costing you, I'll reimburse every cent, I swear."

"You don't owe me a dime, Mitch. Believe me when I tell you this case has touched everyone's hearts. The LeBlanc's have practically adopted Sarah, and they treat the babies like their own grandchildren. She's with good people who care about her; we all do."

"Is she completely healed?" Mitch asked.

"She's recuperated physically, but I can't say she's mentally healed. She's had a pretty horrendous nightmare about Troy getting to the twins. I don't think she'll be able to relax until that S.O.B. is behind bars."

"Or dead, and I'd be glad to do it."

"I sure as hell didn't hear that," Nash said, whistling under his breath.

"Sorry about that, man." Mitch released another long sigh. "This is my fault. I introduced her to that prick years ago."

"What'd you do, set 'em up?" Liam asked him.

"Hell no! He was just one of the punks I started hanging around with after my mom died. I gave him a bloody nose when he said my fourteen year old sister was hot. I told that bastard she was meant for someone a hell of a lot better than him."

"Obviously, he didn't listen."

"He left town for a while, and when he got back they started dating. By the time I heard about it, they were married already. I know I wouldn't have been able to stop them but if I hadn't been hanging around trash like that in the first place, she'd have never even met him."

"Then those adorable twins wouldn't be born and that would be a real shame," Liam replied.

"Are they all right, really, Nash? I've only seen pictures of them."

"Aw man, you're in for a real treat when you do. They're some real beauties."

"I can't wait to see them. That's why I called Sarah, to let her know I've got two weeks leave coming to me. Do you think she's calmed down enough to talk to me now?" Mitch asked.

"Hang on and I'll find out." Nash walked over to Sarah's room and knocked on the door. When she opened it, he smiled into her red-rimmed eyes. "Here, Sarah, someone wants to speak to you." He handed her the phone and quietly pulled the door closed to give her some privacy.

He went back to his room to pace and wait it out. After another five minutes he opened his door to a soft tapping. Sarah told her brother goodbye before handing the phone over to him. He watched her disappear down the hall to meet the others in the living room. "Nash here."

"You have something to write with?" Mitch asked.

Liam picked up a pen and pad from his nightstand. "Sure do; what do you have?"

"These are my contact numbers." He rattled off three different numbers for Nash. "If anything—anything at all happens with that piece of shit, you call me, you hear? I have some retired Marine brothers who live in that area. They'll help if I ask them to."

Liam grunted. "I wondered about that—I know how it is."

"Sounds like you're military, too," Mitch said. "What branch?"

"Navy."

"Aw man, sorry to hear that. You got any specialized training that qualifies you to protect my little sister?"

"Does the fact that I was a SEAL for four years qualify?" Mitch's low chuckle reverberated over the phone.

"It'll have to do, I guess. We can't all be jarheads."

Liam laughed at the good natured teasing. "That's right. Some of us are born with brains to go along with all that brawn." He smiled at Mitchell's burst of laughter as they ended the call.

CHAPTER 21

Angelique surveyed her new digs while sipping on a cup of coffee, satisfied with the results of two full days of unpacking.

"My stuff looks good in here, Sonny," she commented. "I think we'll get along just fine, if you'll have me." She started to say something else then closed her mouth and grinned at her uneasiness. "I guess this takes some getting used to, but I'm trying."

A knock at her door forced her up from her comfortable position of aching feet propped up on the arm of her couch. She set her coffee cup down and groaned as she got up to see who it was.

Mike stood there, holding out a cut crystal vase of fresh flowers in one hand. "Think of it as a house warming gift."

"How beautiful! You're too sweet."

He pulled his other hand out from behind his back to reveal a basket holding two bottles of wine.

"Ooh, is that what I think it is?" Angelique cooed.

"Galvez by Feliciana Wineries. One white and one red."

"Oh baby, you know what I like," she said, taking the bouquet of flowers from him with one hand as she kissed him lightly on the mouth. "These are gorgeous. Thank you so much."

He bowed elegantly at the waist. "You're so welcome."

She placed the vase on the center of her dining room table then turned to take the basket from him.

Mike turned in a slow circle. "This place looks fantastic."

She nodded in satisfaction as her gaze followed his. "It's a great old house, isn't it?"

"Yep," he said, fidgeting with his hat while looking down at his Tony Lama boots. "Y-You aren't still mad at me, are you?" he said, sounding contrite. "I was being kind of a bully at the hospital."

"You were only doing what my mom asked you to. She confessed to me yesterday when I called her. I'm sorry I lit into you like that."

Mike placed his two massive hands around her waist and pulled her to him. "Nothing to be sorry for," he said. "And yes, this is a wonderful place; so convenient and close." He nuzzled her neck softly.

Angelique shivered. "Arret ca, Mike! You need to stop that."

He grinned, but stepped away from her. "I don't want to force you to call your shrink again."

"Oh funny," she said, leaning over to answer her ringing landline. "Hello."

"Angelique dear, is that you?"

"Nan!" she said, meeting Mike's amused gaze. "Yes, it is. How are you? Was your flight okay?"

"I'm fine, now, dear. But that night out in the Big Easy didn't do much for my jet lag. Heed these words, honey. Never play quarters with middle aged drag queens. The more those bitches drink, the better their aim."

"What, no strip club?" Angelique asked, winking at Mike.

"Of course we hit the clubs. As a matter of fact, we lucked out and found one with their version of the Chippendale Dancers. They were quite accomplished."

"Did you get anyone's phone number or address?" Angelique asked as Nan's tinkle of laughter carried through the phone.

"Oh honey, I got more than that. I told you, I'm a huge tipper." She sighed loudly. "Now, how's my Sonny doing?"

"Sonny seems to be doing well. My stuff looks really good in here, Nan. I may not let you back in." Angelique slapped at Mike's hand as he tried to pull her toward him. "Stop it, Mike!" she hissed.

"Is Michael there? Come on, dear. Don't be greedy. Give this old lady some fuel to fire up my imagination," Nan cajoled.

Angelique gave a snort. "Old lady, my foot. You have a better love life than I do."

Nan clucked her tongue. "Well, that's not the way it's supposed to be. What's wrong with that boy?"

Angelique sucked in her breath as Mike's tender lips found a spot on her neck. "Trust me, there's nothing wrong with him."

"Then why haven't you tapped that yet?" Nan asked, loud enough to be heard by Mike.

Angelique's jaw dropped as Mike gave a muffled laugh before leaning over to speak into the phone.

"Believe me, Nan. It's not for my lack of trying."

"Oh, so it's you, then," Nan surmised. "What are you waiting for, Angelique? You know that boy is head over heels in love with you, don't you?"

Angelique's eyes settled lovingly on Mike. "So he says, but it happens he's not the only one."

"Way to work it, girly!"

"Yeah, well, I'm trying to make sure my choices from here on out are based on the right reasons."

"Humph . . . I always thought a screaming orgasm was a good enough reason."

Angelique cringed. "Oh, I cannot believe you just said that." The old woman's cackle echoed around her.

"You've got to loosen up honey, or you'll grow old before your time. Now put my boy on the phone so I can give him a few words of wisdom."

Angel looked in horror at Mike. "Oh, I don't think so."

"Come on, dear, put him on the phone. What are you so afraid of?"

Angelique finally relented and handed the phone to Mike. "She wants to speak to you."

∾∾

Mike took the phone and cleared his throat. "Hey Nan, how's Paris?"

"I don't know yet, Michael. It's taken me all this time to settle in and get over my little escapade in N'Awlins. Enough about me, I've got one word for you, boy."

"What word is that, Nan?" he asked, curiously.

"G-spot!"

"What the hell?"

"Did you hear me?" she asked.

He wiped a hand over his astonished face. "Yes. God yes, I heard you."

"Now, I know a man of your age should know how to please a woman by now, but sadly, countless numbers of men go for years, relying on the old wham, bam, thank you ma'am method, but let me just tell you from experience—"

"No! Don't tell me, Nan. I swear to God you don't have to tell me anything. I'm pretty sure I know." He waved off Angelique as she gave him a questioning look.

"Pretty sure won't cut it, son. You've got to know where that puppy is if you want to make a woman happy."

"I know where it is."

"Are you sure?"

"Uh huh. I'm sure, Nan."

"But do you know what to do with it, Michael?"

"Yes, Nan! I know what to do with a G-spot," he said, sure he was blushing down to the roots of his hair.

∾∾

Angelique gasped, mortified at what she'd just heard. She reached out and grabbed the phone from Mike's hands. "Nan!"

The old woman gave a throaty chuckle. "You're welcome."

Angelique choked on what would have been a laugh if she hadn't been so embarrassed. "I'm hanging up now," she finally managed to spit out as she disconnected and dropped the phone on the couch. She and Mike sat, both silent, staring straight ahead in matching states of too-stunned-to-speak. Angelique chanced a look at Mike and had to laugh at the still-horrified expression on his face.

He blew out an exasperated breath and shook his head. "Un-freaking-believable," he groaned. "Your landlady is something else."

She burst into another round of laughter. "Hell, she was your friend first."

"I had no idea she was such a . . ." He stopped there, and threw his hands up in the air, at an obvious loss for words.

"A free spirit?" she asked.

He cocked his head. "I was going to say loose old broad."

She gasped and looked around as though someone else were in the house. "Not in front of Sonny! Have you lost your mind?"

Mike's brow furrowed as his chest rumbled with laughter. "What the hell's he gonna do? Tell her?"

Angelique bubbled with laughter. "God, I don't know, but I like this place way too much to take the chance." She stood, spreading her arms as she spun slowly around. "Do you hear that, Sonny? I love you and I think Nan is a wonderful, free spirit. She's great just the way she is!" She dropped her arms and leveled her gaze at Mike, who cast furtive glances at his surroundings.

"Yeah," he mumbled. "What she said."

Angelique glowered at him through narrowed slits. "I swear, if you upset Sonny, I'll be very angry with you."

He laughed and pulled her to him for a kiss. "I wouldn't worry about it too much. I'm sure this house is far too intelligent to blame you for something I said." He rested his chin on the top of her head. "I have to go back to work soon, my lunch break is just about up. What do you feel like doing tonight? Anything you want."

"No dancing, my feet can't take it tonight," she groaned.

"How about if we watch some pay per view on my big screen and I cook supper for you?"

The possibility of home cooking immediately peaked her interest. "Barbeque?"

He kissed the tip of her nose. "Sure, if that's what you want. Do you want chicken or steak?"

"Mm, ribs baby. You know how much I love your ribs."

Treating her to his beautiful smile, he reached his hands up under her snug tee shirt. "I'm kind of partial to yours, too."

Always ticklish, she laughed and pushed her shirt down. "Drown them in that fantastic mystery sauce of yours, too."

"Will do," he said. "I should be home by five. Come by any time after that."

"What can I bring?"

"Just bring the wine if you feel like sharing it with me. I've got the rest. I don't want you to lift a finger." He reached down and gave her a bone melting kiss.

Angelique groaned and pulled away before opening her front door for him. "See you later," she murmured. Mike walked to his unmarked Tahoe as she watched, appreciating the rear view of the tight butt and broad, muscular shoulders. She closed the door and leaned against it, placing her hands on her belly in an attempt to control the need his presence invoked in her. She recalled the sounds of a neighborhood cat last night outside her window, obviously female, and obviously in heat. She'd thought the thing sounded like it was in severe pain. Angelique groaned inwardly, amazed at how much sympathy she had for that feline.

∿

Mike worked hard to concentrate on the route back to the department. Anytime he came into contact with Angelique proved to be painful. Especially now that she seemed a little more open to the physical aspect of their relationship. It was definitely a good sign, but he wanted more. Not just the lovemaking, although he grew hard just thinking about it. He wanted the entire frittata, as his grandfather used to say.

He thought of Nash, who'd been so devastated after losing his wife and child. He knew for a fact that Nash wanted the same thing with Angel as he did. He also knew he'd be just as good to her.

What was there to stop her from choosing Nash over him? After all, Liam was wealthy, able to provide so much better for her than he could on a cop's salary. Mike had only a modest portfolio, having lost big in the stock market fiasco that had sucked up the life savings of so many individuals. Luckily, he'd invested half his stock in a safer, lower interest account. He was still better off than a lot of people, but nowhere near where he should be at this time of his life.

He rolled to a stop at the intersection light and raked one hand through his hair as he caught his dark eyed reflection in the rearview mirror. *What would it take to make her choose me over somebody like Nash?* His greatest fear was to be left out in the cold where Angel was concerned. He studied his reflection until the car behind him impatiently blew the horn when the light turned green. Mike shook himself out of his silent musings and drove on to work.

The department's main room was filled with the aroma of freshly brewed coffee, which he headed straight for.

"Harper, how's that lady of yours?" Captain Ted Nichols asked him.

"Beautiful as ever, I just saw her for lunch."

"When are you gonna ask that girl to marry you?"

"As soon as she's decided she wants me to, Cap'n. She's still narrowing down the playing field."

"You mean you've got some competition out there?"

Mike nodded. "Yeah, we were neck and neck, but I think I'm pulling ahead a little more every day. I got a lucky break when a horse threw him."

"Wait a minute," an officer called out from over by the coffee machine. "You're not talkin' about that private detective watching the lady with the twins, are ya?"

Mike nodded. "His name's Liam Nash."

"That's the guy Mel's got the hots for," Hennigan called out.

All eyes in the precinct turned to Mike, who shrugged. "It's news to me."

"Do tell," Captain Nichols demanded of Hennigan.

"It's true. I overheard her when she called that Sarah lady, to let her know she would be on guard duty with her this weekend. I heard her talking about that Nash fella—I'm telling you, man. She was happy as a fat cat with a bowl of cream when she found out he'd be there in the same house with them. Something's up with her and that guy."

"I don't know," Mike said.

"What do you know, lover boy?" Bishop asked him.

He grinned at the large man. "I know Mel's gonna kick all your asses for talking about her behind her back."

"We're not talking about her. We're discussing her non-existent love life," Bishop replied.

"Maybe after this weekend it won't be so non-existent and Harper, here, can breathe a sigh of relief," the Captain said, giving Mike a hearty slap on the back. "Hey son, if you need any advice from a man with many years of wisdom under his belt, just ask."

Mike laughed. "Uh, no, Cap'n; I think I got my quota of that today." He told them all about Nan and the advice she'd given him about the G-spot. Everyone laughed except for Bishop.

He sat there with a puzzled look on his face. "What the hell's a G-spot?" he finally asked.

Raucous laughter broke out in the precinct's main room, prompting several officers to come out of their own offices. The subject got passed around repeatedly, and Bishop asked the question again.

"So what is it? I've heard of it before, but I've never seen one, so I figured it was just a myth."

The laughter in the room grew to dangerous levels as the women officers expressed their sorrows for poor Mrs. Bishop.

Finally, Hennigan stopped laughing long enough to ask a question. "Hey, Bishop, you still live off of Pecan Avenue?"

"Sure do."

"Is your wife at home today?"

"She should be—why?" the tall, lanky cop asked, sounding suspicious.

"I figured I could stop by later and show her where hers is," he said as the entire room erupted in more bawdy laughter.

~~

Mike drove out of the precinct's parking lot whistling along to Jake Owen, singing Don't Think I Can't Love You blaring from his truck's radio. It'd always been a favorite, but more so since it was his and Angel's favorite song to dance to.

He pulled up to the red light, distracted by thoughts of what he'd need to pick up for the barbeque at his local Winn Dixie.

Ribs, of course, apple sauce, honey, brown sugar…

When the light turned green, he took off slowly.

He had potatoes and eggs at home, but was out of mayo…

Too preoccupied, he didn't notice the black Hummer coming hard at him from his right side until it was too late to avoid it.

In the nanosecond before the vehicle hit him, all sense of time and motion slowed to a near stop. He heard a loud ticking in his head and realized it was the passing of time. Not in seconds, but milliseconds. Everything around him began to move in a freeze frame effect—mere fractions of an inch at a time. In that instant Mike saw the driver and passenger of the Hummer and recognized that moment as his own personal miracle. He knew instantly it was God's way of telling him not to give up, that he would live through the accident.

He watched the passenger door crumble inward as the window shattered in slow motion, the spider web of broken glass spreading until it encompassed the entire window.

An instant later his last conscious thought rolled through his mind like a message in marquee lights.

Just get on with it. I've got a destiny to fulfill.

CHAPTER 22

He wandered aimlessly through chambers of random thoughts and memories. It took him awhile to figure out why everything felt differently. He finally realized that he wasn't walking, but floating, gliding effortlessly from one spot to the next. Not slowly, but flitting around quickly, like a Humming Bird, only faster, as though all he had to do was think about where he wanted to be and he was there.

He made an effort to see himself, but couldn't. He tried to raise a hand, a foot, to get a glimpse of any part of his body that used to exist. That still existed, actually...just not here...not now. What should have been a reason to panic couldn't shake him from his perpetual state of calm. He knew, without knowing the how or why of it, that his mortal self still existed. His subconscious, or whatever the hell it was, flitted around the chambers until he came across a memory that pleased him immensely.

He and Angelique together, and judging from their surroundings, he'd cooked for her. He'd barbequed some ribs, just the way she liked them, slathered with his secret sauce, and cooked to sticky perfection. The meal was over and she'd turned up her stereo so they could dance to what he knew had to be their song. It was the same damn song he'd been whistling when he left the station. He could hear Jake Owen crooning in the background.

He watched Angelique close her eyes in bliss as his corporal form held her closely and sang the sweet, meaningful words softly into her ear. From this vantage point, he could actually see her face. She was smiling—the beautiful, sincere smile of a woman who was in love with the man who sang to her. He continued to watch Angel's face as he twirled her around the huge living room, watched the smile light up her face as he sang the last line of the song to her.

But when had this happened? Where had this happened? How was he able to see a memory he couldn't recall happening? His cop senses kicked in and he began to observe things. Like the room they were in…the furniture and other items…the view from the huge picture window.

He gathered information like so many puzzle pieces. Once he'd collected them all, they flew together in one instantaneous conclusion. The discovery filled him with an overwhelming sense of tranquility that flowed freely over him, an absolute certainty that this particular scene wasn't a memory after all. But something else entirely.

∿

Wild eyed and frantic with worry, Angelique burst through the doors of Lafayette General Hospital, with her purse in one hand and her phone in the other.

"Angel! Over here!"

She pivoted toward the voice and headed immediately for Red and Tiffany. "Where is he?"

Red greeted her with a hug. "Mike's in surgery. We just walked in thirty seconds before you did. Luckily, we were in town already when a mutual friend of ours from the department called me for your number. We're going up to the surgical waiting room."

They stepped into the elevator. "Are any of your sisters working here?" she asked, stepping back to let someone else in.

Tiffany answered for her. "No, but I know several doctors working in the trauma wing. Mike's in good hands." She placed an arm around Angel's shoulders. "He'll be fine."

Angelique nodded, too afraid that if she spoke she'd lose control over her closely tethered emotions.

Hours later, a surgeon walked away from the crowd that had gathered in the waiting room, all there over concern for Detective Mike Harper.

Tiffany pulled on Angelique's arm. "Sit, before you pass out. You're pale, Angel. Are you feeling light headed?"

"I'm fine." But Mike could be paralyzed, or a vegetable, or have permanent brain damage. Her terror intensified with every worst case scenario the doctor had come up with.

"The possibilities the doctor mentioned were just that, Angel—he was only trying to prepare you for what could be, not what is. You heard the rest of it. There are too many miraculous stories to mention when it comes to brain trauma recoveries."

Angelique paced, feeling unsettled and overcome by the smell of overheated coffee. "What is a medically induced coma, exactly, and how could that possibly be good for him? I thought the longer a person was in a coma, the less chance they had of ever coming out of it. Wouldn't that be dangerous?"

Tiffany shook her head. "I'm orthopedics, not brain surgery, but I did speak to Tanner while we were waiting to hear something. He'd already listed this procedure as a possibility so I can explain it to you. You see, severe head trauma can cause the brain's metabolism to be altered…off, so to speak, so that parts of the brain aren't getting enough blood supply. Keeping him on Propofol for a while will shut down the brain, and slow its metabolism so it uses very little energy to repair itself. Hopefully, by doing that, it can survive without any serious damage." She placed her hands on Angelique's shoulders. "In short, it repairs itself faster and with less energy while it's asleep. When the swelling goes down enough they'll stop giving him the Propofol and wake him up. That's when we'll be able to see if it's successfully healed itself."

Angel nodded. "I hear the words, Tiff, but I can't seem to find any comfort in that right now. I want him to wake up and know me and everyone else, and to be able to speak, and walk, and . . . " Her voice trailed off as she put the palms of her hands over her eyes. "Oh God, this can't be happening again."

Red walked over to put an arm around her shoulders. "Look, this is the second time I've had a good friend of mine hurt this badly. Mike is every bit as strong as Jackson was then, Angel. And he's got as much to live for. He'll make a full recovery."

Angelique placed one hand over her eyes and released a long, slow breath. "I've got to believe that right now, Red, or I'll never make it through this."

∼✺

Angelique walked to the hospital's atrium and seated herself on a bench, overlooking a fountain. The warmth from the sun-heated, cast-iron seat penetrated her muscles, helping to dispel the chill of Mike's private hospital room. Groaning, she lifted her face to absorb the glorious solar rays of the mid-morning sun.

Almost immediately, her phone rang. She lifted it to view the ID of the caller and thumb swiped the screen to answer. "Hey, Liam."

"How's our boy, Angel? Any change?"

She stifled a yawn. "No change. I guess that's good, I don't really know. How about you? You following doctor's orders and taking it easy?"

"Hell, I couldn't cut up if I wanted to. These ladies would tear my ass up faster than you can say Fat freakin' Tuesday."

Angelique gave him a low snicker "You're in Louisiana now, boy. En francaise, sil vous plait."

"Sorry babe, what is it? Marty Graw?"

"Close enough for a cowboy, I guess. We can't all be gifted with Cajun or Creole bloodlines. It's Mardi Gras, by the way," she said, pronouncing it for him.

"Yeah, well where I'm from we got our own little saying. We can't all be lucky enough to be Longhorns."

"True enough, Liam, but I've been lucky enough to know two of the finest Longhorns this side of the Sabine River. I'd almost forgotten you both attended U of T in Austin."

"Both attended—different years, of course, but neither of us graduated. There was a little too much partying going on. By the time I dropped out, I'd already decided it would be less dangerous to join the Navy rather than face my folks."

"And was it?" It relieved her to talk about something other than the possibility of Mike never waking up again.

"Tough call. My old man was good and pissed, but training for the Seals damn near killed me. It about did my folks in, all that worrying about me."

"I can imagine how rough it was on them," she said, head back, eyes closed and feeling a little like a turtle sunning herself on a river bank.

"I'm gonna let you go, now Angelique."

His unexpected comment had her head snapping forward in shock. "You're giving up, just like that?" His low chuckle let her know her judgment was off.

"All I meant was that you sound tired, so I'm going to end the call. You need to get some real rest, Angel. I bet you haven't slept since it happened."

"Oh," she said. "I've been napping but I'll admit it's been awhile. That couch in his room isn't much to brag about."

"I wish I could take your place."

"I wouldn't let you, just like I wouldn't let him when it was you in the hospital. Besides, I start at the clinic in Lafayette tomorrow. All day long I'll be worried sick about him, as well as you and Sarah."

"Don't worry about Sarah. Between Mel and me, she's fine."

"Who's Mel?"

"She's the cop that helps out on her days off. Apparently, she and Sarah got close during her hospital stay."

She lowered her chin, her interest in the current conversation at an all-time high. "Oh, reddish hair? I've met her. Is she good?"

"Harper says she is. I haven't had the opportunity to see how good she is yet."

"What the hell does that mean?" she said.

"We haven't had any incidents to test her skills yet . . . and I mean her police skills. What the hell did you think I meant?"

Angelique remained quiet, biting her lower lip at her second major screw up concerning another woman.

"Angel, you have no reason to be jealous of Mel."

"I'm not jealous," she fibbed. "But don't you find her attractive?"

"Well, sure I do. I'd have to be blind not to see how beautiful she is. But she's not here for me. She's here for Sarah and the babies. I guess I should be flattered, but oddly, I'm a little insulted."

After a moment of personal contemplation, she released the breath she'd been holding. "You're right."

"Especially since you've got both Mike and me chasing our own tails over you."

"You're right, and I'm sorry."

"I am?" He sounded doubtful.

Her own burst of laughter took her by surprise, and Liam joined in. "Yes Liam, I'm wrong…you're right."

"Hmm, strangely enough, I find it disturbing that you're not more upset."

"I'm tired, sweetie."

"Maybe. Regardless, I know you're under a lot of stress over there."

"Listen, I need to get back to Mike."

"I know you do. Tell him I said hi, and tell that son of a bitch he better get his ass back up and running soon. There is no honor in winning by default."

"Winning? I'm not a prize, you know."

"Hmmm," Liam said, his voice lowered in a seductive growl. "That's your opinion."

CHAPTER 23

Troy hoofed it to the far side of the pasture where he'd hidden his car, the blare of the big house's alarm system still ringing in his ears. How the hell would he get to that bitch now that she and those brats were in a big, fancy house with a security system? How the hell had she rated that, not to mention her own damn bodyguard?

What had only taken a minute to reach his car, felt more like several by the time he tore out of there. With the lights off, he headed down the shortcut to the river, where the boat waited for him. The same boat that was supposed to carry his wife with him. Hell, he'd have even left the brats for the Ritchie Riches. Who the hell pops out two kids at a time, anyway? Just his shitty luck to hook up with a broad who carried that twisted gene. She never had time for him anymore. Besides, they cost a fortune in diapers and formula. Who needed it?

He figured he'd done enough damage to give that stars and stripes jarhead fucking brother of hers something to gnaw on for years. The day that high and mighty son of a bitch had bloodied his nose over a comment about his sister's fine ass, it'd stirred a fire in him. He'd backed off then, because no chick was worth getting his ass thrown in jail for statutory rape. But he knew if he ever had the opportunity to tap that ass, he would take it.

Years later, on his first night back in town, he'd seen her. Had to have her. Unfortunately, the bitch wouldn't give it up without a ring on her finger. At the time, he'd figured it was a small price to pay. Even then, her dick of a brother had been too busy saving the world to make it home. So, he'd married her.

Looking back on it, he should have just slipped the bitch some Special K or a Roofie and left her ass with something to remember him by. He smiled to himself, thinking about an all-nighter he'd had with Miss Too Prim and Proper to do it any way other than boring as hell. He'd had the best night of sex in his life, courtesy of a particularly high grade of Liquid Ecstasy he slipped in her glass of water. After that bitch woke up the next morning, she couldn't sit comfortably for a week. She never did confront him about it, but he figured she suspected something. Her refusal to drink from anything other than bottles or cans she'd opened herself after that was a pretty good indicator.

From then on his goal was to control her, own her, break her.

Ah, well, it looked like he'd have to make his great Mexican escape without her. He'd made some enemies here, skipped out with all the profits of a huge drug deal to front this little venture, so staying wasn't an option. He suddenly pictured her—smug, smiling, and laughing in his face. He allowed himself a low chuckle, knowing she was smart enough to figure out sooner or later that she'd never be able to let her guard down—not as long as he was alive and free. He would be back for her.

∽

Sarah and Leah sat together in the center of Leah and Daniel's huge bed, each holding a baby in their arms. Daniel paced back and forth, still seeming irritated at Liam's shouted order to "Stay here and lock the door behind me."

"That son of a bitch has got some balls snooping around my place in the middle of the night like this. That's good. I'll use 'em to hang him from, when I get my hands on him."

"Daniel," Leah hissed.

He turned to his wife, who cocked her head toward a clearly worried Sarah.

"Don't be afraid, Sarah. He'll never get through any of us to get to you or the twins. If I've gotta beef up this whole damn system to keep his ass off our property, I damn sure will."

The corners of Sarah's mouth turned down in a worried frown. "If they don't catch him tonight, he'll go underground. Troy's always been so good at slithering out of trouble. If he gets away there's no telling where he'll go or how long it'll take for him to surface again. But I know…he'll be back."

Leah rocked Sammi in her arms. "And that will mean more waiting, wondering, and worrying for all of us"

"He loves keeping me off balance, looking over my shoulder. God forbid I ever get the chance to enjoy life again," Sarah added, in a tortured whisper.

Daniel swore under his breath as his cell phone rang suddenly. "Liam! Please tell me you got him." He closed his eyes as he listened, nodding slowly. "All right, then. Keep us informed." He lowered his phone and turned to Sarah. "They found an abandoned car by the river and think he got away by boat. Mel just called the Coast Guard in case he makes it out to the Gulf."

Sarah buried her nose in Danni's soft curls to hold back frustrated tears. "Oh God."

"Now, don't jump to conclusions, sweetie. It'll be fine," Daniel said. "I bet they get him by morning."

"I'm sure you're right." Sarah gave Daniel a pert nod, trying not to let him see how wrong she thought he was.

∽◡◠

Sarah spent the next day at the office, thankful for the work that kept her mind off Troy for a while. She could afford to relax some, knowing her girls were safe and secure with Leah and Daniel at the ranch, while Liam set up camp in her office. Weekends spent all day at the ranch with her twins were heaven.

Things ran smoothly enough, but Sarah couldn't fully relax, knowing her brutal ex could show up any minute.

One week after his disappearance, she got a house call from a couple of State Troopers asking to see her. Once she'd introduced herself to the two men, she stood waiting, arms crossed tightly across her chest.

"Mrs. Richa—"

"Hebert. Please, I've gone back to using my maiden name. Call me Sarah Hebert."

The officer nodded as though he understood her dilemma. "Ms. Hebert, we're working a joint investigation with the U.S. Coast Guard on a vessel they found capsized about fifteen miles south of the opening of Sabine Pass. No registration number or name on the boat. They dropped a rescue swimmer to check it out and recovered a waterproof box secured inside it with some items we're thinking you can identify." He pulled out a container, marked 'Evidence' and opened it up in front of her. Inside were several items, all tagged with bright yellow labels. Among the items was an IPhone covered in a Grateful Dead case.

Sarah covered her mouth and nodded. "That's his phone. I remember when he bought the case." She picked through the other items and pulled her hand back. "I don't recognize anything else."

The officer nodded. "The card had been removed and all other info has been wiped out, so we don't have much to go on. We'll be sending it to our tech specialist to see if we can get anything back."

"I'm sorry I can't help you with the other items," she said.

"You did fine. To your knowledge, does he have any friends or relatives in that area? Someone who may have met him out there? He could have abandoned the boat and a few of his belongings, to keep the authorities off his trail."

"The only relatives I know of are his aunt and uncle in Nederland, Texas, but they're in their seventies or eighties and in a nursing home now."

"Did they have children?"

"Yes, but last I heard, his cousins are in northern California and Oregon. That's why the old folks are in the nursing home."

The trooper nodded while taking down some notes then handed her a card. "Please, if you can think of anything else that may help us with the investigation..."

"I'll be sure to call you. No one wants that maniac caught as badly as I do, officer," she assured him.

"If you don't mind me asking," Daniel spoke from behind her, "what kind of a boat did the Coast Guard find?"

"It was a nice boat. A cabin cruiser type, thirty-five footer. The kind with a galley, sleep space for four, head with sink and vanity. Just what I want for my retirement. What a damn waste."

He tapped his pen on his pad before tucking it into his shirt pocket. "The diver was able to get into the cabin, and said that thing was pretty well stocked. It looked like he was planning to lay low on it for a while, and not by himself, either. He even saw a couple of packs of disposable diapers inside. One more thing. He had padlocks on the outside of the cabin. Whoever he planned on bringing along with him wouldn't have been a willing passenger. Since he's got three felony counts of kidnapping on him they've decided to haul the boat in for further investigation."

"Good Lord," Leah whispered. "Thank God for security systems."

Sarah clutched at the table, suddenly feeling dizzy at the trooper's last bit of information. The thought of her and the twins being his prisoners again, this time completely isolated out in the Gulf of Mexico, made her nauseous. One hand on her belly and one covering her mouth, she made a heaving run for the powder room.

CHAPTER 24

Angelique watched the REM activity under Mike's closed eyelids, a good sign according to the doctors. They'd backed off the drugs that had been keeping him in the coma, as all signs of brain swelling had diminished. All he needed to do was wake the hell up.

When a long run of lowly muttered profanity interrupted her thoughts, she glanced up at Melanie Finley, the one responsible for the offense. Angelique placed her foam coffee cup on the tray. "Problem?"

"I'd say so," Mel said, dropping her phone into the shirt pocket of her uniform. "They found a boat abandoned and capsized in the gulf. A cabin type, and they think Sarah's ex was planning to escape in it to Mexico." She explained how it was found and the investigator's reasons for thinking it was Troy Richard's.

"Oh God. Padlocked cabins."

"Yeah, apparently her ex isn't happy unless he's keeping her locked up and under his thumb. The son of a bitch," Mel fumed.

Angelique stared at the female cop who seemed to care about the welfare of Sarah and the twins as much as anyone. "So, there's no sign of Troy? What do they think happened to him?"

"They don't know, and that's the really awful part of all this, isn't it? Nobody knows if the sadistic bastard is dead or alive. Poor Sarah."

Angelique shivered as a feeling of cold dread filled her. "What if he planned it to look like he's dead so everyone will think he's not a threat anymore? She'll never be able to let down her guard. Ever." She glanced over at Melanie, who'd begun to pace the floor like a caged animal. "Mel?"

"Hmmm?" she answered, clearly distracted.

"You said you'd seen cases like this before. How'd those particular cases turn out?"

Melanie slowed her pacing and came to a gradual stop. "Never in a good way."

"I won't ask what happened, but in your professional opinion, do you think it's possible Troy could have planned something like this just so he could get to her?"

"Professionally, I know it's possible. Personally, and this is just my gut instinct talking, I'm leaning more toward probable."

Angelique crossed herself before speaking. "You know, Ma Mere Antoinette always said the devil reserved special places in hell for people like him." She jumped at the hoarse croak that erupted from Mike's hospital bed.

"I sure as hell hope y'all aren't talking about me."

"Mike!" Angelique threw herself at his head while Mel went to find a nurse. "How do you feel?"

"Fuzzy, and thirsty as hell." He tried to lick his dry lips.

"Here," Angelique said, as she dabbed at his mouth with a wet washcloth. He caught the cloth between his teeth and sucked at the moisture.

"Need water," he croaked.

"Let's wait until the doctor says it's okay." She drenched the cloth in cold water before raising it to his lips again. "Oh God, it's good to hear your voice. Do you remem—" Her question was cut off as the doctor rushed into the room.

"I hear sleeping beauty has awakened."

Mike's reply was quick but raspy. "Yeah, and he's thirsty. Can I have some water?"

"Well, sure you can." The doctor sounded downright jovial.

"Here you go." Angel brought a glass of water with a straw to his lips. Mike's eyes drifted shut as he pulled hard on the straw. She handed the nurse the glass at his doctor's quiet request to clear the room, and walked out with Melanie.

"All right, Mr. Harper, I'm Dr. Moore and it's time to see what we've got going on. Do you know why you're here?"

"Accident. The Hummer ran the light and hit me."

"Excellent."

Mike continued to answer questions about who was president, the year, the month, the two women who'd been in the room with him. He heard a click near his head and turned toward the sound.

"Mr. Harper, I just need to check your eyes for pupil dilation."

A few seconds passed in silence before Mike answered. "I'm ready when you are," he slurred, still trying to shake off whatever drugs they'd given him. "Think you could remove these bandages firs—" The rest of the sentence froze on his lips, replaced by a horrified urge to scream as the doctor's hands encountered the fleshy area around his eyes.

He wasn't wearing bandages.

∾

Angelique paced, trying to brush aside the feeling that something was off. She barely registered Melanie's cheerful chatter through several phone calls telling everyone that Mike was awake.

Awake, yes. But was he fine?

An agonizing fifteen minutes later, the nurse hurried out, followed by the doctor, looking pensive. Angelique stopped her pacing to face him while he jotted something on a note pad. He finally looked up and smiled at her.

"His memory seems to be fine. He knows both of you and what happened. He's still in a bit of a fog but that will lessen as the drug continues to fade from his system. No sign of paralysis in either upper or lower torso."

Angelique crossed her arms tightly as the doctor took a deep breath, seeming to brace himself. Oh, God. Give us all strength.

～～

Mike barely registered the door opening and the following footsteps as he stared out the window. Or rather, at the one fuzzy area of dark gray in the otherwise complete sea of blackness.

"Hey Babe, how're you feeling? You need more water?"

"Right about now I'm thinking I could use a shot of something a little stronger. Guess I'll settle for water." He reached out suddenly and knocked the glass out of Angelique's hand. He cursed low in his throat at the sound of water splashing and the bounce of plastic cup upon the tile.

"Oops, looks like we need a little synchronization," Angel said, trying not to sound as disappointed in him as she obviously was. How could she not be? He was blind, and helpless.

"Angel."

"Don't you dare apologize, Mike. I should have let you know I was handing it to you."

"Just, go home."

"Wh-What?"

"I said go home. I know you've been here the entire time and you need to go home and get some rest. Besides, I need to sort this out in my own mind."

"Sort what out?"

"This blindness thing and what it means for me and for the rest of my life."

"I don't know about you, but the doctor just told Mel and I there's a good chance your loss of sight is temporary."

"And all that means is that there's an equally good chance it's not."

"Hey Harper!" Melanie's voice cut in. "Since when did you become such a pessimistic asshole?"

He swung around to face her, for all the good it did him. "Since I woke up from a coma blind as a fucking bat."

"Oh no, he dropped the F-Bomb. I'm so scared," Melanie said, her voice oozing with sarcasm.

"Kiss my ass, Finley," he growled as she burst into laughter.

"Oh please. You know I'm a crack shot, so give me something a little more challenging. Considering that you're acting like a complete ass, you make a seriously big target."

"Why don't you show some respect and get the hell out of he—"

"Enough!"

Mike's jaw snapped shut at Angel's tightly spoken command. He waited, jumping slightly when she spoke again, this time directly in front of him.

"We're not going to play this game Michael Harper. No one who gives a crap about you is going to leave you alone so you can wallow in self-pity."

"I'm not wallowing, dammit. I'm just trying to adjust to the fact that I could be like this for the rest of my life."

"And we're trying to make you understand that it may only be for a few days," Mel threw in.

Mike exploded off of the bed. "How the hell do you know?" Dizziness had him grabbing for something to hold on to. Angel's voice came to him like a song, a gentle melody of compassion and reason to soothe his aching heart.

"Michael, I'm here. I'm with you. I will always be here for you. We will get through this and you will be fine."

He collapsed onto the bed like a cheap tent in a hurricane. "Okay. Okay. So, maybe I missed some of what the doc said due to the screaming."

"What screaming?" She brushed his hair back from his forehead.

"The screaming that was going on inside my own head." He grabbed her hand and brought it to his mouth. "I think I need a hug, babe." He didn't have to see her to know she was smiling when she answered.

"What's it worth to you, big boy?"

"Just about anything, but what did you have in mind?" He came the closest he had been to a smile since he'd woken up to a world cloaked in darkness.

She stepped up, wrapping her arms around him as he pulled her close. He lifted his face for a kiss then remembered they may not be alone. "Is Finley still lurking around here?"

"She left after your little temper tantrum a couple of minutes ago."

"Just as well," he said, pulling her down for a thorough and much needed kiss before she slipped out of his reach.

"That's enough, Harper. You hurt more than just your head, you know."

He tried to flex his right shoulder, winced as pain shot through him. His left wrist was sore as well. "I am sore as all get out, now that you mention it. At least my legs are okay. So tell me," he said, patting the mattress beside him. "What did the doctor have to say about all this?" He felt the mattress sag as she settled herself next to him, surrounding him with the subtle scent of her perfume.

"Dr. Moore seems confident your sight will return. He's ordering another MRI to see if anything else shows up, but as the pressure to your optical nerves continues to dissipate your eyesight should begin to return gradually. At this point, they can't tell to what degree it will return, but they're putting you on high doses of steroids to speed the healing process."

"How long does he think it'll take before we know?" He sensed her choosing her words carefully.

"If it hasn't begun to come back after two weeks there's a possibility that it won't."

He released his breath in a loud huff. "I can't accept that."

Angel spoke in a desperately tight voice. "You'll accept whatever God has given you, and you will learn to be as grateful as the rest of us are that your life was spared."

"Yeah, I guess you're right." Even as he spoke the words she wanted to hear, he held on to the one thought that ran through his mind like a marquee banner. No way...No way in hell would he saddle a woman, any woman, with a blind husband.

CHAPTER 25

"Thanks for the ride, Niki," Mike told the student nurse returning him to his room.

"No problem, Mr. Mike. Let me know if you need anything. I'll be on duty until six. Heads up. Looks like you have company."

Mike tilted his head, hearing the clump of boots and the sharp click of a woman's shoes on the tile. "I'd know the sound of Nash's size elevens anywhere, but I'm not sure about who's with him."

"It's me, Detective Harper, Sarah Hebert. I'm Liam's American Express these days. He can't leave home without me."

"Hey!" Mike said, generally pleased to hear her voice. "Well, I can't tell by looking but you sound excellent."

"I am," she said. "The LeBlanc's were a God send, and the twins are crazy about them."

"We're all crazy about them," Nash added. "How you doing, Injun Joe?"

He shrugged the one shoulder that didn't hurt like a mofo. "Well enough. Still blind as a mole rat, and I just found out I'll need shoulder surgery for a seriously torn rotator cuff in my right shoulder, but I've been ordered to be thankful for just being alive. So, I'm thankful I'll be blind and crippled for a while."

"Fun, fun…"

"Oh, it's not that bad," Sarah commented. "Your shoulder will heal, and once your eyesight returns, at least you'll be able to go grocery shopping alone. The difficult part is accepting that sometimes you really do need help."

Mike nodded, forcing a smile he didn't feel. "It's even more difficult when you're usually the one giving the help." The uncomfortable silence surrounded them like a vacuum, sucking all the air out of the room.

"Um, mind if I use your restroom?" Sarah asked.

"Go ahead." Mike waved his hand. "Make yourself at home." He waited until he'd heard the door close before he spoke again. "So what's going on with the investigation?"

"They can't find any sign of her ex, either dead or alive. We have no way of knowing if it's a setup to throw us off or if it's legit."

"And until you know for sure, she can't be left alone."

"You got it, Chief."

"Man that sucks for her, having to be stuck with your ugly mug until this is over with."

"Pfft. With my good looks and charming personality? I don't hear her complaining."

"She will now that she's seen you next to me. There's nothing like a side by side comparison to realize she got the bum deal."

Nash burst into laughter. "You must not have looked in a mirror lately, dude. You look like shit!"

Mike twisted his mouth, waiting for it to hit him. He didn't have to wait long.

"Oh. Oh, damn, Harper. I'm a dumbass."

"No arguments here."

"Really man, I'm sorry about that, but you really do look like shit."

This time Mike burst into laughter. "Nobody's said a thing to me but you. How bad is it?"

"Well, you remember that old riddle 'What's black and white and red all over'?"

"Yep."

"Well, that's you if you add a little green, yellow, and purple to it."

Mike snorted. "Asshole."

"Same to you, buddy."

After a few seconds of laughter, Mike sobered. "If it doesn't come back, I'm screwed, Nash."

"It'll come back. You just had to go and one-up me, didn't ya? Here I thought I had Angel in the bag with the old falling off the horse act. I knocked myself out for a day and everything. Then you go and land yourself in a week long coma. She'll be putty in your hands after this."

"I've known that girl long enough to know she wouldn't base her decision solely on something like this," Mike said. "Besides, if I don't get my sight back I'm pulling my name out of the hat."

"What the hell are you talking about? I thought you loved her more than to hurt her like that."

"I love her enough not to tie her down to a blind man for the rest of her life." Mike cleared his throat as Sarah re-entered the room. "I don't want to talk about this anymore."

∾

"Yes sir, I understand," Sarah said, shaking her head at Liam. "Please call me if there's any change in the situation. Thank you." She laid the phone gently on the table, resisting the urge to throw it across the room. "Still no sign of him, dead or alive." She clasped the back of her neck to ease the build-up of tension that always occurred at the thought of Troy.

"He'll turn up, and if he's alive, I'll get him for you. If not, so much the better."

She let her hands drop to the table. "Sooner or later, you'll need a normal life again, and I'll have to learn to live without constantly looking over my shoulder, never knowing if he'll turn up one day. It's a depressing thought, but I'll adjust."

The sound of the doorbell caught her by surprise and within seconds, her hostess entered the room, followed by a bit of eye candy to lift her dour spirits.

"Look who I found."

Sarah smiled up at the breathtaking good looks of Tanner Collins. "Oh, hello." The brilliant smile he gave her had her fighting off a sudden urge to blush like a prepubescent girl. "Are you lost?" Maybe he was looking for Red and Tiffany's house instead.

"I don't think so." He held up two gift bags from an exclusive baby shop in the Lake Coburn Mall. "I came to fulfill my tooth-finding obligations. I got twelve month, is that going to fit?"

"It depends what it is." She gasped when Tanner reached in the bag and pulled out two of the most adorable outfits she'd ever seen. "Oh. My. Gosh!" She grabbed for them to study the exquisite hand stitched detailing on the two suits, made identically except for the color. "This is going to be perfect on them right now. The pink will be perfect on Sammi and that light green looks so good on Danni." She clapped her hands together. "I can't wait for them to wake up." Tanner's face exhibited genuine disappointment.

"They're sleeping already?" He looked at his watch, frowning. "Isn't it kind of early?"

Leah laughed. "Not for the night, silly. It's their afternoon nap. They should be up soon, though."

As though planned, first one squeal, then another travelled through the hallway from the nursery.

Tanner's eyes widened in delight as Leah headed for the babies.

Sarah held up the outfits. "Let's go see how these look on them."

He swept out his arm with a flourish. "Ladies first," he said, following her down the hallway.

Sarah paused just inside the doorway. "Hey, my babies. Did you have a good nap?" She walked up to one crib where a curly topped Danni grinned sleepily at her with upraised arms. "Come here sweet girl." She lifted the child easily and held her close as she covered her face with soft kisses. She turned toward Sammi, all cuddled up with Leah, and showered her face with kisses, turning the child into a single, stump-toothed, bundle of grins and giggles.

Sarah pivoted, searching for Tanner and froze at the look of unadulterated awe on his face. "Are you okay?"

He stammered his reply. "Yeah, I'm just-I-I've never seen babies just waking up before."

"Really? What do you think?"

"It's kind of amazing. I didn't think they could get any cuter than they already were."

"Wow. That is one great answer." Leah handed a baby over to him. "Here's your prize."

Tanner took hold of Sammi and held her out in front of him, as though he wasn't quite sure what to do with her. The two stared at one another, both smiling, sizing each other up. Sarah knew the second her daughter's face turned red what she was trying to accomplish. Before she could open her mouth to warn Tanner, Sammi gave one loud grunt and released a liquified diaper full.

∾

One package disposable diapers: $10.00

Generic baby wipes: $2.00

Boudreaux's Baby Butt Cream: $3.00

The look on bachelor doctor's face at his first poop-filled diaper: Priceless.

"Good God!" Tanner's cry came deep from his diaphragm.

Sarah attempted, but failed, to keep her amusement to a minimum as he held her child out and away from him. The look on his face said that if his arms had been two feet longer, he'd have used every inch.

Leah didn't even try to hold back her snort of laughter. "Eat, sleep, and poop, in that order, Tanner. We have a rule around here. Whoever's holding them when they poop gets to change the diaper. Lucky you."

If Sarah had bet that Tanner's expression couldn't possibly have turned anymore horrified than it already was, she would have lost. She handed Danni over to Leah and reached out for Sammi. "Let me have her."

"But, the rule."

"I wouldn't hold you to that. This one could scar you for life." She smiled as he gratefully handed over her daughter. To his credit, he stayed at her side and watched her change Sammi's diaper, despite the greenish hue of his face.

She cast another glance in his direction and giggled as she pulled the diaper's second Velcro tab tight. "You aren't going to pass out or anything, are you Doctor Collins?."

He turned his head to take a breath then faced her, frowning slightly. "I'm a brain surgeon, Sarah. I never deal with that particular end of a patient."

She laughed and raised Sammi's shirt over her had then kissed her daughter's belly. "Well, he doesn't know what he's missing out on, huh Sweet Pea?" The infant broke into a fit of belly laughs that had all three adults chuckling along with her.

"Let's see how these girls look in their new threads." Sarah and Leah proceeded to change the babies into the clothes Tanner bought for them.

Once the babies were all snapped and buttoned, they sat them up in their new duds.

"Look at that." Tanner beamed, clearly pleased at how they looked in his gift.

"Adorable, and perfect fits. You have wonderful taste, Tanner," Leah exclaimed.

"I picked up a few other items for them. I hope you don't mind. The saleswoman at the shop informed me that accessories are a girl's best friend." He placed another bag on the bed containing two sets of elastic headbands and tiny pink and light green cowboy boots, every item a perfect match with their new dresses.

"If the boots don't fit, I can exchange them for you. That saleswoman guessed at the size, according to their ages."

The accessories drew squeals of delight from both women as they gushed over them.

"They should fit." Leah compared the boots to the girls' chubby feet. She pulled them on over their socks.

Sarah contained their abundance of golden curls in the headbands. "Pictures! We've got to take pictures of this."

"This is too adorable." Leah scooped up Danni to support her in a standing position.

"Look at this. My little cowgirls love their boots." Sarah picked up Sammi and lifted her to face Tanner. "Girls, say 'Thank you, Doc Collins.'"

Sammi studied Tanner for several seconds before she cracked a big grin at him and patted his face affectionately with both hands. "Ta...Ta . . . " she cooed.

"Hey there, beautiful. You like your new duds? Did I do good?" He ignored the super long string of drool that fell to the front of his shirt.

"Oh..." Sarah pulled her away and wiped his shirt with a burp rag.

"No worries." Tanner smiled down at the child with her arms outstretched to him. "Can I hold her?"

"Sure you can, just be warned, there's plenty more drool where that bit came from." She leaned forward and Sammi practically jumped from her arms to Tanner. Finding it difficult to pull her gaze from Tanner and her daughter, she finally forced herself to turn away. "I'll get the camera," she said, leaving the room.

By the time she got back, Tanner was holding both her daughters, somewhat awkwardly, but looking comfortable enough. Who was this man? He sure didn't seem like the same self-centered, egomaniacal, womanizer Tiffany had described. Of course, Tiffany also said he'd changed lately. No kidding.

She took some shots with her camera then got a few more shots and a bit of video with her phone. She sent pictures to Tiffany, Melanie, and Angelique via text messaging. Within moments she got replies back from all of them, gushing over the clothes. Within moments after that, Melanie had called her.

Tanner tried to look casual as Sarah quietly discussed his gift buying abilities with someone over the phone. Once her short, cryptic answers seemed too frequent, accompanied by a slight blush, she ended the call.

"Who was that?" he asked.

"Um, that was Mel."

"Is that the cop? The redhead?" She nodded, but looked away, making him wish he knew what those two had been talking about.

"Let me take one off your hands." Sarah reached out, relieving him of Sammi.

He leaned in to touch his forehead to Danni's. "It's just you and me, kid." Danni grinned, lifted her face to kiss him on the mouth, and passed gas a split second later. He laughed and turned to Sarah. "At least it was just a fart this time."

She lifted her brow indignantly. "Everyone knows that little girls don't fart, Tanner. They fluff."

"Pfft! Yeah—that didn't sound like a fluff. And neither did what Sammi did in her diaper a while ago."

"Oh well, that was something entirely different. We introduced a new baby food, so that's to be expected every now and then."

He nodded. "Understandable. So, what were you and Officer Mel discussing?"

"Aw, she was curious as to how you learned about accessorizing those two outfits."

"I had some help," he admitted.

"From who?"

"The saleswoman at the boutique I went to yesterday afternoon suggested them." He turned away from her. More to hide his own shame, than anything else. The twentyish saleswoman had actually suggested more than that. As per his old, predictable self, he'd taken her up on it. He'd given himself a royal verbal reaming afterwards. Too late, of course to do anything about it but have regrets. It disturbed him to think he was addicted to anything, whether mentally or physically, even if it was one-night-stand-pick-up-sex.

"I bet you spent a pretty penny on these. You didn't have to do that, you know. An outfit from K-Mart would have sufficed."

He frowned. "K-Mart sucks."

"Okay, Rain Man…" she said.

He reached out his finger so that Danni grabbed hold of it, swinging it back and forth. She brought it to her mouth and began gumming it in earnest. He smiled at the minor pinch of her sharp stump of tooth as she bit down hard. "I wanted to do this." And that was the truth.

Something about these girls, all three of them, tugged at his heart strings. He lowered his head, filled with shame at the memory of what he'd done the night before with a complete stranger, all the while thinking of the woman beside him. He was overcome by the sudden urge to go. To get away from the pureness, the innocence of these two children and their mother before he contaminated them.

In an instant, his entire upbringing became open for review. All his life, his parents had tried to raise him to believe he was somehow superior, better than anyone else, and that others should consider themselves fortunate to be in his presence.

Five minutes with these three precious human beings and he suddenly knew better.

"I need to go." He placed Danni in her crib and turned away from Sarah, toward the door. He didn't want her to see him for what he was—a fraud—an asshole trying to act like a decent person. "I've got things to do." Changes to make.

"Oh, okay." Her voice registered genuine disappointment. "I understand. You're a brain surgeon, for gosh sakes. Of course you have more important things to do."

He stopped, halfway to the door, something telling him this would be the first truly important step toward a new life. He turned slowly back to face her.

"Just things that need to be done, Sarah. Nothing more important than you and your girls." Never that. He wanted to tell her how they'd touched him. Wanted her to know how special they were. Could hear himself screaming that he wasn't worthy to be in their presence. Not yet. He turned away from her.

"Tanner."

The sound of his name from her lips halted him at the door. One hand on the doorjamb, he answered without facing her. "Yes, Sarah?"

"You're welcome to visit us here anytime."

He tensed, fighting the urge to tell her he wanted that more than anything. He swallowed and braced himself. "Thanks. It-It might be awhile." He walked out. Left like the coward he was, before he spilled more than he wanted to.

CHAPTER 26

"Come in, dammit," Mike growled at whoever the hell was knocking on his door.

Angelique breezed inside. "I come bearing baked goods from my mom. How's that shoulder today?"

"It hurts like hell." Wincing, he tugged on the sling supporting the shoulder he'd had surgery on two days ago. "Not only can I not see a damn thing, I can't even wipe my own ass anymore. Just shoot me and get it the hell over with."

"Oh, babe, come on. You know none of this is permanent."

"How the fuck can you say that to me?" he barked.

"Look, most people have to go straight home after a surgery like this. At least you get to stay here in the hospital to recuperate."

"Most people have their eyesight to rely on when they go home. Or have you forgotten?"

"Of course I haven't forgotten."

"Well, it sure as hell sounds as if you have."

"How could I possibly forget? How could anyone forget with your insufferable attitude and you treating us all to a bitch, moan, and groan fest every time we visit? Not to mention your foul mouth? You need to quit feeling sorry for yourself. Don't you know how close you came to dying?"

"I wish I had," he said, barely above a whisper. He heard her heels hitting the floor in staccato rhythm as she approached.

"What did you say?"

He lifted his gaze, did his best to aim for the general area of her eyes. "I said I wish I had died," he bellowed. "Is that loud enough for you?" He heard her exhausted sigh. He'd hurt her yet again. Hurt them, and any chance they had of making a future together.

"Mike, calm down," she pleaded, the sound of her voice low, level with renewed patience.

"Just go, Angel. I don't want you here. I don't want anyone here."

"Michael—"

"Leave. Now."

"I'll leave when you're not being so ridiculous."

"I don't want you here!" He waited for her comeback, trying to come up with something new. Something more convincing. By the time she spoke again, he knew he'd hurt her good.

"All right, I'll go" Her voice quavered with tears. "I'll be back tomorrow. I bet you'll feel better by then."

"Don't come back." He bit the inside of his mouth to keep from taking it back. It was time to let her go. Without another word she left the room.

Mike let his head fall back on the pillow and rubbed his face with his left hand. Then rubbed his eyes, hard, willing them to see. Just to see anything at all.

"What in the hell is your major malfunction, Chief?"

Mike jumped at the sound of Liam Nash's voice. "Shit, man! You ever heard of knocking?"

"Didn't have to, the damn door was wide open. I could hear you bellowing like a pissed off bull halfway down the hall."

"You by yourself or is American Express with you?"

"I'm alone. Melanie relieved me today. It was either come visit you or see someone pleasant. Guess who she picked? You know, everybody at the nurse's station is talking about what a pain in the ass you are now. You've got them all dreading coming in here for a damn thing."

"Yeah? Well, Fuck 'em. Fuck 'em all!"

Liam snorted. "Yeah, you keep that up. That's a good way to make damn sure you never get chocolate pudding again in this place. Or, hmm—what do we have here?"

Mike heard the crinkling of a plastic bag at the foot of his bed then the sound of some kind of storage container being opened. It wasn't long before the aroma of baked sweet dough and fruit flooded his senses.

"Or fig tarts from Ms. Marceline, either." Nash made no secret of taking a bite and groaning with unconcealed delight. "Damn, that woman can bake, can't she?" he said, his mouth half full.

"You son of a bitch. She brought those for me." Mike reached out for them.

"Oh, hell no. I know Angel's mom well enough to know she wouldn't want you rewarded for upsetting her daughter the way you did. These babies are coming home with me."

Mike threw the covers off of his legs, and got another good whiff of his favorite pastry in the world. "Fine. Just take 'em with you when you get the fuck out of my room. And close the goddam door on your way out."

Liam's tone revealed his disappointment. "Are you really stupid enough to risk losing Angelique for something that may remedy itself any day now?"

"It's been nearly two weeks, Nash. If I was ever gonna see again, it would have happened by now."

"You don't know that, and besides, even if you don't see again, it doesn't mean you can't have a normal life."

"Normal?" He wished he could hit something. Hit it hard. Hell, he wanted to beat the shit out of it. "Not being able to earn a living is normal?"

"Who the hell said you can't do that?"

"How am I going to be a cop when I'm blind?"

"Big boo hoo…"

Mike jerked a fist back at the sound of Nash's voice right next to his ear. "Would you stop that? Make some fucking noise when you move around this room."

"You get trained to do something else. It's called occupational therapy, you dumb shit. And you need to need to watch that foul mouth of yours. You know how bad Angel hates it."

"Fu…"

Nash cut him off with a low growl. "You even think about saying that, I will kick your ass. I'll wait until you're more of a challenge, of course—blind, bum shoulder, and feeling sorry for yourself and all—I'd prefer some competition when I knock you flat."

Mike clenched his jaw and stood, felt for his surroundings. The bed, the table next to him, and concentrated on the exact location of his former friend. "Even like this I could kick your ass," he said, sniffing the air like a hound dog. "That shit you bathed in last night makes for a hell of a stench, and I'm ambidextrous as all hell when it comes to fighting a pussy like you."

"Oh, so you can fight with one hand, but you can't wipe your own ass?" Nash burst into laughter.

"Just how long were you eavesdropping on our conversation?" He grew more pissed by the second.

"I heard enough. Like I said, everyone could hear up and down the hall with that bull horn voice of yours."

"Get the hell out of my room."

"Make me, asshole."

Mike swung so hard with his left hand he heard the whoosh as it reached nothing but air.

"Not even close. I think when I leave here I'll go pick up the pieces of Angel's broken heart. She's probably home, crying her eyes out by now—"

He talked just long enough for Mike to get a good read on him. He swung again and connected this time, taking Nash by surprise, as well as himself. He waited for some response, his one fist up in front of his face, his stance ready for a fight.

Nash burst into laughter and slapped Mike's good shoulder. "You see, asshole? I knew you still had some fight left in you. Anybody with enough guts to swing at a man like me when he's in your condition can make it through any damn adversity life throws at him. Do you see that now, Harper?"

Mike rubbed his stinging knuckles on his shirt. "I'm not bleeding, am I?"

"Uh, nooo, but I am, jerk off. Thanks for the concern."

"Oh, man. Really? Rreally? I didn't hit you that hard. Must be that glass jaw of yours."

"S'just a busted lip. Only a scratch, lucky for you. Humph, lucky for me, 'cause the ladies love my lips."

"Oh, please," Mike snorted, holding his stomach. "I think I'm gonna puke."

"That's what Angel tells me all the time."

"That she's gonna puke?"

"No, jerk. That she loves my lips."

"Whatever..." Mike waved him off. "No shit, man. Are you all right? You don't need stitches or anything, do you?"

"No, I'm fine, but what about you? No more stupid talk. Deal? Life's too damn wonderful, and short, to walk away from it without a fight."

Hearing the honest to God concern in his friend's voice, Mike realized he'd crossed a line he had no right to cross with Nash. This man had lived through real loss. True adversity. Overcome by a feeling of pettiness and shame at his behavior, he extended his hand. "Deal. And I'm sorry. About a lot of things."

"It's all good, Harper. Just don't let me down again."

"I won't." Mike succumbed to a huge yawn. He came out of it flinching at the sudden headache. "Ow...fu . . . I mean shit!" He rubbed at his head.

He heard Nash's guffaw from the doorway. "Good effort, but you better work a little harder if you want Angel's approval, Chief. Later!"

Mike settled himself back in his bed, thinking about the conversation with Angel, and wishing he could take everything back. What a royal ass he'd been. What was it Nash had said?

Life's too wonderful, and short, to walk away from it without putting up a fight. The guy could be a major pain in his ass, but sometimes he spoke with pure genius.

∼✷

Angel opened her door on the first try, thank God. She didn't quite know how she was going to handle it if Sonny had decided to play hard to please with her today. She plodded to her bedroom, exhausted and depressed at the disastrous visit with Mike.

Determined to cry herself to sleep and stay that way until morning, she dropped her purse on the mattress and threw herself facedown beside it. She'd barely had time to clear her mind when the shrill ringing of the landline sliced through the silence of the room.

She reached over to pick it up and brought it to her ear, keeping her eyes closed. "Hello…" After a short connection pause, Nan's cheerful voice carried through the earpiece.

"Angelique, are you all right dear? I got this sudden urge to call you."

"Really? Why?"

"I have no idea, but when I get this feeling that Sonny's trying to tell me something, I've learned not to ignore it. It's been proven too many times over the years."

"Ah…Well, the truth is, I'm not okay, Nan. Our boy's in trouble."

"Michael? What's wrong? Is it a complication from his shoulder surgery?"

"His shoulder is fine, Nan. It's been thirteen days since the accident and he still doesn't have his eyesight back. He's determined it won't come back and told me he doesn't want me back over there. He's angry at the world right now."

"Oh phooey, that's his male bravado talking. It's easier for a man to show anger than fear. They think it makes them weak. Foolish pups. You'll have to do what you can to get through to him."

Angel sniffed loudly. "You didn't see him, Nan. He's given up."

"When you live as long as I have, you realize that life is a series of storms. This one will blow over just as many others already have. Next time you see him you grab those BVDs by the waistband and give those balls of his a good, solid jerk. That'll get his attention. Then tell him Nan said to get his ass in line."

Angelique burst into laughter at the mental image of that. "God, I'm glad you called."

"Me too, if I could make you laugh. Now how are coming along with that decision of yours?"

"I'm not. I still love them both."

"Well of course you do, but it's not fair to either of them. If you're going to do this thing then do it!"

"It's not that simple."

"Sure it is, and if you'll be honest with yourself just once, you could see it. You have a choice to make. Don't drag it out any longer that you have to. Think about which man you can't see living without and tell the other one, so he can begin putting his life back together without you in it as anything more than a friend."

Angel sighed. "I'll try, Nan. I really will. Now I need something to take my mind off of all this. How's Paris treating you? Met anyone interesting?"

"Oh, yes, dear! Paris is full of men. Young, old, of all shapes and sizes. Loads of promise here. I did have an encounter of the sexual kind yesterday. Want to hear about it?"

"Uh…sure. Why not?" Angel figured she could use a good laugh.

"This little man approached me at a sidewalk café, within sight of the Louvre. We talked for a bit then he showed me what he was hiding in his pocket."

"Nan! Ew. Is it too late to change my mind?"

"It was a pill bottle full of little blue pills, dear. Viagra. I wasn't even sure they sold Viagra in France. Imagine my delight."

"Oh, God. Do I have to?" Nan's laughter carried over the lines.

"He said he'd gotten the prescription filled a month earlier but hadn't seen anyone he wanted to try them out on until me. Isn't that the biggest line of bullshit you've ever heard?"

"Sounds like a line, all right."

"Sure it was. I told him he needed to update his pick-up lines, and then I took him to my hotel room. I gotta tell ya, honey. When I got my first glimpse of his tiny little package, I thought I'd made a terrible mistake."

Angel covered her eyes and groaned. "Oh my God."

"But within minutes of popping that little blue pill, 'Mr. Wrinkles' overcame his shyness."

"The Frenchman's last name is Wrinkles?"

"No, dear, that's the name of hi—"

"Ohhh! Don't say it. I get it now."

Nan's laughter rang out again. "Gilles and I had a lovely afternoon together," she said, with a satisfied purr. "Wish I could have an experience like than in the Louvre. Now that would be a memory of a lifetime. Love in the Louvre…"

Angel heard someone speaking in the background as Nan answered. "Is that him?"

"Him? Gilles? Oh no, dear. I never see the same man more than once, anymore. They become quite attached and it's too stressful to give them the boot."

"Of course. Silly me."

"They have to accept the terms before we ev…"

"Yes, I get it. I understand." Angelique cut her off, feeling a tad queasy in her belly. "Nan, I really must go now, but thank you for calling. You really have cheered me up."

"I know dear. You try to ease up on yourself, a bit, would you? I'm sure you're causing my Sonny undue concern."

"I will Nan. Goodbye now." She ended the call and lay there, trying to picture some of the things Nan said. She found herself smiling and realized that, despite everything, she did feel better. "God bless that little old lady," she mumbled. "She may be a loose old broad, but she certainly is lovable."

∿

"What kind of pain are you experiencing now, Mr. Harper?" The neurologist hovered around his face.

"My head is killing me, and my eyes—my eyes hurt like hell."

"How's this? Does this cause any discomfort?"

"Yes," Mike hissed, closing his eyes and turning away from whatever his doctor was doing to cause the pain slicing clear through to the back of his eyeballs.

"Hmm. That's actually quite good news. It's the light from my penlight that's causing pain. That means the pressure is releasing from your optical nerves. As they become more efficient, they get sensitive. It's like when your foot goes to sleep. As circulation returns, you get that pins and needles feeling, right?"

"Yes." Mike nodded, in agreement.

"Well, it's the same thing with your optical nerves. They're being bombarded by all these signals they haven't been able to receive in nearly two weeks, and they're somewhat oversensitive."

"Does this mean I'll get my sight back?"

"It means your optical nerves are trying to recover. I can't promise to what degree they'll come back. We're still in wait and see mode, unfortunately."

"I understand." Mike refused to jump to any hopeful conclusions. Better to accept at least partial blindness now than build his hopes up only to have them shatter later on. "Thanks, Doc."

"Try to get some rest now. You'd be surprised how much healing goes on in the human body while it's in deep, restful sleep mode."

"I was about to take a nap before you came in here. For some reason, I can't seem to quit yawning today," he said, covering his mouth one more time.

"Get to it, then, and let me know if there's any change."

Mike nodded as he heard the door close upon the doctor's departure. He settled back on his pillow, eyes closed, trying to rest, with thoughts and memories of Angel invading his mind.

~~~

He had no way of knowing how long he'd slept. He heard a nurse or someone moving around in his room, and opened his eyes by habit. "Who's here?"

"It's me, Mr. Harper. Julie. I'm your nurse until six a.m. Is there something I can get you?"

"Can you tell me what time it is, please?"

"It's two in the morning. Would you like some water or anything? I'm sorry if I woke you."

"That's okay. No water. I'm fine. But, you could do me a favor."

"Sure. What do you need?"

"Could you tell everyone how sorry I am, that I've been a grumpy horse's ass lately? I had no reason to take anything out on all of you. Everyone here has been wonderful to me."

"I'll do that," she said, "But…wait a minute."

"What is it?"

"You're following my clipboard with your eyes. Can you see it?"

"I supposed it's because you're moving around the room and I hear your footsteps."

"What footsteps? I'm standing still. The only thing I'm moving is the clip board and you're following it."

Mike concentrated, realizing he could see a shape, blurry, light, and undistinguishable. But a shape none the less. He could see it, could follow it with his eyes. "I'll be damned."

"That's a good sign, Mr. Harper. A very good sign. Good for you. I'll leave a message with your neurologist's answering service for him to come by. He said to be sure to alert him with any changes in your condition. All right!" She left the room on a cheerful beat.

"Yeah." Seeing a blurred shape was better than seeing nothing at all. But it was a far cry from being anything close to normal."

CHAPTER 27

Angelique braced herself, smoothing down her blue skirt before opening the door.

Liam stood before her, looking as handsome as he ever had in his lifetime, she was sure. His thick locks somewhat longer than they had been upon his arrival and spiked up a little with some kind of hair product. The day old stubble, inviting her to run her fingers over his chin. His jeans, just right tight, paired with an emerald and blue print button down shirt that brought out the green of his eyes. What a beautiful man.

She smiled at him. "Hey. Come on in."

He entered, stopping to envelop her in a bear hug that ended with a soft kiss on her cheek. "How's the man today? Have you spoken to him?"

"No," she said, as the intoxicating scent of Yves Saint Laurent's L'Homme Libre wafted over her, making her mouth water. Damn. He knew how much she loved that cologne on him.

"I plan on going there later." She closed the door and asked him to sit on the couch. She sat beside him and let him take her hand in his.

"What's wrong, Angel?"

His voice, heavy with concern for her, had her struggling to hold back the tears. "I can't put this off any longer, Liam. My heart can't take it anymore. So..." She took a deep breath. "I've made my decision, and I have to go to the hospital later this afternoon to tell Mike. It'll be the most difficult thing I've ever had to do. I'm hoping you'll come with me."

∿

Mike rubbed his eyes. They were good and sore now that his nerve endings were firing on all cylinders. His eyesight hadn't improved since this morning, so he still wasn't ready to cry victory. "Come in," he said, at the soft knock at the door. He knew her by the soft click of heels, her subtle, yet provocative scent of whatever the hell perfume she wore, before she ever spoke.

"Hey Angel."

"Can you see?" She sounded surprised.

He shook his head. "No, but I don't need sight to know it's you." He reached a hand out to her. "I'm sorry for yesterday Angel. I had no right to speak to you that way."

"It's okay."

"No. No, it isn't okay, and it won't happen again." He pulled her close for a hug, noticed a slight vibration pulsing through her, as though she were afraid of something. "Hey," he said, putting her at arm's length. "What's wrong? Did something happen that no one's telling me about?"

"No. It's just that I'm here to tell you something."

Mike's heart did a nose dive to the pit of his stomach. He had to stop her from speaking, from saying the words he couldn't hear right now. "Now's not the time for this, Angel."

"Mike—"

"I mean it, babe. Don't you do this right now." He stepped back and pivoted to face the window.

"I choose you, Mike."

He froze, wondering if he'd heard correctly. Slowly, he turned to face her again. "You can't be serious."

"I love you, Mike. I want to build a life with you."

"You'd have a better life with Nash."

"Not if I'd be regretting that he wasn't you."

"I can't let you do this."

"Do what? Love you? You can't stop me from loving you."

He shook his head slowly. "Maybe not, but I can sure as hell stop you from throwing your life away. Marry Liam, have some kids, and be happy together."

"I won't marry him. I love him, but not the way I love you. You're the one, Michael. You've always been the one, even if you won't have me. It makes no difference if you get your sight back—partially, fully, or not at all. It won't change anything."

"Well that's too bad, because I won't marry you unless my sight returns enough to be a cop again." He snapped his mouth shut to form a hard, firm line.

"I knew you'd have this attitude," she said. "What'd I tell you?"

"Yep, you nailed it."

"Nash? What the hell's going on here?" Mike turned to see a shape walk through the door opening.

"She asked me to come with her for moral support because she knew you'd be an asshole about this. You just can't help yourself, can you? She's one smart lady, our Angel."

"I thought she was, until this." He turned to where she last stood. "You picked wrong this time." He searched for and found the blur that was Nash's again. "And she's not our Angel anymore, she's yours. Now, take her home and close the door on your way out, please." He turned back toward the bed. The room filled with an overbearing silence as he waited to hear the sound of the door close.

"I'm sorry," Nash said. "What was that last bit you said?"

Mike turned around, searched for him again and finding him. "I said she's no..."

"You son of a bitch. You can see me! I moved locations after I spoke and you found me. You can see, can't you?"

"Is this true, Mike?" Angelique burst out in that high-pitched thrilled squeal of hers.

"No reason to get excited," Mike admitted. "I see big blurred shapes, and that's all I may ever see. Nash," he said, waving his hand in his direction. "Take Angel and yourself out of here, would you?"

"Don't be an ass, Harper. Why won't you accept that this could be the beginning of something good for the two of you?"

"Because I won't let it be. Not now—and maybe not ever." He walked to the door, opened it and held it open for them. "Now leave, please—both of you." He stood at the door, head down and fighting off a feeling of shame, mixed with the knowledge that he was doing the right thing for her. He heard them walk down the hallway where Angel's voice carried to him, her words making him smile to himself even as he fought back the urge to cry.

"I told you he'd be a jerk, didn't I? He just can't help himself—big freaking he-man. Nan's right. Men find it easier to show anger than fear. Nothing but huge walking egos with a set of balls."

It's good she's pissed—better she be pissed now than hurt later on.

∽◡∾

How odd that he was at the same red light again, thinking of his shopping list for the barbeque. The light turned green and he accelerated slowly just as he had that day, and things began to happen, just as they had the first time he'd lived out this scenario. The Hummer, its driver, and its passenger, and the sudden feeling that God was trying to send him a particular message: *Don't lose hope...*

Every nerve ending snapped to attention as he realized what he was seeing. Damn! How could he have forgotten this part? How could he have let this feeling of absolute well-being slip right out of his memory banks when it was so important? It could have made life so much easier the past two weeks if he'd just held on to it.

Mike woke with a start, pain radiating from his shoulder as he thrashed in his bed, mimicking the moves that had torn his joints in the first place.

Everything came back to him in a flood of sensations. The accident. The reason he was here. Partially blind, banged up, with his shoulder in a sling. The dream—re-living the accident. And finally, the memories— the mental images that had the thud of his heart taking center stage in his chest. A deep rooted feeling of restlessness warred with serenity for domiciliary control as he tried to regulate his breathing.

"Oh God!" He relaxed his shoulder in an attempt to ease the pain.

The door opened and his nurse entered. "Mr. Harper, are you in pain? You slept through your last dose."

"Oh shi-i-itt. I'm sorry!" He gasped an apology to the nurse, still fighting the pain.

She laughed. "It's fine."

"Yeah, I was dreaming and tried to move it, I guess. It hurts like a son of a bitch now. Sorry."

"I'll be right back with your meds."

"Please hurry. Aw shit! Sorry."

"I will."

Mike heard her chuckling as she left the room. Still fighting the pain when she returned a few short minutes later, he winced as she flipped on the night light to administer the pill to him. He took it and thanked her before she left, and waited impatiently for it to take effect. Finally, it began to thread its way through his system, seeping into the muscle tissue and easing nerve endings. Relief. Sweet relief washed over him as he began to drift off.

In the last moments of sweet bliss, just before being overcome by unconsciousness, he realized something. The nurse. He'd seen her face. Not clearly, of course, but he'd seen two dark spots for eyes and the blur of her mouth moving.

He allowed himself an honest to goodness smile just as the pain medication took him completely under.

∽∽

"How many fingers am I holding up?"

"Two."

"Good. How clear?"

"Still blurry as hell, Doc, but I definitely see two blurs and not just one big fuzzy blur. Is that good?"

Dr. Moore's boom of laughter filled the room. "That's very good. Your pupils are beginning to react as they should to the light, Mr. Harper. You understand, of course, that there's still no indication your eyesight will come back a hundred percent."

Mike nodded. "It will, I know it will." He smiled, thinking of the gift he'd been given. The knowledge of a life with Angelique, seeing, and with something else he'd dared not even acknowledge until recently. A future.

It took another week for his eyesight to return to normal. By the time he left the hospital, he was able to call his own cab. He gave the driver his home address and asked him to wait for him as he went inside to change into something decent.

He returned to the cab several minutes later, breathless with excitement. "One more stop," he said, giving him directions to Angel's place. He paid the man and walked cautiously up to the door to ring the bell.

She answered, gasping as she stood there, in her work clothes. He gave her a careful inspection from head to toe, noticing she was in her stocking feet.

"The shoes are always the first to go." He laughed as her face lit up with delight.

"You can see?"

"I can see everything, even more than I could before," he said, reaching out to smooth her furrowed brow with his thumb.

"What do you mean?"

"Let me in and I'll explain."

She pulled him inside and closed the door before walking into his open arms. "I've missed you, Mike."

"Me too, baby, but I couldn't face coming to you until my eyesight was back to normal. Now, come over here." He pulled her to the comfortable sofa. "I want to tell you about something that happened to me just before the accident."

"What is it? Did you remember something? Was there someone else involved?"

He settled next to her, pulling her close against his side. "I think it was God, but hear me out. Have you heard how people say their life flashed before them right before an accident? Well, in the moments just before that Hummer hit me, I caught a glimpse of my future. It's almost like time stopped for me. I saw that rich kid behind the wheel, the same punk who hit Sarah and the girls, he just drove right through that damn red light."

Mike wiped his forehead and steeled himself, wondering what she'd think when she heard the rest of the story. "Now here's where it gets strange. I remember blinking, and when I opened my eyes again, it wasn't him behind the wheel anymore." He turned to face her as she sat, seeming to be totally absorbed with his story. "I was behind the wheel."

She blinked twice and shook her head. "You saw yourself driving...what? The Hummer?"

"That's exactly what I saw, and you were my passenger in the front seat. You were wearing a white blouse and your hair was loose, blowing in the wind, because the windows were down. Babe, you were laughing and looking at me with such love." He lowered his forehead to hers and released a long, deep sigh. "I know now that God showed me this glimpse of our future so I wouldn't lose hope," he said.

"But you did, Mike. You made yourself and everyone else around you miserable. I don't understand why you did that."

"I know I did, and I'm sorry. I couldn't remember it, Angel. It wasn't until you and Nash left after your last visit that I dreamed about the accident again, and it all came back to me." He smiled down at her, kissing her lightly on the lips. "In the dream I could see even more detail and this time something in the backseat caught my attention. Something I hadn't noticed the first time."

"What did you see, Mike?"

"There was a seat in the middle—a toddler's car seat. It was carrying a child. I couldn't tell if it was a boy or a little girl, because all I could see was a head full of dark curls. But Angel, instinctively, I knew that child was ours."

CHAPTER 28

"Liam, pass the pasta salad, please," Sarah said for the second time, again with no results. "Nash!"

It finally snapped him out of his daydream. "Yeah? Did you say something?"

"For the third time, could you pass the pasta salad please?"

He gave her the bowl, along with an apologetic look. "Sorry about that. My mind was somewhere else."

"No kidding. Where've you been?"

"Hmph, somewhere between purgatory and put me out of my misery," he said. "Wherever I end up, it looks like I'll be there alone."

She sucked in her breath, sending him a sympathetic look. "You know how badly Angelique didn't want to hurt you, right?"

"Yeah, I know. That's probably why she put it off for so long. Harper's a good man and he'll be good to her. I sure as hell can't complain. She gave me a second chance when most women wouldn't have let me in the door."

Sarah placed a spoonful of pasta salad on her plate. "Angel's a good person. She gave me a second chance too. God only knows what I'd be doing if I hadn't gotten the job with Dr. Maze and his staff." She took a bite and chewed thoughtfully. "And if you love her as much as you say you do—"

"I'd let her go, I know. What a stupid damned cliché."

"Well, damn, Nash. I was going to say you'd be happy for her, but you've kind of ruined that for me, since it's even more of a cliché." She waited for him to face her then crossed her eyes until they both burst into laughter.

"I am happy for her, and him too, for that matter. They make a great couple, but that doesn't mean I won't be miserable around them for a while. There are two things I want right now. First, to know that you and the twins are safe and sound from your ex-asshole for good, and second, to see Louisiana in my rear view mirror." He took a sip of tea and wiped his mouth with a napkin. "When are Daniel and Leah coming back from Houston?"

"They should be back by tonight. They'll probably be loaded down with gifts and clothes for the girls. God, I wish they didn't do that. I already feel like I owe them so much."

"Just let 'em. They love all three of you like family. They've told me that on numerous occasions."

"But, it's not necessary."

"It makes them happy," he said, reaching for the cell phone in his pocket. He looked at the screen and frowned as he answered. "Nash here." He walked into another room to speak.

Sarah cleaned her plate and loaded her and Liam's dishes into the dishwasher. She was humming a country hit to herself when Liam's voice broke in from behind her.

"Sarah."

She turned to face him. "Yeah?"

"I need you to take a look at this picture—it's a tattoo." He walked over to meet her and manipulated a photo on his phone screen. "Does this look familiar?"

Her heart pounded, as though sensing how important this call could be. She stared at the screen. A picture of a tattoo, a familiar one of a snake all coiled up and beginning to swallow its own tail. The tattoo seemed to be located on a man's back. "Where on the back is this located?" she asked, knowing how much this answer was worth to her and her daughters.

"It's on his left shoulder blade."

Sarah's hand flew to her mouth. "Is he . . ."

Nash nodded. "Yeah, he's dead. The face," he stopped. "They, uh. Well, he can't be identified by his face. The body washed up on a beach just across the Texas line."

The glass she held fell to the floor, filling the room with the sound of shattering glass and the floor with shards of crystal. "Oh God."

Nash pointed in her direction. "Don't move." He backed out of the room to finish the phone call.

Sarah stood frozen in place until he returned.

"Are you cut anywhere, Sarah?"

"No, I'm just-I'm . . ."

"Look, he's the father of your daughters. It's only natural that you'd be sad at his passing, no matter the circumst—"

"I'm so relieved!" she cut him off in a rush of breath. "Oh God, I feel like this slab of cement has been lifted from my chest." She approached him cautiously, stepping around broken glass. "Are they sure it's him? Are they sure he's dead? Is there any possible way he could show up where the girls and I are? At any time?" She rang her hands. "I need to see him. I have to see all of him. I have to know if it's him."

"You can't see all of him, Sarah."

"Why the hell not? I can take it if it'll prove to me that it's him."

"Because, there is no body," he said calmly. "There are body parts, all found in a large cooler someone found washed up on a beach. Texas state police suspect they used at least a couple more coolers because, well, all they have is a torso and his upper legs."

"I don't care. That's enough to prove if it's him or not. Can you arrange it for me, Nash?"

"I suspect someone from the Texas troopers will be calling you soon enough to make some kind of arrangements. They'll be sending more photographs soon of any distinguishing marks they find."

Sarah felt herself nodding. "Fair enough." She looked around at the broken glass on the floor. "Dammit, look what I did." She step out of the room and returned with a broom, a dustpan, and a small shop type vacuum; between the two of them, they had every splinter of glass cleaned up in a few short minutes.

After checking on her sleeping babies, she returned to the kitchen to find Nash pouring himself a cup of coffee. He looked up, his eyes questioning.

"You want a cup?"

"Sure." She accepted the mug of coffee he'd prepared the way she liked it and they made their way to the den. Settling deep into the comfy leather couch, each on opposite ends, he spoke what had been on her mind.

"It looks like I won't have to wait long to head back home."

She thought of one person who'd be disappointed if he left. "Why don't you stay here, Nash? We like you and you have connections and friends here. I mean, I know you're my bodyguard, but we're friends, right? Leah and Daniel like having you around and the twins are crazy about their 'Uncle' Liam. Annie, Drake, Tiffany, and Red…" And Melanie. "You could have a good life here."

"I have a good life in Lubbock. I have connections there too, and friends. Grant it, they're a little different from you guys. Not nearly as friendly, but they have my back. I have a history there."

"From what you've told me, what you have there is a past. Maybe you should stay here and make a future."

"A future alone."

"Just because you won't have a future with Angelique doesn't mean you'll be alone."

"Sarah, stop." He placed his hand on her forearm. "What I don't want is to see those two together and feel bad about it. I can't handle that. I need to go back home. I want to go back home, at least for a while, anyway."

She studied him closely, and could tell he was being honest about the situation. It took a big man to admit he was hurting, and he was both—a big man—and hurting like hell.

∿

"I'll get the door, babe."

"Thank you," Angelique called back to Mike, as she put the finishing touches to her clean kitchen. She smiled, hearing the two masculine voices of the men she adored. She knew now, that one would remain a dear friend while the other would eventually be so much more than that.

"Hey beautiful." Liam spoke fom the doorway of the kitchen.

She turned, beaming up at him. "Hey you." She grabbed a dishtowel to wipe her hands and met him for a hug. "How are you?" She peeked around him. "Is Sarah with you?"

"Nope. No Sarah. We just got back from Beaumont. She positively identified the remains of Troy Richard. They're running a DNA test, just to be sure."

"Oh my God. Really? When did they find him?"

"Texas State Police called last night, and sent me images of identifiable marks on his body. They eventually found all of him in three separate containers either washed up on a beach somewhere or still floating in the gulf. That old boy must have pissed somebody off pretty damn good before he made a run for it."

"Drugs?" Mike asked.

Liam shrugged. "At this point, we can only speculate. Anyway . . ." He slapped his black Stetson on his leg nervously. "I came to tell the two of you I wish only the best for you guys. And goodbye."

Angelique felt her heart drop a bit although not enough to dispute that he was making the right choice. She suddenly remembered how sick she'd felt the first time she saw Red and Tiffany on the dance floor together, and she hadn't even been in love with Red. He must be hurting terribly, and if she knew anything about the man, he was feeling guilty as hell about it.

She and Mike exchanged a look of complete understanding before she met Liam's uneasy gaze. "You know how much we both care about you, right?"

He nodded. "I do know that, and that's why I have to go."

"I know you do. For now, anyway. But I also have a feeling you'll be back here one day. You're like Mike, you know. You may have been born a Texas Longhorn, but we'll turn you into a halo wearing, New Orleans Saints fan one of these days." Nash shook his head and laughed, as he made his way to the front door. "Maybe one day, Angel. I figure I got at least a year or two of season tickets to buy so I can watch my 'Horns' whip up on those LSU Bengals."

"Pfftt. In your dreams, cowboy."

"We'll see." He shook Mike's hand then crossed the threshold out to the porch. He swung around, a trace of a smile on his face. "But until then…" He held up his right hand, his index and little finger extended with his thumb holding down the ring and middle fingers. "Hook 'em, Horns!"

"Yeah, right!" Angelique snorted. "We'll see you in Death Valley next fall, cowboy. Our Bayou Bengals just love cooking up a good ol' Longhorn stew."

Liam laughed again as he looked at Mike. "Is she always that serious about her college football?"

"God, you should here her during a Saints game."

"She gets 'Who Dat?' fever, too?" Liam groaned.

"You bet your ass I do, and I've got the number nine jersey in my closet to back it up." She grinned up at him.

Nash clucked his tongue. "Hopeless."

"Just waiting on another Black and Gold Super Bowl, baby," she added.

Nash tipped his hat and turned toward his truck, muttering "Damn Crazy Cajuns."

Angelique stood arm in arm with Mike, watching their friend climb into his truck and back out of the driveway. She closed the door and leaned against it, staring up at her choice for the rest of her life. She smiled into his sexy eyes, knowing she'd chosen wisely. "I hope he comes back one day. I know someone who's dying to make him a good match."

"Yeah, Mel's gonna be real disappointed when she finds out he's gone."

Angelique cocked her right brow curiously. "You know about that?"

"Mmmhmm. I know a lot of things." He pulled her close with his left arm.

She linked her hands around his neck. "Is that so? You got anything you want to share with me tonight…Cowboy?" she purred into his ear before nipping at his lobe.

"Something big." He pressed his thick, hardness against her.

She shivered at the promise of what was hidden behind his tight, zipped jeans. Taking his hand, she pressed a soft kiss upon his palm and led him to her bedroom.

"Seriously?" He lit up like a kid with a season pass to Disney World. He halted, jerking her to a stop. "What about Sonny? You don't think he'll get angry or jealous or anything, do you? I'd hate to have your doors start sticking because of me."

"I've already explained it to him, just in case," she added in a whisper. "Besides, I hardly think he'd be shocked, given his owner's past sex-capades." She gave a gentle tug and they restarted the trek to the bedroom.

"What about your therapist? Won't she disapprove?" He sounded somewhat doubtful.

She couldn't keep the smile from her face. "I called her this afternoon. She said I'd made my decision as that of a mature woman, using all the criteria available to me, without the use of sex as a crutch to sway my opinion one way or the other."

"Okay, so that means—"

"She basically told me to go for it."

"No kidding? We have your shrink's blessing?" He still looked as though he was afraid to believe it.

"Oh babe, we have more than that." She pulled him through the door of her bedroom and then turned him, pressing him gently down onto the mattress. "We have doctor's orders."

EPILOGUE

"Honey…I'm home!" Angelique called out, kicking her shoes off at Mike's front door. She lifted her face, sniffing at the delicious aromas permeating the air. "Something smells wonderful." She entered the kitchen and peeked inside the black iron Dutch oven he loved to cook in. "Mm, beef stew." She closed her eyes and inhaled, catching the subtle scents of several different spices, as well as a fine wine in the thick gravy. "Mmm, that's gonna be so good." The sound of her voice barely covered the growling of her stomach. She'd chosen the perfect day to work through lunch, what with the overabundance of calories this meal promised.

"Mike?" she called, wondering why he hadn't made his usual appearance by now.

"In here!" he called, from the back of his house.

Resisting the urge to sneak a taste or two, she covered the pot and made her way to his voice."

"Where are y—" Angelique stopped inside the doorway of his bedroom, shocked into silence at the room's transformation. Muted light from dozens of candles bathed every surface in a soft, luminous glow.

"Oh…" she breathed, as he appeared before her, sexy as hell in black jeans and a white dress shirt, buttoned down just enough to show a little of that sexy, broad chest of his. Her gaze travelled to his bare feet. Ah, that's good. No boots to remove.

He walked up to kiss her then handed her a half-filled glass of wine.

"What's going on here, Mike?" she said, taking the wine, her stomach filling with butterflies at the sight of him, all sexed up with his engines revving and vibrating. Or was she the one revving and vibrating?

"We're celebrating," he said, lifting his right arm to tap his own wine glass to hers.

"No sling!" She only just realized he'd been holding a glass of wine in each hand. "Oh, baby, that's wonderful."

"It is, isn't it?" He placed his glass of wine down on one nightstand next to his massive bed. "I figured now that I can use both arms, it was time to do something I've wanted to do for over six months."

He let her have one more sip from her wine before taking her glass to set it beside his. Both hands flew to her mouth as he produced a small, deep blue velvet box and knelt before her.

"Oh...oh." She struggled to calm the rapid thud of her wildly beating heart.

"Angelique Therese Baptiste, would you do me the honor of becoming my wife?" He opened the box to show her the emerald solitaire, flanked by a cluster of diamonds totaling at least a half carat on each side.

"How did you know?" She squealed, truly delighted with the gorgeous ring.

"You answer my question first, and then I'll answer yours."

"Oui, monsieur. Absolutely! Of course I'll marry you." She squealed again, covering his face with kisses.

"Bon. Now as to your question," he said, taking the ring out of its dove gray satin lining and slipping it easily onto her finger. He stood up, holding both her hands in his own. "You remember when we dropped off your watch to have it repaired in October?"

"Yes, and you picked it up for me a week or so later."

"That's right. The woman who's owned that shop for twenty years said you went by often and always stopped in front of the emeralds. Now, she said you'd told her, on countless occasions, that if you ever got an engagement ring, you wanted the main stone to be an emerald. She also said that a few months earlier you'd seen this particular ring and fell in love with it."

He brought her hand up to kiss the finger with the ring on it. "What I need to know is if that woman was just feeding me a line of bull to make a sale, or is that really how you feel?"

"It is absolutely true, Mike. The second I saw this ring I hoped it would be mine one day."

He nodded, seeming to be satisfied with her answer. "And now it is, along with my heart, Angel." He lowered his mouth to cover hers in a heart melting kiss.

Stop here for Sweet ending…
Continue for a tad more Heat!

She let him kiss her, waited for the kiss to work its usual magic on her by turning her insides to mush. Within seconds she wanted him...needed him as near to her as possible. She pushed him gently to a seated position on the bed, ever mindful of the incision from his surgery, while unbuttoning his shirt. She pulled it away from his shoulders and down his arms, in a rush to have him bare-chested and at her mercy.

"Someone's in a hurry today." Mike laughed as she pushed him back on the bed and tackled the snap and zipper of his jeans. "It took me hours to get myself ready for tonight, but does she notice? No! She just commences to ripping my clothes right off of me, without even a 'Looking good tonight."

She paused, letting her hands fall away from the waist-band of his jeans, already half-way down his hips. "Do you want me to stop?"

"No." He grimaced, pushing down the front of his jeans, she suspected to relieve the throbbing erection inside his boxer briefs. "Hell no. I'm dying here, babe."

She grinned down at him and proceeded to pull his jeans down his hips so he could kick them off his legs. His erection, now free from the confines of the tight jeans, bulged invitingly behind the briefs. "Mm, baby. Looking good tonight," she said, before licking her lips.

Mike groaned then sat up to pull her close. He slipped his hands under her dress. "Now you." He took the time to caress both her silk-clad butt cheeks with his hands before lifting the clingy black knit of her dress over her head. His arms dropped to unclasp the front closing black lace bra, freeing her glorious pale orbs from their bondage. Leaning forward, he covered one nipple with his mouth while brushing his thumb lightly over the other.

Angelique's breath released in a quick rush of air as Mike growled low in his throat, sending a frisson of need coursing through her.

In one quick movement, he had her on her back as he leaned over with his weight on his left elbow. He kissed her again, letting his right hand familiarize itself with all the parts of her body it had missed out on up until this moment. "Mmmm..." he growled. "You're in for a real treat, lady."

"I seem to remember you treating me a couple dozen times over the last month," she said.

"Yeah, but I've got my right hand back now," he said, slipping off her black silk panties with one swift movement.

"Oh...oh...my..." Angelique sighed with pleasure as he began a skillful exhibition of manual dexterity. Within a few short minutes he brought her to the precipice of need and over the edge. "Oh...Mike," she moaned low in her throat, before her insides clenched and shattered from the monumental climax.

"Geeeeze…" she groaned, with a last prolonged shudder, panting and straining for enough mental capacity to regain her power of speech. "What were you doing down there?"

His laughter rumbled deep in his chest. "It's a matter of having the touch. Kind of like when you make a wine glass sing."

She whimpered as he kissed her, starting the slow burn all over again.

"Hey, babe?"

"Mmm?" She indeed felt like a fine crystal wineglass he'd 'played' perfectly.

"I'm good with my left hand…"

"Yes indeed," she purred.

"But with my right, I'm better."

"Mm…you are…perfection…is what you are," she said, reaching over to remove his briefs before straddling him.

"I'll take that," he said. "And I'll take this, too." He placed both large hands around her waist to pull her forward. "You have no idea how badly I've wanted to touch you like this…to do this with both hands over the last month," he said, lifting her until she'd settled around him, encompassing the considerable length and breadth of him.

She sighed with satisfaction, loving the feeling of him deep inside her. "Oh…I think I do." She began to move slowly, gliding over skin slick with her own pleasure, riding him until they were both panting, both grasping—reaching for release—and finding it together.

Afterward, they lay entwined, snuggling close, as heartbeats calmed, gasps reverted to deep, even breathing, their needs satisfied, and sated…for now, at least.

"Angel," he whispered.

"Hmm?"

"I doubt I'll ever be a rich man."

"No, huh?" Her face registered feigned surprise.

"Smart ass. This is serious business."

"Why would you think I'd ever want to be rich?"

"Doesn't everybody these days?"

Her fingers toyed with the dark silky hair on his chest. "In my younger days I may have thought that was important. Now I know better." She craned her neck to see him, to touch the face of the man she adored. "I just need love, and everything that goes along with it."

"Like what?"

"Honesty, trust, fidelity…"

"Oh, you mean I can't go chasing skirt with the guys anymore?" He made an attempt to look upset about it.

"You can try, but you may want to think twice."

"Why's that?" He raised himself on one elbow to gaze down into her beautiful green eyes.

"Well." She traced her nail gently along his jawline. "I hear male castration is quite painful, especially without anesthesia." Laughter rumbled in his chest, causing a deep, stirring need in her to be as close as possible to him.

"Just as I thought."

A moment later her mouth found and melded with his in a lingering kiss.

She pulled back slowly, finished the caress with a gentle tug and nip at his lower lip.

He rolled onto his back, using his left arm to bring her with him. She rose above him again then lowered her head so that her dark hair fanned out across his chest. "What was it you were thinking?" She purred, enjoying his reaction to her kiss.

"Like I was saying, I always suspected my Angel had a little devil in her. Are you gonna be one of those wives who gives her husband trouble?" He groaned, as her long, silky locks skimmed the super sensitive skin of his chest, abs, and belly.

She lifted herself to stare into eyes the color of rich dark chocolate, thankful for the fates that had brought this man to her.

"Some, I'm sure. But I'm willing to bet it'll never be more than a man like you can handle." She trailed her finger over his chiseled abs. "So, what do you think, big man? Are you worried?"

Mike slipped his hand to the back of her neck and gently tugged her closer. He gave her a devastatingly handsome grin before answering in his deep, rich rumble of sexy baritone.

"About you and me? Not even a little."

Thank you for letting me share Green Eyed Temptation with you. I hope you enjoyed reading all about Angelique, Mike, and Liam. I'd be honored if you would consider leaving me a review on Goodreads or other review websites.

Other Work by LORI LEGER

La Fleur de Love Series
Book One: Some Day Somebody
Book Two: Last First Kiss
Book Two and a Half: Hart's Desire (Novella)
Book Three: Brown Eyed Girl
Book Four: Heaven in Your Eyes

Halos & Horns Series
Book One: Green Eyed Temptation
Book Two: Sarah Smile
Book Three: Meagan's Marine
Book Four: One Year to Forever

Seasons of Love Series
(Multi-Author Anthology Series)
Book One: Hearts, Hearths & Holidays (Bells Will be Ringing)
Book Two: Spring Promise (Loving Cat)
Book Three: Sweet Summertime Love (Still Loving Cat)
Book Four: Christmas by Candlelight (Baby Blues Christmas)
Book Five: It's a Summer Thing (Full Circle Summer)

Full Circle Love
(The four part collection of Cat & Zach novellas combined)

Prime of Love Series
(A series dedicated to mature characters finding love and laughter
through the everyday twists and turns of growing older)
Book One: Running Out Of Rain
Book Two: Hanging On To Hope
Book Three: Spring of 2016

Read Cathryn & Zachary's four-part love story first . . . Then meet Zach's dad, John Michael. Sexy is as much a part of his DNA as those Ferguson-blue eyes.

Sometimes you need to lose all hope in order to find true strength...

HANGING On To *Hope*

PRIME OF LOVE: Book Two

LORI LEGER

About the Author

Photo of Ms. Leger provided by Joan Granger of
Simple Memories Photography in Welsh, LA

Lori Leger is a wife, mother, doting grandmother, and Mistress of
Procrastination. She lives in Louisiana with the love of her life, her
very own Studley-do-Right. He's earned his spot in the Keeper
Husband's Hall of Fame by allowing her to walk away from an
eighteen plus year career as an Engineering Technician in Road
Design to stay home and write.

She adores writing stories set in her beloved southwest
Louisiana, where good Cajun cooking, helping your neighbors, and
saying y'all is as normal as hurricanes, heat, and humidity. She
figures as long as she's not tunneling through ten feet of snow to get
to her car, it's a perfectly acceptable trade-off.

Lori has ten full-length novels, and one novella published in
three series: La Fleur de Love, its spin-off, Halos & Horns, and her
latest, the Prime of Love series. She has also contributed to, as well
as published, short stories in each of the five Seasons of Love
anthologies, an author collaboration series. She's compiled four of
the short stories about one particular couple, Cathryn and Zachary,
into a single book called Full Circle Love. It acts as a prequel to the
Prime of Love series.

She's contributed to the Sweet & Savory Cookbook of Amazon Authors, published by Top Ten Press. Lori also has an article published in the non-fiction book Writing After Retirement: Tips From Retired Writers, published by Rowman and Littlefield Publishers, and edited and compiled by Carol Smallwood and Christine Redman-Waldeyer.

Hanging On To Hope is the Second book in her Prime of Love Series, novels dedicated to mature characters finding love and laughter through the everyday twists and turns of growing older. She has a third planned for the spring of 2016.

www.CajunflairPublishing.com
www.lorilegerauthor.com
cajunflair@lorilegerauthor.com
lleger641@yahoo.com

Join me on Facebook, Twitter, Goodreads and Pinterest.